THE
AMERICA
GENE

THE AMERICA GENE

By Michael Nesmith

Cover design by Randy South

ISBN 1-56111-000-0

First Edition Online: June 2009
First Edition in Print: October 2014

*Dedicated to the loving memory
of my dear friend Douglas Adams, whose
encouragement for me to write this book
was the last straw.*

Chapter One

The old weathered boards in the derrick groaned as they warmed in the pre-dawn air. The moist, corrosive wind from the Gulf swung the rusted pulley atop the crown-block platform of well 517A and made it clank and creak.

A faint light.

Cash Carruthers, eyes closed, leaned his back against the railing of the platform. All night he had been thinking, half asleep, half awake, sitting atop the abandoned derrick.

He opened his eyes as the new summer sun lit the sky with its early rose, lit the pampas to a yellow-green, lit the sandy, scratchy roads to buff, outlined Cash's form with the first bright orange of the coming day.

This dry well, number 517A, was the only nonproducing well of the fifty he owned, and over the years the platform perched high on the old rusty drilling rig had become his meditation retreat. He had never spent the entire night here before, but this time he had plenty on his mind.

The first glimmerings of an idea had awakened, and while he was smart enough to know he was under its influence, he didn't know what it was or what to do about. He had no precedent for it, no way to understand it; only to know that it was there, powerful, and his life was about to change. That was all he knew, but he knew that to a certainty.

Time to go home.

Cash was extraordinarily handsome by the standard of the time. Tall, with broad shoulders and narrow hips. His brown eyes, bright, were set deep under wide, full eyebrows, and he had shiny dark hair with more than a hint of gray. A high forehead perfectly balanced his jaw. His face was always in a relaxed smile, so when he did smile he expressed all the joy in the world, and people around him couldn't help but smile with him.

He was popular and rich, lived casually for one so wealthy, and lived mostly alone. He had just turned fifty years old.

His ranch stretched for miles across the immense, flat

coastal plains next to the Gulf of Mexico, from Corpus Christi Bay on the north to Brownsville on the south, from the littoral backwaters of the Intracoastal Waterway on the west to the vast citrus orchards of the Rio Grande Valley on the east.

Cash raised grapefruit on some of it and had oil wells on some of it. He started making money in college, turned that into more, and kept on. From pizzas to computers to bio-tech, then everything-tech, then just everything, including the oil and grapefruit, all finally under the heading of the Sandra Corporation.

Back at his comfortable, large and rambling ranch house, he stepped from the shower, shook his hair dry, shook the stiffness of the night from his bones, and then gazed out the window in his bedroom, across his property toward the Gulf of Mexico. He could not see the water from here, but he felt it in the distance, a few miles across the flat, treeless country.

He slipped into fresh blue jeans, a rough denim shirt, boots and a hat and walked outside into the heat of the morning and stood still for a second. He rubbed his knuckles over his closed eyes and yawned. The air was humid and heavy, the sky clear and cloudless—the beginning of a very hot day.

In his open Jeep—no doors, top, or windows, only a windshield—he drove toward the Gulf. The wind tousled his hair. The sun shone warmer and warmer, and finally hot.

Ninety-four degrees in the late morning.

He drove along the shoreline and wondered at the attraction of an oceanfront. The shoreline, like all of Cash's property, was flat, easing out into the water for great distances. One could wade the shallow, sandy shoals for three miles into the gulf water in some places and never get more than waist deep.

Inland, the elevation rose only a few feet above sea level. Even looking away from the Gulf, there were no distant mountains. The horizon was one long flat line.

Standing on the beach looking toward the Gulf, the line was silver and straight along the top edge of the water, marking the eastward horizon; looking from the same place to the west, the line was glowing white along the land, again perfectly straight.

Tourists who came here all remarked on how flat the land was, how the indeterminate distance to the horizon was disconcerting and indefinite, defeating any sense of depth. It was the same vacant comment as "how green Ireland is," or "how tall the buildings are in New York." The Texas Gulf coastland was flat, the land disappearing into the distance without a ripple over the unseen curve of the earth.

He turned the Jeep along an inland road and felt the incessant breeze from the Gulf blow at his back. He pulled his hat low to keep it from blowing off and drove toward Helensburg.

Helensburg was a town of a few hundred permanent

residents, most of whom worked on the ranch for his oil company. The town's eponym, Helen Unger, the first sheriff, died in the line of duty in the late 1800s. It looked and functioned like the other towns of the area, except its only real tax base was the salaries for the work in Cash's Gulf Coast Oil Company's oil fields.

The town consisted of a small cluster of worker houses and mobile homes raggedly arranged along asphalt streets crumbling from the heat. In the center was a gas station, new and shiny, an old bank building now a minimart/hardware store, a cleaners and laundry, and the Partaway restaurant, bar, and nightclub.

Cash drove into the lot next to the Partaway, parked, and walked from the blazing, humid, diamond-clear Texas day into the dry, dark, neon ruby-red light of the shockingly cold air-conditioned bar. The wood floor squeaked as he stepped inside.

Henry Biggins, the bartender and part-owner, an ex-roughneck, was more than surprised to see him. He quickly grabbed a rumpled menu and escorted him to one of the booths by the windows. The windows were darkened by blue sun tint on the glass, and hung with blue-and-white-checked curtains that shut out most of the light.

Cash slid onto the blood-red Naugahyde banquette and asked Biggins for iced tea and a chef's salad.

When Biggins returned with the food, normal by all estimates except for the size of the iced-tea glass, which held over a liter, he said, "Surprised to see you, Cash. Glad. But surprised."

Cash smiled graciously. "You O.K.? Business good?"

"Umm, business is fun. Don't know how good it is. Had a band in here last week I almost ran away with. Good music these days."

"Kind'a band?" asked Cash.

"Tejano. Tex-Mex Oompah Country Western. Out of Corpus. Sparkle suits, a great female lead singer. El or Los something. They're coming back in four months. Can't wait. Git ya anything else?"

"I'm good," Cash said. He looked around the room. He was the only one there. He studied the signs over the bar, the tiny dance floor with traces of sawdust, the bandstand where the chrome mike stands reflected the neon beer signs in coruscations of blue and red and transformed themselves into colorful crane-like birds.

Cash ate in silence, the only sound the clatter from Biggins as he cleaned the bar glasses.

When Cash was through, he motioned to Henry, who walked back to the table and began clearing the dishes.

"*Los Bomberos.* The Firemen." Henry said. "Don't know how the girl fit with the name. She was the whole act, if you ask me. Maybe she was the fire. Tomatoes good?" he asked.

"Yeah. Sweet." Cash said.

"Teresa grows 'em," Biggins said "I'll tell her." He started to walk away, but Cash stopped him.

"Hank, you mind if I come in here and play?"

Biggins was at a loss for words. This was very strange. He stared at the table a second longer than normal, then finally back at Cash.

"Play?"

"My guitar. I'd like to come play and sing."

"Well, sure, I guess. I didn't know you—."

"I might not be any good. I'd like to try, though. How 'bout tonight?"

"Saturday? Uh, there's a band comin' over from Corpus. Blues band I think. You want—."

Cash stood up from the table. "Blues band would be good. Think they might let me play a number?"

"Yeah, if you want to play, that's, you know, that's fine. I'll just tell 'em you—uh—" Biggins raised his eyebrows, stretching a mask across his face to hide his incredulity.

Cash laid a twenty on the table. "O.K. Thanks. If they don't mind, maybe—?"

Henry nodded.

"So. O.K. Done. See you tonight." Cash smiled and gave Henry a short clumsy bow, then turned to the door and walked out.

Outside the sun was glaring. One o'clock and hot. The bright light of the day, in contrast to the darkness of the bar, blinded him for a few seconds. Cash held his hand over his eyes as a visor, to adjust to the light and the heat.

He hopped into his Jeep, stared at the front of the Partaway, and tapped his fingers on the steering wheel. As he started the engine, a hot blast of air and sand billowed from beneath the car. Cash made a decision to go talk to his dad, and drove toward Port Aransas via Corpus Christi.

Corpus Christi had lost itself to the frenzied growth of the late 1990s, surrendering its early character to malls, freeways, and franchises. The tiny downtown area of bantam buildings, in glass, granite, and aluminum, was a miniature of any big city caught in growth. What there was of the past was punctured, flat, rendered out of date and useless.

The causeway out of Corpus and away from the mainland led only to a road at the south end of Mustang Island, a barrier island with wide sand beaches in front of pampas-covered dunes between the Gulf of Mexico and Corpus Christi Bay. The road went north thirty miles along the narrow island and ended in the little town of Port Aransas, a sport-fishing and oil-drilling-and-distributing community.

Cash drove the roads as fast as his old Jeep would go, about fifty miles per hour, and forty-five minutes later in Port Aransas he turned into the drive of the small Sportsman's Motel, where his father, Leland, lived.

The motel, built in the 1940s, once a whorehouse and gambling hall, was now a simple tourist court, usually only occupied on weekends by teenagers on a bender.

Leland lived in the very end unit, next to the manager's cottage. The motel was modest but well-maintained, and Leland's apartment was exceptionally large and very nice, a combination of rooms that used to be the honeymoon suite and a secret casino. It had a large living room, a bedroom that was almost as big, a bath, and a handy kitchen/dining area that opened to a veranda covered by a green-and-white-striped awning.

Leland had moved there when Cash left for college. After Cash became rich, one of the first things he tried to do was get his father to live more comfortably, to take advantage of the money, but Leland never would.

Cash finally bought the whole motel on the condition that the owner continue to manage the property and keep the purchase a secret, which Cash thought would protect his father's pride. Cash then made sure the Sportsman's Motel stayed in perfect condition, paying for a series of remodels and upgrades to the buildings, including his father's apartment.

But it wasn't pride that caused Leland to refuse Cash's generosity. It was because Leland had no desire for or interest in the trophies of success. He was a comfortable man, happy in essence, assured, and no more influenced by a rogue desire than he was by a rogue yawn; both passed unnoticed.

What Cash didn't know was that Leland knew of the purchase, so the final secret was Leland's and not Cash's.

Cash stopped his Jeep in the driveway outside his father's apartment and jumped out. Leland ambled out of the front door and gave his son a welcoming hug.

"Biggins just called," Leland said.

"About tonight?"

Leland nodded.

"I've been thinking about this for a long time," Cash said.

Leland turned sideways to him, gesturing. "Want to come in? Want me to come out?" he said.

"Let's take a stroll on the beach," said Cash.

The two men walked along a shale and gravel path toward the beach.

"What did he say?" Cash looked at his dad.

"What you said. That you wanted to come play with the band there tonight. I think he was wondering if you could play well enough. He didn't ask the question directly, but I answered it."

"And...?"

"I said I didn't know."

Cash and Leland had perfected their strolls over the years. They would saunter slowly, hands clasped behind their back, more or less in step, side by side. Sometimes they walked so slowly that leisurely hours could pass and they would cover almost no distance. These walks were communion between them, when they shared unspoken thoughts as they each gazed out from the same perspective, at the same speed, in the same direction. Cash had come to depend on them. They provided an implicit guidance from his father.

They turned from the path and onto the beach, which was dotted with umbrellas and trucks.

From Port Aransas to the south, the beach was a scythe, like the mirage of an infinite image from two mirrors facing each other, curving away into limitless distance, beyond any point of focus.

On weekends it was full of little children who ran in and out of the gulf water, men with beer bellies and white legs who leaned back in aluminum chairs next to campers and cars, and women with loosened halters who stretched out facedown on beach towels and soaked in the sun. A big, lazy beach.

Leland looked toward the sea, drew his gray hair back from his forehead, then shoved his hands into the pockets of his short pants.

After a while he asked, "How do you play in a band you've never rehearsed with and whose songs you don't know, or anything?" Leland asked.

"Henry says they're a blues band, which makes it simple. Not that the blues are simple, but the songs are all sort of the same structure and easy to play. And I'm going to play a song I wrote."

"A blues song?"

"Kind of. Yeah."

Cash nodded yes and looked at his father but saw no reaction. Leland looked away to the sea.

"What's your net worth these days?" Leland asked.

"Maybe six and change. I dunno, exactly."

"So you're going to sing the blues?"

"I know, I know. But it's—something I would like to do." Cash studied his father for more clues of what he was thinking, an inkling of his dad's opinion. Leland looked straight ahead, revealing nothing.

"You gonna play your guitar?"

Cash nodded.

"And sing?"

Cash nodded again.

"Is it O.K. if I come?" Leland asked.

"That's why I came by. To get you."

"Think I can I go like this?" His dad held out the sides of both legs of his shorts with his thumb and forefingers. Cash shrugged. Should be fine.

The late afternoon stretched into the sky above the Gulf beach, long shadows and changing light announcing the close of the day. They came to the path leading back to the motel. Leland stopped and looked to the Gulf once more, then to Cash.

"You hear from…? Lost her name."

"Diana? Diana Copeland, head of Copeland Lines. Cruise ships. Sure. We stay close."

"Haven't seen her in a long while. I remember her as pretty."

"She was. Is. In her own way. Very pretty, I think. She's been in Italy for the past few months, her office's there."

"Pulled together, too. Was she smart? I remember smart."

"Yeah. Very. We've spent a lot time together. But—" Cash

rocked his hand back and forth. "but—it's not—I wouldn't call it—I dunno—"

"Authentic?" Leland smiled at Cash.

Cash smiled back, then looked down. "I suppose."

They were back at Leland's motel now.

"So you sure I can go like this?"

"You look fine to me, Dad."

Cash climbed into the Jeep as his dad settled in the passenger seat, and the two of them drove toward Helensburg in the onrushing hot Texas night.

The transformation of the Partaway from its daytime presence to its nighttime one was intense. The glitter of the neon beer signs bounced from the shiny trucks in the overflowing parking lot. The usually prosaic freestanding frame building, a simple large square with its sagging wraparound porch and saloon-like corner entrance, had become exotic and beguiling, an oasis lighting the dark.

Leland and Cash parked down the street and walked to the entrance. During the walk, Cash began counting the cars and trucks. He stopped counting at fifty. Cash was overtaken with a strange new sensation. He did not like it. It made him physically uncomfortable, anxious.

The band was playing loud, funky blues when Cash and Leland walked in the door of the smoke-filled room. Biggins saw them and waved from behind the bar as he pointed directions to a booth.

There were over a hundred people in the place, half of

them on the dance floor, most standing still, listening at the edge of the small stage.

When Cash saw them, the new feeling deepened, and he thought his idea about playing tonight might be a bad one, that he might not be able to do it at all.

Performing was new territory for Cash. He had played infrequently in public, at a few parties after lively encouragement, campfire-type sing-alongs, where he controlled the song selection and played the guitar. Most of the time he played and sang by himself, at home.

This was very different. His emotions were in turmoil, and his palms were sweating. When he realized he had not brought his guitar—that he had nothing to play—he was petrified.

He knew he had no reason to be. He could easily go home, get his guitar, and be back in time to play, but he felt something awful was at work.

Cash had made cold sales calls, had introduced himself to strangers on the street. He was not afraid of being noticed. He was familiar with the fame of wealth, the reactions of the awestruck and envious, the disingenuous, the sycophantic. He was not afraid of rejection, failure, even bodily harm. This was not like any of that. It was a type of steady, creeping discomfort. Something was not right, but he had no idea what.

To Cash, fear was usually meaningless, like a moment of cold wind, a shudder, something to be brushed off. Why now, he wondered, was he so shaken? Why were his palms sweating? They had never done that before. He stopped at the edge of the dance floor and stared straight ahead into nothing. To an observer, it was the stare of immobile panic.

Cash's concern was abruptly torn apart by the overpowering sound of a woman's voice, low in tone and pitch, and fierce, filling the room. For the first time since he walked in the door, Cash looked at the band.

Standing in front was Amber Fanfare, her hand wrapped around a microphone on a stand, pulling it into her face, her eyes closed, her head forward—an attack.

She was barely over five feet two inches in height but with the figure and carriage of someone tall. Her legs were long in relation to her torso, her hips were small, her shoulders wide. She was wearing a loose T-shirt that hung just to the curve of her back and jeans that were tight enough that one could see the shape of her legs, every muscle as they moved and flexed. She was sultry, sexy, her whole body expressive of every word she was singing—words unintelligible through the pounding blues-band beat, except to those who knew the song.

The microphone made it almost impossible to see her face, and her eyes pressed tightly shut distorted her features further, but Cash didn't have to see much to know Amber Fanfare was a stunning beauty. Had he been able to see her clearly he would have seen the well-defined jaw, the slight, sad fall at the edge of her eyes, the perfect nose.

At the end of a verse, Amber opened her eyes and looked

directly at Cash, who was standing in her line of sight. As she looked at him, she overtook him in her assurance and her control, and at that moment all the fear left him. Amber was able to compel the song to obey, the band to follow, the audience to listen. It was not personal to him—he was only a face in the crowd to her—yet her unquestioned authority silenced his fear as it silenced the crowd's, by bringing everyone into her truth. In all the corporate boardrooms and halls of political power, he had never seen such command. His reaction was to smile his famous smile, all the joy in the world. Amber did not notice.

Her eyes shut once more as she silently waited for the band to play until her next refrain. Cash looked around the room for his father. He weaved through the crowd to the booth where he crumpled in next to his dad.

"I forgot my guitar," he said.

"Freud would be proud," said Leland.

"Freud would be wrong. I really want to play. But there is something—something else. Weird anxiety—something. Don't know what." Cash looked at him.

"Stage fright?" Leland said.

"Really? I'm not afraid of these people. I like these people," Cash said, surprised.

"Hmm. Is stage fright real fear?" Leland asked the question to himself. "I don't know. I think it's a form of excitement. I've never had it."

"It's trouble. What can I do about it?" Cash looked at his

dad, who shrugged.

Leland pointed to Amber. "She keeps closing her eyes."

The song was coming to a close, and Amber had stopped singing. She was turned sideways to the audience and the band. Head bowed, eyes closed, she swayed her hips forward and back to the rhythm as she stamped her heel in time. When the song finished she turned her back to the audience, walked to the back of the stage, and took a drink from a plastic cup, indifferent to the cheers. It was an unstudied move, as real as rain.

Leland cocked his head to one side and studied Amber. "Although that doesn't look like fright management. She's very good, I think."

"Look at this." Cash held his hands palms up. They were glistening with sweat.

"Stage fright." Leland nodded. "That's my call."

Amber returned to the microphone.

"Like to introduce a special guest. Gonna come up and play a number with us. Give it up for Cash Carvers." Amber put her hand above her eyes and turned inquisitively to Biggins at the bar, who pointed to Cash.

The single follow spot swung around to Cash, encircling him in a ridge of blue light. Cash thought it could have just as easily come from a guard tower.

Biggins yelled out, "Carruthers!" as a correction for all to hear, and everyone did except Amber who was looking for a place to sit on the stage and wait out whatever was coming.

Chapter Two

Cash stood on the stage, sweat pouring from his forehead into his eyes, hands shaking so badly he was almost unable to play. The guitar player from the band had happily lent him his ax, jumped immediately from the stage, and headed for the bar, relieved to be out of any line of fire. Cash turned to the band and said, "Twelve-bar blues in E, a shuffle about here..." He snapped his fingers in tempo, "One, two, three, four." The band started a lazy shuffle somewhere behind the tempo Cash had stated, and Cash began to sing.

It was clear the moment he opened his mouth that he was terrible. His voice was thin and weak, and he was slightly off pitch. The band members looked at each other, winced, and stared at the ceiling or some other neutral spot in the club.

Henry Biggins maintained an expression of indeterminate nature as he looked at Earlene, a snuff queen at the bar, and watched for a clue from her. Earlene rolled her eyes, shook her head, took a swig from a longneck, shifted on the bar stool, and spun away from the stage with a kick of her toe against the bar front.

The crowd turned listless. The few that had been dancing sat down, the few that wanted to keep dancing folded their arms across their chest and stayed still, hoping this would be the only song. The disaster of Cash Carruthers rolled like a tsunami across the room and left not only destruction in its wake, but worse: discomfort. Everyone but the morbidly curious avoided looking at the stage. Everyone was uncomfortable. Everyone squirmed in their place, such was the dis-ease.

Everyone, that is, except Amber Fanfare.

Amber stared at Cash like he was a miracle. If she had ever seen a more fascinating creature in a more amazing moment, she could not remember it. She gawked as Cash careened through the song. Not only was she not uncomfortable, she was excited, interested, and captivated. Amber Fanfare, whose life consisted largely of saying no to a dozen hits a day from a dozen men, took a moment to close her mouth.

She had encountered people dealing with stage fright before, but the way Cash dealt with it mesmerized her. It was simple stage fright, to be sure, but simple stage fright can obliterate people, and it obviously had almost reduced Cash to blither. And yet he pressed on, kept his head up, stayed with it. With utter absence of approval from the audience—in fact, complete aggressive rejection by the audience—Cash still moved forward, standing there in a kind of dignified mortification. Amber thought he was either crazy or more courageous than any man she had ever seen.

After what seemed like hours to the crowd, the song mercifully collapsed to a halt. Polite applause popped erratically around the room, but the main sound was the squeaky scrubbing of wood chairs against the wood floor, confirming the confused silence of embarrassment.

Cash fled from the stage through a side door, a welcome escape. The band immediately launched into a provocative solid blues shuffle, the dance floor burst to life again, and Earlene spun the bar stool to face the stage, tapping her long purple nails against the counter through a soggy cocktail napkin. Henry Biggins poured her a free double Jack Daniel's, neat, as recompense.

Amber watched transfixed as Cash dove for cover, and then she seized the microphone, connected, and sang. She could feel her legs shake up through the small of her back.

Outside, Cash was walking in small circles in the gravel and dirt behind the Partaway, staring down, hands deep in the rear pockets of his jeans. When Leland came around the corner, Cash raised his hands in surrender.

"I'm sorry. I'm sorry. I'm sorry," he said over and over.

Leland patted him on the back, then gave him a side-by-side one arm shoulder hug, a loser hug, a "we still love you" hug.

"I've never been that scared. I've never been scared like that. I was—" Cash held out both hands for his father to see. "Look."

His hands were fluttering like crepe ribbons attached to the grill of a department store fan. "This never happens to me. What the hell?"

"It was grim, son, true," Leland said. "But admirable. I never saw fear like that outside a foxhole. But you pushed on."

"That was some other thing, something new," Cash said. "I've never been that bad at anything before. I got up there, and some strange chemical started through my veins, some—some—I don't know, liquid fear. I thought I was going to faint, scream, and laugh hysterically, all at the same time."

Cash was calming down. The sweat on his hands dried. His breathing came back to normal.

Cash looked at Leland. After a few seconds of complete silence, Cash exploded into a laugh. Leland knew what it meant and laughed too, happy for the release. The two of them were laughing like escaped convicts when Amber walked outside from the stage door in front of the rest of the band on a break.

Amber walked up to them and smiled the biggest uncontrolled smile she had smiled since she started singing the blues.

"That," she said, "was awesome!"

Cash tried to respond but instead disintegrated into more laughter. Leland was right behind him, laughing hard, until Amber got infected and laughed as well, though she had no idea why.

"What?" Amber said.

"Noth—oh, n—nothing," Cash said through the tremors. "Thank you. That was really sweet."

Amber slowed down, darkened, and shook off the virus. Sweet was not funny to Amber. She stopped laughing.

"Did I miss something?" she asked, pleasant but wary now, not smiling, not frowning.

"No, no, no. It was the moment. I was, just—" Cash saw Amber in the shadows. Tenebrous. He steadied, too.

"Please. No. I'm sorry, that was precisely the right thing to say, and for me to hear. Really. It was funny because of where—when—it came in the scheme of things. I was feeling suicidal about my performance just as—what you said, and I—and, thank you. It was perfect, just the right thing to say. Thank you."

"Suicidal?" she said.

"No, no, no. Figure of speech. I still don't quite know how to deal with how bad I was." He looked at her with a grimace and smile combination. At that moment Cash made his first real contact with Amber, through her translucent brown eyes. He drew a sudden short breath.

Leland saw this from a father's perspective. Amber's presence was something extraordinary for Cash. She was not like the other girls. She was also young enough to be his daughter.

"I'm Leland." He extended his hand to Amber.

Amber glanced away, awkward. Then she shook Leland's hand.

Leland smiled quietly, knowingly, carefully.

"And you know Cash." Leland gently formalized the moment, re-established the social order.

Amber nodded and stared straight at Cash. "O.K. But you were straight. Truly right. You were," she said.

"Well. I—I thought the crowd was going to kill me."

"Crowds don't know anything. They never know what's going on. Don't sing for anybody but yourself anyway. I sing to myself and watch the show I see from up there." Amber moved a step closer to Cash. She put her hands in her hip pockets, like Cash, and looked up at him.

The air was warm from the heat of the ground, humid from the ocean. There was a faint smell of gasoline, Gulf water, booze, cologne, and a tinge of marijuana. Leland knew he was in a closed room full of combustibles. Time to go.

Leland gave his son a parting shake around the shoulder. "Well. Cherry blossoms, huh?" he said. "Amber. Pleasure. I'll be inside."

Amber and Cash stood closer together than ordinary conversation called for, their combined shadows etched against the rough wood of the Partaway building, their bodies backlit and rimmed by purple and orange rings of neon from the Partaway sign and halogen from the streetlight.

Cash was surprised for a moment by the sudden departure of his father, but the surprise did not sway his attention, now focused entirely on Amber.

The gravel crunched under Amber's boots as she moved a baby step into his space.

"Yeah, cherry blossoms. Did you make that up?" she asked.

Cash looked down at Amber, who was close enough to embrace. He backed up a step. Make it up?

"Yeah," Cash said. "I was in D.C. It was spring. So I thought I'd write a song about the trees."

He was far enough away from her that he could see her full figure.

"Hey, look. It was so odd how you said, 'It's cherry blossom time,' over and over again," Amber said, breaking the silence between them. "That took guts. O.K., not odd, exactly, but true enough. I knew what you were swinging at. That was you. You were tough. You stuck with it. And that was good. That was easy to watch. Crowd didn't get it. So what."

Cash now knew the song was idiotic. He thought it avant-garde when he wrote it, when he sang it to himself at home. As a real song in a real band, it became ludicrous.

He had stood on the stage and sung "It's cherry blossom time" fifty-three times in a row while the band played a blues dirge, the crowd becoming more hostile at each repetition. So he had had to reach down into an unexplored part of himself, conquer the fear, and go forward. He had not suspected by trolling the waters of an uncharted section of his soul for courage he would attract Amber.

"Well," he said, and then went silent. He was not at a loss for words, but he was intimidated by any that came to mind. "I don't know. It was spooky."

Somehow he was standing close to Amber again.

"Are you married?" Amber asked him. She assumed he was old enough to be her father, but she asked anyway.

"I have eight children," said Cash.

"Whoa." Amber blinked.

The sides of Cash's eyes crinkled. He shook his head. No.

"Kidding. Never married, no kids. Only me. You?"

"Not that I know of," she said and crinkled right back at him.

"Hey, Amber, we're back up," the band leader called as the members filed back inside.

"That mean you have to go?" Cash asked.

"Yep. You gonna stay?" Amber asked. "Sing another song?"

"Sure," Cash said. "I'll just run home and slip into some protective headgear."

"Hey," Amber said mildly. "Most of it sucked. But some of it didn't. No reason to quit yet. Right?" Amber took a step toward Cash.

"Amber! Come on!" Insistent.

"Maybe I'll see you in the show," Amber said, and turned and walked through the stage entrance. She did not look back at Cash, but she wanted to.

Cash thought about following her in, but Amber's allure was not enough to make him go back in the Partaway. Not tonight. The thought of going back inside and mingling with an audience he had just dragged through one of the worst episodes of their lives was unbearable.

The band was into a grinding roadhouse blues when Amber burst onstage and took the mike. When she sang, the song moved up exponentially in power.

Amber scanned the Partaway crowd for Cash, to see if he had followed her.

This made her singing slightly different. Her usual sexy and appealing manner of delivering the message of songs—oblivious to her surroundings, lost in the song—was hiding in the shadows of longing. As she looked around the room, the song took a second place to her search.

Of course, Cash was not there. However often Amber's eyes flashed across the undulating crowd, Cash was not there.

By now he was standing on his front porch looking up at the hot Texas night sky, the stars above like a ceiling with no depth, a picture of stars. Amber was not exactly off his mind, but she was off to the side for now.

Cash was dealing with another blunt force that had nothing to do with her. The evening was causing his self-confidence to give way, his mystical, almost miraculous, self-confidence. Cash felt a little lost, a little confused, but worst of all and first of all, embarrassed.

Cash did not know this embarrassment was a normal down-side of performing in public. Every performer at some time or other has embarrassed themselves onstage. Public humiliation is an occupational hazard.

Professional entertainers deal with it routinely. The amateurs who came off stage and burst into tears of self-loathing never make it.

The real pros, the thundering, on-top-of-it pros, nurse the wounds, pick up the shards of their self-esteem, put it back together, and head back out to the stage to try again. Those were the rules of engagement.

Cash, of course, did not cry or burst into sobs of rejection. True, he did not know he would shake with fear in front of the Partaway audience, and he had not known how bad the song was or his singing would be. He had some theories as to the reason for tonight's fiasco: no one had liked his song, his singing was poor, and he was unprepared and unaware of what was expected. He understood the failure well enough.

What confused and concerned him was that he had no standard for success. It was mystifying. The only person that seemed to understand it at all was Amber Fanfare, and if he was to be honest with himself, he had only a limited idea of what she was talking about.

He turned and went inside his house but did not turn on the lights. He stood for a moment after he pulled the doors closed behind him, staring into the darkness. Amber's words after the show came back to him again and again. Soon the only thing he was thinking about was Amber Fanfare.

* * *

Henry Biggins stood in the stark yellow incandescence of the single, unshaded bulb that hung over the stage entrance to the Partaway.

The last of the band's equipment was being strapped into an old, bruised van. The various band members had gotten in their cars and driven off, leaving behind Lane, the bassist and the van's driver, and Amber. The club was empty and dark, and except for the stage door, which Henry held open as Amber came out, locked.

Amber walked outside, stopped next to the open van door, and looked back at Biggins. Biggins set the alarm, shut off the light, and closed and locked the door. His back was still to the van when Amber said, "Mr. Biggins. You know that guy who sang tonight?"

Biggins turned and walked to her. "Cash? Yeah. Why?"

"Know how I could get in touch with him?" she asked.

"I got an office number. Is there a problem?"

"Problem?" Amber said, surprised. "No. I, uh…like the way he sings and was thinking about getting in touch with him."

To his credit, Henry was at least diplomatic, leaving his own opinion of Cash's singing unspoken.

"Oh," he said. "Well, like I say, I got an office number if you want that. I just set the alarm, though. Can you call me tomorrow?"

Amber's life was a constant parade of men who would do anything she asked, who wanted to take her to dinner, take her to Acapulco, or just talk to her. Amber was unaccustomed to wanting anything from men. It was always offered.

She didn't know how to say to Henry she wanted Cash's number right now.

"That's O.K.," said Amber. "I'll call you tomorrow then." She got in the passenger side of the van and stared out the window with her brow furrowed, intense.

Biggins drove away as Lane put the van in gear and drove away, too, holding a joint in his lips as he fumbled with the broken radio knob in the van's dashboard.

Amber looked at him and thought about Cash, about the difference. She stared down the road, straining to see past the high beams. She wanted Cash. Somewhere out in the darkness, he must be waiting for her.

* * *

Horton Callaway slid his empty chair under the table for one at the Arrow Club and went outside for a smoke. He had finished dinner and was looking forward to smoking a cigar.

Horton was an habitué of the Arrow Club, one of the smaller, more exclusive Houston clubs for the wealthy, because it had a dining room and an outdoor terrace that suited him, he liked the food, and there were usually a number of attractive single women there. Horton walked across the terrace and leaned against the rail, looking across the lawn toward the tennis courts. The high bright lights were swarming with bugs, the night sky a blue-black to their white frenzy. Horton took some time to light his cigar. He was unsteady from too much wine.

He did not know at this moment that Cash was in the grips of one of the strangest failures of his life. He did not know this, but even if he had, it would not have changed his decision to leave the Sandra Corporation.

He tried to think of the right way to tell Cash he had decided to quit.

He had been running the Carruthers empire, Cash's fortune, for fifteen years, and in that time he felt he had made no appreciable difference to Cash's assets or wealth. If Horton thought an idea of Cash's was bad, it was usually good, and if he thought the idea was good, he never knew why. Horton was so far out of sync with Cash that the two men hardly ever spoke outside the purview of the professional relationship that bound them.

If Cash was sui generis among wealthy bachelors, Horton was stereotypical. Married once when he was young to a trophy wife, he now lived alone with the emotional detritus of that divorce and had slowly turned into everyone's expectation. He dated starlets and wealthy widows, gave lavish gents-only parties for private prizefight screenings, and lived globally between five mansions and apartments usually filled with weekend guests. Once a year or so, he would toy with the idea of purchasing a professional sports franchise, but he never liked the numbers.

During his tenure with Cash, Horton had amassed great personal wealth and was grudgingly respected among his peers. It was clear to Callaway that for all his apparent personal success, he was impotent and had never really mattered at all to the overwhelming success of the enterprises he was running. It was as if they were all operating autonomously. He was a broker, a manager, an exploiter of someone else's talent and good fortune.

Horton was not without his own luck and ability in this endeavor, but that didn't matter to him right now.

What mattered was that while Cash seemed inspired, astonishing everyone with one excellent idea after another, Horton himself plodded, somewhere behind and to the left, keeping the business ordered and organized, and then gathering the harvest. He watched with awe, envy, and dismay as almost every move Cash made scored perfectly. It had become unbearable.

He stubbed out the butt of his cigar in a crystal ashtray and crumbled the remaining leaves into a pile.

"There is a phone call for you, sir," said Tom, the maître d', as he handed him the remote phone from the front desk.

"Yes?" Horton said into the receiver, curious who would call him on this phone rather than on his mobile, which was constantly on and constantly with him.

"Horton?" The female voice was talking loudly above a bad connection. "It's Diana. The damn satellite phone is acting up. Can you hear me O.K.?"

"Well enough. Where are you?" Horton knew Diana Copeland could be anywhere, and it was always the first question he asked when he heard her voice on the phone.

"Right off Cabo San Lucas. I'm going down through the canal, repositioning to the Gulf. For the Caribbean and Mexico."

Diana Copeland inherited a freight shipping company from her father and doubled its size by going into the cruise-ship business. Right now she was in the owner's stateroom of the flagship of her fleet, the 525-foot, 16,800-ton *Marianna*, looking out over the stern.

The faint thump of the disco four floors down was muted, blending with the sound of the water as it curled over the hull, the slight vibration of the huge engines like a distant air conditioner hum.

Diana was always onboard whenever one of her ships went through the Panama Canal. She had flown the company jet from Teterboro to Santa Monica and then chartered a helicopter to pick her up and bring her on board the Marianna at sea anchor just off Long Beach. Everything had worked well so far except the damn phone. She was worried she would lose the connection.

"Are you with Cash?" she asked Horton.

Interesting way to phrase the question, Horton thought. Why didn't she say "Is Cash with you?" This distinction was another reason for leaving Cash, even though it existed only in his mind.

"No. I haven't seen him. He's at the ranch, I think. Did you try there?"

"No. I really just wanted to talk to you. I'm coming back up to the Gulf with the boat. I'm thinking of putting the *Marianna* out of Houston for a bit. I have some ideas about setting up something new, and I wanted to talk to you about it. Privately."

Diana Copeland had long been in love with Cash Carruthers. They had met some years before at a political fundraiser in D.C., where they both contributed heavily to a presidential candidate who eventually lost. They became friends, then lovers, then real friends, and finally, business partners.

Through Sandra, Cash had early invested substantial money in Diana's cruise business. That had been several years ago, and Horton had finally sold all of Cash's interest in Copeland Lines, once the business was healthy and there was a good profit in it.

Horton and Diana had remained cordial.

"How did you find me here?" Horton asked.

"A hunch. Will you have some time for me next week? I want to talk about commerce," she said.

"Commerce? Are you building more ships?"

"I'm always building ships," she said. "But that's not this. I don't want to talk about it over the phone, and especially one that isn't working right. We'll be up there in a few days, and I'll give you call. You're planning on being in town, though, right?"

"I'll be in town, but—," Horton said, thinking at the same time he might not be with Cash any longer.

There was a squeal, then static, and then the line went dead. Horton laid the handset down on the table and signaled to Tom he was through.

He walked to the bar and ordered a fifty-dollar glass of brandy. He settled down in an overstuffed leather chair to watch the people in the lounge who were, it appeared to him, mired in mediocrity.

* * *

Amber pointed to an approaching off-ramp.

"This is me," she said.

Amber jumped from the van seconds before it rolled to a stop outside her house. With the halting high steps of a crane, Amber crossed the dirt and gravel yard of the house, past the pickup truck parked on the would-be lawn. The bassist called out, "Bye." The cry echoed once, then drifted unanswered across the rows of deteriorating double-wides randomly laid along the twisted streets of Amber's neighborhood.

Amber rattled open the bars of the flimsy security door covering the front door, slipped inside the dark, musty trailer, and closed the door quietly behind her.

She walked into the kitchen area of the double-wide and turned on the fluorescent light in the fake vent over the stove. There was a lingering smell of propane, beer, and fried-chicken bones, and stacks of greasy paper plates coming from an open garbage can next to the sink. She opened the refrigerator, pulled out a beer, and unscrewed the cap as the light went on in the bathroom.

"How'd it go?" the voice called out.

Amber sat at the particleboard counter that separated the kitchen area from the living room and took a swig from her beer. "Fine, I guess," she said.

Chastity Fanfare padded in from the bathroom in slippers and a red nightgown, hair in curlers, face shiny from night cream. She was an older version of Amber, beautiful, still trim, and exotically sexy. She lit a cigarette off one of the burners of the stove and peered out the window over the sink into the night.

"Time's it? Did you come straight home? You didn't get in any trouble, did you?" she said.

"It's three, Mom. I got off at two. Do the math." Amber took another gulp and looked at her mother.

Chastity looked up and made a face. "Don't be a smart aleck."

She took a long drag from her cigarette, walked to her daughter, and sat down next to her with a loving stroke of Amber's hair.

Chastity picked Amber's bottle cap off the counter, held it between her thumb and little finger, and tapped her cigarette ash into it.

"Show go O.K.?"

"It was O.K. Yeah."

"How much'd you get paid?"

"Twenty-five bucks."

"You sing good. You could make some good money at it. Do what you're good at. Make money at it. That's what it's all about."

The two women sat silent. Amber finished her beer; Chastity finished her cigarette and went to the refrigerator. "'Ja eat?" Amber shook her head.

Chastity pulled out the almost empty box of takeout chicken, opened it, and set it in front of Amber. "Here. We had chicken. Cap'n Bob brought it home from work."

"Is Cap'n Bob here?" Amber asked. This troubled her.

"No, he left about an hour ago. He's gotta go out tomorrow with some guys down from Houston. After Marlin. They're leavin' in...look at that." Chastity pointed to the clock over the oven. "They're leavin' in an hour. Let's go to bed, honey." Chastity stood up and dumped the empty beer bottle and her cigarette ashes in the trash.

Amber walked into the living area and unfolded the bed from the couch. A single sheet was wadded in the corner. She straightened it out as best she could, but it was like the skin of a cantaloupe, permanently wrinkled.

Amber sat on the edge of the bed and started to take off her jeans. Her mother sat next to her on the edge of the foldaway bed and tried to help Amber undress.

"Let me help you, baby," Chastity said. "Let me tuck you in. You're still my little girl, aren't you?"

Chastity reached out to grab her daughter's jeans. Amber violently pulled back and pushed her mother away at the same time.

"Mom," Amber whined. Her mother backed away, hurt.

"I was wanting to love you a little, that's all. Help you get ready for bed, like we use ta. For Christ's sake. Suit yourself. Good night." Chastity turned and huffed from the little living area into the back bedroom and banged the door shut.

Amber pulled off her jeans and pulled on a pair of jockey shorts from under the foldaway bed and a T-shirt from the same stash, her preferred nightwear. She walked to the kitchen and turned out the light.

In the darkness she walked to her mother's bedroom door. She tapped lightly. There was no answer. She knocked again, louder.

"What?" came a petulant response.

Amber opened the door, crept in, and slipped into bed with her mother.

"You can't sleep here. I'm mad at you."

"I'm sorry. I know." Amber gave her mother a hug and snuggled next to her in a spoon. "I wanted to say good night. I love you, Mom."

Chastity rolled over to face her and brushed the hair from her daughter's face. "I love you, too, sweetheart. Did you have a good time tonight? You never said."

"It was O.K."

"Honey, you sing great. And you look great, too. That counts, you know. I've got a lot of things go my way from being something of a looker. And you're lots better 'n me. You could get any guy you want."

"Like Cap'n Bob?"

"Now you know you like Bob. He's treated us real nice. I think a lot of him. That boat he's got's worth a lot of money, too. You should give Bob more of a chance."

More of a chance? If Chastity only knew what she had been through with Cap'n Bob, she would murder him in his sleep. Amber could never tell her mother, but not being able to do so was painful. Bob had never gotten to Amber, but it wasn't for lack of trying. The last thing he needed was "more of a chance."

"As long you like him, I guess, and I don't have to live with him."

Chastity drew her daughter toward her and hugged her tight.

"You're a good girl Amber. I do love you so. Let's go to sleep now."

"I'll go back to the couch. I need to unwind." Amber kissed her mother on the forehead.

"O.K., honey. I want you to have whatever you want. G'night."

Amber pulled the bedroom door shut behind her and walked softly to the folded-out couch. All at once, Cash's face filled her thoughts.

That he hadn't come back to the club confused her. She was never rejected. The slightest hint of interest from her would send any man instantly into the chase.

Why hadn't he come back?

Chapter Three

C ash was up early. He moved from the couch to his reading chair and propped his feet on the ottoman. His house was friendly and lived in, with no sign of a decorator. Cash's own eclectic tastes were reflected throughout, united by his appreciation of things beautiful and fine.

From his reading chair, a large, low, overstuffed armchair, he had an expansive view through floor-to-ceiling windows on the south and east walls, past a few close trees, across a well-tended lawn and low shrubs, to an open grassy plain dotted with mesquite. The lawn, the shrubs, and the trees were not formally landscaped, but they were well cared for and had the human hand about them. There were no fences, not another building in sight, only the open countryside and the immense Texas sky.

The first light of the sun painted the eastern plains pink. Then, shortly after 6 a.m., Cash reached for the phone and called Leland.

"Hi there," he said when Leland answered.

"Are you alone?" Leland asked.

"Did you think I was going to take her home with me?"

"There were odd winds blowing. What do I know?" Leland was up, ready, a morning person.

"She was a gem, that's true," Cash said. "But have you ever known me to do anything like that?"

"No. But so what," Leland said. "I've got some grapefruit. Did you eat at all yesterday?"

"Salad at Henry's. I'm starving. You wanna come over here or want me to come over there?"

"Why don't you come on over here," Leland said.

"O.K. I had a hard time last night after I got home. I kept thinking about what happened when I played. I know I was terrible, and the crowd didn't like it. But usually I have some idea how things should have gone right. You know, how they should have worked if they were going to work at all. But when I got home and was sitting here, I realized I only had an idea about how things were wrong, no idea what would make them right. You know what I mean?"

"Mmm," Leland said. "Not yet."

"The only salient point of the night was what the singer, Amber, said. She said it was all about the show you see from the stage. And I think she's right. That is probably the measure. Which made me realize I didn't have any idea what was supposed to happen if it had gone well. I had no idea about any of that."

"She's no fool. Come get some grapefruit, and we'll keep going." Leland knew Cash listened carefully to what he said, so

Leland was careful about what he said.

"I'll be over in a few." Cash hung up the phone and stood up from the chair.

Leland Carruthers took his morning walk along the beach. It had populated overnight with families in campers and tents, side by side, facing the Gulf. It looked to him like a miserable way to spend a weekend, but these were city-trapped folks, for the most part, who were grateful for anything outdoors.

Leland walked along the makeshift road that had grown between the campers and the gentle rise of the dunes.

He was puzzled by this present turn of events, and about Amber especially. She had put a topping on the affairs of last night. It was the first time Leland had seen Cash without a base, like a leaf in a creek, bouncing here and there. He understood Cash's discomfort but didn't understand the reason.

* * *

Horton Callaway looked at himself over the solid brass fixtures in the mirror of his paneled-mahogany and green-marble bathroom, a markedly masculine and elegant bathroom.

He had an industrial-grade hangover from the Cognac and felt like he had been in a 24-hour airplane crash. Inside the medicine drawer, he found some pain relievers and took three. He was nauseated, his head hurt, and he was irritable. He soaked a towel in hot water and draped it over his nearly bald head, and then he walked to his clothes closet. There was a knock at his bedroom suite door.

"Raymond?" Horton called out.

"Yes, sir. Are you going to want breakfast?" Raymond, Horton's house manager, asked as he waited and listened at the door.

"I suppose. I feel rotten. What do you do for a hangover?"

"It goes away after a while, but there is some colorful lore, as well as fancy recipes, for dealing with it. Would you like to try any?"

"Yes. All of it. I'll be out in a minute."

"There are some pain relievers in the medicine drawer."

"I found them. Thanks. Did Charles stay here or did he go home?"

"He went home. He said he'd be back late morning."

"O.K. I'm thinking of driving to Corpus, maybe see Leland Carruthers."

"Driving to Corpus Christi, sir? Today?" Raymond caught himself just before he gave away his surprise.

"I thought I might enjoy it."

"I'll give Charles a ring, then."

* * *

Amber called the Partaway house at 8:00, again at 8:15, then at 8:20, then 8:30, then 8:35.

"Who do you keep calling, Amber?" Chastity was barely up, shuffling along in her robe and slippers. "I couldn't sleep, you pounding on the phone every five minutes."

"I woke you up by my hitting the keypad on the phone?"

"I'm a light sleeper."

"I'll say."

"Who are you calling?"

"I'm calling the club I played at last night."

"Why?"

"My, uh, wallet, ID. I left it. But the owner's not there. He said he would be in this morning, though." Amber pressed the number again without looking at the phone.

Chastity opened the refrigerator door and took out two grapefruits. "You want something to eat, honey?"

* * *

"These are fresh. Ruby Reds from the valley. Off your ranch." Leland sliced the grapefruit and laid it on a plate on the dining table in front of Cash.

The kitchen/dining area of the apartment was cozy. Leland loved to cook, and Cash had expanded his father's motel kitchen and filled it with expensive commercial-grade appliances by having the manager pretend it was an ordinary upgrade for the motel. The ruse was transparent, but no one said anything about it.

"This is the time for them." Cash covered the grapefruit with a layer of sugar and pulled the meat out with a serrated spoon.

Leland salted his and began to eat. "I'll make some toast in a minute." He waited for Cash to speak.

After a few seconds Cash said, "So, when Amber said that—about watching the show from the stage—I thought, she has a solid idea of the way this is supposed to work, and I don't. I'm not saying I agree with her, you know. Only that it was obvious I was missing something. And what I missed might very well be what she understood."

"She was good," Leland said.

Leland walked to the sink and put his empty grapefruit rind down the 2.5-horsepower commercial disposal in the sink. It pulverized in three seconds. "She had real power," he said.

"So when I got home I kept thinking about her. And, I—it made me want to get back up onstage again. See if she's right. So. Do you think I should call her?" he asked.

Leland looked quizzically at Cash. "If all this 'I'm missing something' is a cover for wanting to call a pretty girl, then no. Otherwise—"

"No. Yes. O.K. In a way, it is. It is. I take the point. But it's more about performing. Learning to sing. Amber could be a big part of that, I think." Cash pulled out the last bit of the grapefruit and looked at it on the end of his spoon.

* * *

"My gosh, this is delicious. Please have one," Diana Copeland said. She was standing on the bridge of the *Marianna*, twenty-two miles off the west coast of Mexico, eating from a platter of grapefruit slices that the galley had sent up with toast, coffee, bananas, and orange juice.

"We took them on in San Diego. They came out on the chopper with you. They're from Texas, down in the Rio Grande Valley. Ruby Reds, they're called." Captain Lars Heldstrum helped himself to one of the slices on the platter. The bow of the *Marianna* pierced the cobalt waters of the Pacific. The beautiful all-white, yacht-like cruise ship was cruising at 20.5 knots on a calm sea in a clear sky.

"Lars? What's the biggest ship you know of?" Diana ate another slice of the grapefruit.

"Aside from the *Titanic*?"

"That's sailing now," she said.

"Well, I don't know all of them. Someone tells me they're building a 250,000-tonner, with eight stories on her and rooms for 5,600. That may be the biggest I heard of. You thinking of building the world's biggest ship, ma'am?"

Diana gazed to the starboard porthole. They were surrounded by the sea, no land in sight. "No. Not a ship, Lars, not exactly a ship."

Diana took another grapefruit slice and salted it with the silver shaker on the tray. "I think Cash has Ruby Reds on his ranch somewhere," she said as she popped the bite into her mouth. "By the way, the satellite phones were awful last night, I meant to tell you. Very frustrating."

* * *

Amber held the receiver to her ear and let the phone ring twenty times.

"God. Why doesn't he have an answer thing?" she moaned as she put the phone down.

"What was in the wallet?" Chastity ate a spoonful of grapefruit. "Are you upset?"

"That guy told me he would be there this morning, sure."

"I know, honey, you just said that. But he's not. Maybe he forgot it was Sunday. I did. Eat some of this. It's really good. They're fresh in from the valley." Chastity held out the grapefruit to Amber.

"You mean you think he may not be coming in at all?" Amber could not hide the tension in her voice.

"Well, sweetie, it's Sunday. Lots of clubs don't open on Sunday."

Amber slouched down in the chair and absently took the grapefruit from her mother, took a bite, and swirled it around in her mouth, not swallowing for a long time. She pushed the rest of the grapefruit around the plate with her index finger.

* * *

"I really can't eat this," Horton said, as he pushed the grapefruit away and shoved his chair from the table. He leaned the chair back on its two rear legs as Charles came in through the servants' door.

"Morning, Mr. Callaway, sir. How you feeling this morning?"

Horton looked at Charles through "don't ask" slits for eyes.

"Could I make you a drink? A mimosa, perhaps?" Raymond asked. "A bit of the 'hair of the dog?'"

"Oh God, no. I don't want to ever drink again. Have we got some toast or something? Here, take this grapefruit away, will you? It's about to make me throw up."

Raymond bused the bowl with the grapefruit in it. "I'll put on some toast."

"Charles, how far is it to Corpus from here? By car. I mean, in time, how long a drive is it?"

"Corpus? We could be there in three and a half, maybe four hours. It's a couple hundred miles, but the road is good all the way. Did you want to go along the coast?"

"I don't know. I was thinking of driving myself."

Unseen by Horton, Charles looked at Raymond, who looked back as if to say, Don't ask me what he's thinking. The only time they had seen Horton drive had been down to the beginning of the long circular drive on the estate grounds, where he had smashed the front of the car into one of the massive pilasters that held the gate. The idea of Horton driving himself two hundred and ten miles to Corpus Christi was unimaginable.

* * *

"It's intriguing," Leland said as he took the empty grapefruit rind from the table. Cash went to the bread bin, took out two pieces of rye, and began to butter them.

"Intriguing?"

"I expect you're serious about the singing part." Leland dropped the rind in the drain and zapped it.

Cash put the bread in the toaster. He knew Leland's lingering question.

"Pop, I could have a daughter her age."

"So, that's a problem?"

"Not by itself. But she would have to have a lot to say."

"She had a lot to say last night." Leland took the hot toast from the oven, juggling the pieces on his fingertips as he went to the counter. "Jam?"

Cash nodded. "True. In her own way, yes, she did. Like I said, smart."

* * *

"How can I be so stupid?" Amber stood up suddenly from the table and paced around the tiny kitchen. "Of course he's not going to be there on Sunday. I should have made him go get it right then. Can you take me out there, Mom?"

"I told Bob I would meet him at the wharf around noon. I could take you after, but if he's closed ... what ...?"

"He may be there but not answering the phone. Maybe cleaning up or something." Amber was trying not to plead.

"O.K. O.K. If you really want to go, I can take you after I meet Bob at Cap'n Jack's on the wharf."

Amber gave her mother a disproportionate thank-you hug,

then a big kiss on the cheek.

* * *

"Where's the phone down here?" Horton looked around the servants' kitchen, unfamiliar territory.

Raymond pointed to a wall-mounted phone next to a large pantry door. Horton spread some jam on the toast, walked to the phone, and dialed Leland Carruthers, who was standing next to Cash's Jeep, saying goodbye, when he heard the phone ring.

"I'm going out to 517 for a while," Cash said as he started the Jeep. "I'll catch up with you later." Leland waved and darted for the phone.

"Leland, it's Horton," Horton said, as he took a bite of toast.

"Hi, Horton. You're up early of a Sunday." Leland took off his flip-flop sandals and settled into the couch in his front room.

"I want to come down there and see you. Excuse me for eating this toast in your ear."

"Is something wrong?"

"No. But I want to talk to you sooner rather than later. Can I buy you lunch?"

"Sure, I suppose. I was gonna go down to Cap'n Jack's on the wharf. You know that place?"

"Can I get the chopper in there?" Horton took another bite. Raymond and Charles looked at each other, relieved.

"Well, no Horton, you can't get the chopper in Cap'n Jack's, but…"

"I know that, Leland. I mean somewhere close."

"The heliport at the derrick yard. I'll pick you up."

"No, that's O.K. I'll send Charles down with the car."

"It's only a half-mile away from Cap'n Jack's, I could—"

"No. I might want to go out and see Cash anyway."

Charles looked at Raymond and rolled his eyes. This was more like it—crazy and extravagant.

"What time?" Horton asked.

"Suit yourself," Leland said. "Anytime around midday."

"O.K. I'll see you between 12:30 and 1:00 at Cap'n Jack's there on the wharf."

"Good. It'll be fun then. That's when the boats come in with the morni—" Horton had hung up. Leland looked at the phone and smiled, shook his head, and put the handset back on its cradle. He had no sooner put it down than the phone rang again.

"Leland, Hank," Henry Biggins said through the phone.

"Good morning Mr. Biggins. How're you?"

"I'm good. I was gonna come out to PA in a bit, wanted to see if you wanted to go out to Cap'n Jack's, get some peel-'em-and-eat-'ems?"

"Shoot Hank, just made a date for lunch. But it's at Jack's, so maybe I'll see ya. What'd'ja think of the boy last night?"

Henry paused. "He was, ummm, that took a lot of guts. I don't think I could have done that."

"I thought the other singer was good. Amber." Leland nodded slightly, acknowledging Henry's meaning.

"Right, Amber. Yes, she was. Well, so, I'll see you around

lunch at Jack's and wave," Biggins said.

* * *

"God, it seems like we only finished eating and another meal starts," Diana said, as the steward took the breakfast tray and announced brunch in the main salon. "That's what amazes me about this floating hotel business. All people want to do is float, eat, and walk around."

Lars Helmstrund called the first mate to the wheel.

"Are you going below, Ms. Copeland?"

"I really get tired of all this food, don't you, Lars?"

"Sometimes, yes, ma'am."

"There's a place Cash and I go sometimes in Port Aransas, in Texas, not too far from his ranch, called Cap'n Jack's. They bring shrimp in from the bay, boil them up, and serve them in paper baskets. You peel the skin off and eat them with a big glass of beer or iced tea. You think our passengers would ever go for something like that?

"Actually, no, ma'am."

This made Diana laugh. "It's as if life goes from meal to meal, then people book these cruises that are nothing but a nonstop meal. Those Ruby Reds were a welcome relief. It's good to have the occasional love affair."

Diana's owner's suite was immediately below the flying bridge and spanned port to starboard above the two luxury suites immediately below it. Only a bit smaller than Cash's ranch house, it was professionally decorated with fine carpets and furniture, thematically nautical to the extent that it all blended perfectly with the ship's curved walls, low ceiling, and rounded windows.

Diana sat at her desk and fired up her computer. It was her link to her offices in Fort Lauderdale, Houston, and Genoa, Italy. She checked her email, read the *New York Times* and *La Repubblica*, and then pulled up the plans for the largest floating structure ever built, "The *Mariner*: A Seagoing Superstructure."

The idea had come to her over the past five years, as she became more familiar with the habits and patterns of the sea-cruise set. She decided all the patrons wanted to do was float and eat, to drift aimlessly. She had learned the ports of call were secondary. Many times only a handful of the passengers went ashore. They preferred the protection of the boat, the casino, the pool, reading in the sun, or strangest of all, shopping.

When she started the cruise line with a boat she converted from a freighter, she installed state-of-the-art theatres for movies and live acts, casinos with the full complement of gaming and dozens of slot machines, and lush, overstuffed restaurants serving world-class food. There was only a small shop for incidentals, such as toiletries and the occasional item of apparel.

To her surprise, she found the little store was a regular habitat for the passengers, a social gathering spot, so she began stocking more and more items and increasing the size of the store. She added more goods and amenities and finally started adding more stores. Soon almost one complete deck was taken up with various shops offering everything from jewelry to electronics. She thought sometimes, only half-kidding herself, she might even be able to sell gardening supplies.

That notion grew until she dreamed up the *Mariner*. She thought if she could launch a huge vessel somewhere in the Western Hemisphere, one that could follow the currents of the ocean, drifting around and through exotic waters and places, while always staying outside the twelve-mile limit, it wouldn't be so much a ship as it would be an island, one with a bit of control over where it went. This floating hotel-apartment could be home to tens of thousands of people—maybe even hundreds of thousands. The ocean would impose almost no limit on its size.

Theoretically, the number of people would be limited only by the vessel's structural integrity. Since she intended the craft to drift, many of the usual problems of naval architecture were irrelevant. It would not need to slice through the waves. It would ride like a cork, with three quarters submerged. It would never need to maneuver close to a dock—it would be a dock. It could carry great volumes of different fuels that might last for years, especially with solar and wind additions. It could serve as a refueling station for her other ships if needed and create new routes. It could even have a landing strip for small planes. All in service to its center of apartments, casinos, and shopping malls. She had dreamed repeatedly of all she could do with such a magnificent idea.

Copeland worked diligently in secret with a design team, and after two years, she finally had a plan for building the enormous barge/island. That plan sat before her now on her computer screen.

She looked at the architectural drawings showing a silhouette of the floating condominiums drawn against a low sun across the water. To her it was beautiful. A floating world. Limitless possibilities. Now she needed to raise the money to get it under way.

Her first pass at the numbers indicated she needed somewhere around $500 million U.S., but the business plan kept growing until it was close to $800 million. If at $500 million the project was extravagant, at $800 million it was pure folly.

When Diana proposed the idea to her chief financial officer, she laughed and then became concerned when she realized Diana was serious. The CFO showed Diana the impossibilities of the venture's economics and the peril to the existing enterprise, but Diana did not retreat. Instead, she called Horton Callaway.

She knew Horton had made close to a billion dollars, personally, by staying shoulder to shoulder with Cash as he managed Cash's fortunes, but it wasn't Horton's wealth that Diana was interested in. She was looking for someone to say yes to her.

With his business sense and his capacity for raising money from a group of investors, Diana was sure Horton could put together a plan. She did not know of Horton's decision to leave Cash, but if she had, it would have made no difference.

* * *

Chastity Fanfare changed her name and her life when she found out at thirteen that she was pregnant with Amber. Chastity was christened Sue Ellen Bindleford, part of an itinerant family that worked the citrus groves in the Rio Grande Valley of Texas.

Her sex life began at twelve with the boys of the fields, and she actively dated, as she euphemistically called it, every weekend. Like Amber, she was a young beauty. Amber's father, a Mexican farm worker, disappeared quickly back into Mexico when Chastity told him she was pregnant.

Chastity's mortified parents were cruelly abusive emotionally, so at thirteen and a half, Chastity ran away and set up a living space in a house trailer that had been left behind, along with a little money, by one of her boyfriends, in the town of Falfurrias. It was close enough to the citrus groves and her farm worker friends but far enough away from her mother, father, and sisters to make life livable. She learned to smile broadly when in danger and to remain still. She also changed her name to Chastity Fanfare and fiercely maintained its verity in the face of incredulity. That change, along with kerosene lamps, a water well, no phone, and a wood-burning stove, kept her off the grid, and out of sight to anyone she wanted to avoid.

Because of her beauty and her bright, toothy smile, she attracted many men, all of whom paid regular visits to her trailer. These young men always gave her a bit of money, enough for Chastity to get by. It never occurred to Chastity that such a life would be looked upon as prostitution. She could not have thought of herself that way.

When Amber was born, Chastity, in all her youth, moved into motherhood. Fortunately for Amber, Chastity loved being a mother and showered her daughter with constant affection and encouragement.

Amber was a lovely child, mild in temperament, alert, responsive, happy, and trustful. She had her father's sad eyes and her mother's sensuous lips, her father's square shoulders and her mother's curved hips. The most beautiful aspects of the Latino and Caucasian had come together in her.

There was from her first consciousness something special about Amber that was unique to her. When she walked across a room, it was a fluid, nonstop motion that looked almost like a dance. Her small but perfect figure made her carriage agile and quick, but her ease and confidence imparted an effortless slow-motion glide and a calm, secure, and precise balance.

Amber did not jiggle, titter, or bounce like her mother; she was relaxed and mysterious, always beyond reach, like smoke slowly rising. Instead of a wide, bright, come-hither smile, she had a knowing, simple, seductive grin. Her huge brown eyes conveyed a mischievous sophistication that was playful and alluring.

The two women looked more like sisters than mother and daughter as they bumped about in the dilapidated pickup truck on its way to Port Aransas.

"So where is this Partaway House?" Chastity asked.

Amber was staring out the window at the windsurfers hopping the small waves in the shallows of Corpus Christi Bay.

"Not house. Just the Partaway. House makes it sound like a drug rehab center."

"O.K. The Partaway. Where is it?"

"I think it's over there." Amber pointed out the window to the southwest.

"Just 'over there?'" Chastity was exasperated by her own incompetence.

"Well, I don't know. I was riding, so I wasn't paying...I mean, it's in this kind of town place, sort of by itself." Amber didn't know. She was hoping her mother could figure it out for her. Such a reasonable expectation was, in this case, wildly misplaced.

Where Amber's disorientation was a shrinking aspect of her youth, with Chastity it was a continuous worldview. The two women had as much chance of finding the Partaway as they did of levitating.

"Don't worry, baby. We'll find it." Chastity said, calming herself as much as Amber. "We'll go there after we go to Cap'n Jack's. Somebody there'll know where it is."

* * *

Cash was sitting atop well 517A, looking toward the gulf, thinking.

He wanted to use the quiet contemplation to decide whether to pursue singing and playing, whether to call Amber Fanfare, and whether to join a band, all notions that, in the context of who he was, were bizarrely irrational, if not to Cash, then to everyone around him. Absurd in the extreme.

But it was his father who came to mind.

As Cash stood on the stage last night, he had felt his father's powerful influence. And afterward, when he was standing outside, when Amber Fanfare had joined them, his dad looked at him in a way that conveyed an understanding of the forces at work.

The rails pointed into the sky, and the clack of the machine as the car pulled forward made a little thump on the bottom of the tub and his hands held the chrome bar in front of him and he looked skyward and then the tracks were gone and there was nothing but sky and they were perched looking out at all the horizons and land and then they were looking straight down from a hill of wooden lattices of peeling white paint and the car picked up speed and hurled down in a clatter with screeching steel wheels. Leland's arms reached around and held him as the gravity started its increase, then the bottom was there and the speed and it was like the feeling you get on an elevator and Cash laughed then and he laughed now and then he was trembling on a precarious perch and he was standing on his father's shoulders and looking into a pit of fire and burning debris, hot, molten, glowing with white sparks drifting up into the hot afternoon and across the pit, on the other side looking down was another young boy, three years old and standing on his father's shoulders, looking into the same pit and the father made a motion as if he were going to throw him into the pit, a feint, a tease, and the young boy was terrified and screamed and grabbed the crown of his father's head so the father was embarrassed and walked away with the screaming child, away from the crowd, dropping the child from his shoulders with a lariat swing of one arm, untwisting to the ground, to walk like a man. Leland held his son's hand and his fingers were enormous and wrapped around the little fingers and Cash could see what it meant to be good and have good, that his dad was not giving something that could be turned into a joke, a tease, a taunt, but that it was a complete and unobstructed gift and when they came to the top of the next lattice-work hill and the car slowed a bit there was another feeling in his stomach as the car came over the top and the next hill was shallower and not so terrifying and the car was floating on gravity instead of being pulled down. Leland lifted a bit in his seat as they rounded the top and then there was the smell of automobiles, and beer, and perfume, and caramel popcorn, and hot dogs, and his dad's smile, that went out and down and across the next little valley in the roller coaster as it coasted and rolled to a stop when his dad picked him up and looked into his eyes and there was that loving connection, wise and clear and bright like a sling reaching under his arms, powerful hands lifting and holding him and taking him out of the car, laughing and laughing and laughing. There was no "My, aren't we getting heavy," but an "I will lift you up and you will fly and never coast to a stop, you are the light of my being as I am the light of hers and his before her, and it is the light we are seeing that is shining from the tiny cracks, opening them, dissolving them, prying them apart and shining out, and this light is not a collection of light but a reflection of light."

Cash drove the white Jeep along the streets of Port Aransas, surprised to see a helicopter, much like his own, he thought, beginning a descent into the derrick yard beyond the wharf about a mile from Cap'n Jack's.

Chapter Four

Cap'n Bob Reno backed the thirty-three-foot Bertram Sport Fisher into the slip adjacent to the pier seating area that jutted from the rear of Cap'n Jack's Seafood Restaurant. Most everyone on the pier knew Bob and his boat, the *Dolphin*. No flags were flying from her this midday, which was unusual for the *Dolphin*. It meant the whole morning's fishing had produced nothing. Bob was out of sorts.

He cleared the bilge and shut the twin diesels off as his deckhand jumped from the ship and lashed the stern to the pier cleats.

Leland, who was watching all this from one of the tables at Cap'n Jack's, was familiar with Bob Reno and made it a point to stay away from him.

Leland was more interested in the arrival of the helicopter as it disappeared behind a row of buildings and landed in the derrick yard. From the corner of his eye, he saw Cash walk through the open door into Cap'n Jack's.

Leland gave his son a wave.

As Cash walked up, Leland said, "Horton's on his way in."

"Here?" Cash sat down at the table.

"Yep. Did ya see the chopper?"

"I thought that was it. What's he want? You know?"

"Nope. That was him calling when you left. Said he was comin' down, wanted to talk to me."

"To you? Think I should leave?" Cash stood up again. "How's he getting here from the yard?"

"He had Charlie drive the Merc down. I offered to pick him up, but he—Horton baffles me. Yeah, you should probably get lost. Lemme see what's up."

"You goin' back home after this?"

Leland nodded. "Plan to, unless Horton comes up with a showstopper." Leland pointed to the front door. Horton's black-windowed Mercedes slithered up and parked across the street.

"I'll go through the bar," Cash said and quickly walked away.

The restaurants and bars lining the bay-water marina were contiguous, each with their own bay terrace, so it was easy to see and travel from one into the next. In the next-door bar, Bob Reno and his two customers sat at a small table. He poured a pitcher of beer between the three of them and watched Leland and Cash.

Reno recognized Cash from around Jack's but didn't know—or care—who he was, and he avoided contact so he wouldn't have to say hello. Behind Cash, Reno saw Horton Callaway coming through the front door of Cap'n Jack's. If he made Cash for a local nobody, he was sure that Horton Callaway was somebody important, seriously rich, and looking it. Light gabardine pants, tight-knit monogrammed polo shirt, alligator loafers and belt: all meant money to Reno. He watched as Callaway went over to Leland Carruthers and exchanged hellos. He wondered which of the two men was the most powerful.

Cash stood outside the bar entrance next to Jack's and looked up and down the street. It was loaded with tourists carrying beach gear and heading for the Gulf or else wandering aimlessly in and out of T-shirt and souvenir shops. Despite its setting, Port Aransas was not a pretty town, and the tourists and cheap shops added a tawdriness.

The transient nature of the townsfolk was due to Port Aransas's location as much as its history. The Texas Gulf Coast, one of the most corrosive environments in the world, had a constant breeze from the east that carried salt and rust-breeding moisture. This, combined with regular hurricanes, ensured that no building lasted long. As a result, buildings were designed to "fall down and not be bothered with," as the saying went. It was easier and cheaper to remove and replace a collapsed tacky prefab than it was to try to fight the environment by maintaining an expensive high-technology dwelling. Port Aransas was thus a cluster of low-rise, essentially disposable structures housing everything from residents to the fire station.

Tourists tortured the town further with disrespect and constant litter, rococo on the ubiquitous rust and rot. Everything was dinged, bent, broken, or falling apart. Cash had once tried to instill a community spirit in the locals, but he eventually gave up. The locals didn't care, and most of them weren't that local.

There was no Cap'n Jack. It was a conceit of a migrant couple from Boston who had come to south Texas to escape the harsh northern winters and make money running a generic bar and restaurant that could have been anywhere. The couple happily gouged as deep as they could for grade-B hamburgers and sandwiches. Even the local Gulf shrimp, the peel-'em-and-eat'-ems, although delicious, were not actually fresh or local. They were frozen on the boats that caught them and then routed through New Orleans.

The town could have been at least a charming, if not a beautiful, seaside resort. Instead it was grimy and depleted by the tourists, by the wind, and by the town's main industry, the construction of offshore oil derricks that drilled in the Gulf.

Cash jumped and backed close to the wall of Cap'n Jack's to avoid a pickup truck that came a touch too close to him as it turned into a lot and parked.

Inside the truck, Chastity and Amber gathered a few things together to make their exit. Both women put on their respective faces for dealing with the stares they were sure to encounter. They had refined two modes of social intercourse: attract attention, or avoid it. Today they would use the latter. Dressed in jeans and shirts, they were still more provocative than the local beach bunnies who bounced around in their tiny bikinis.

It took the two women a few seconds to rev up their unique countenances to operating speed. Chastity's armor was the disarming smile she flashed, strobe-like, along with a quick disconnect that reduced everything to a casual encounter. Amber's was a distant stare, making no contact at all, focusing on an unseen planet. As the two women alighted from the truck, heads turned. Women were startled; men were interested.

They crossed the street and walked toward Jack's. Cash recognized Amber, smiled, and walked toward her.

Amber had perimeter radar she monitored to know when people, especially men, were approaching. She saw a hazy, unidentifiable image of Cash from this sensor, and as an avoidance, turned to her mother and pretended to be deep in conversation.

"Amber?" Cash called out.

Amber and Chastity stopped. Amber blinked twice. She did not recognize Cash. This was an adult, far from a contemporary. What could he possibly want? She stood disconnected, child watching grownup, as he approached. It must be someone for her mom. How did he know her name?

As Cash walked toward the women, he was backlit from the sun and its reflection on the water. His long legs in lanky stride had the same grace Amber possessed when she moved, and Amber instinctively recognized it, recognized part of herself coming toward her, something familiar. She blocked the sun from her eyes with her hand.

Then she saw him. She was surprised. This was a grown man, a grownup man, old enough to be her father, maybe even her grandfather.

"I thought that was you," Cash said, now fully revealed by

Amber's shading hand. Amber was motionless, held in the awful realization of her fondest desire, coming true in exactly the wrong place, at the wrong time.

"Hi," Chastity said, much to Amber's dismay. "I'm Chastity Fanfare." The remark was carefully inflected to imply kinship with Amber, but not to clarify it. Chastity wasn't sure she wanted to be a mom right now. She could see this was no ordinary stranger, no usual man. She grinned her broadest, most outsize grin, and extended her hand.

Cash shook Chastity's hand. When she felt Cash's smooth hand, a gentlemen's hand, she was certain he was someone special but could not identify the reason. Her grin was pasted on now, connected to nothing, and she would leave it there until she got to the next need for response.

Cash looked at Amber. "You remember me from last night?"

Amber was not hiding behind her mother's legs and sucking her thumb, but she may as well have been.

"Sure. You were great." Amber realized just how tall Cash was, just how much he towered over her. She saw a look in his eyes and remembered why she had been so taken and what was so familiar. Power.

"I'm Cash," Cash said to Chastity, looking directly in her eyes. As he looked he saw a confusion, a deep carefulness behind her eyes, saw the smile as a mask.

Cash had long depended on his insight into the likes of Chastity to offer help when it was needed or to stay out of trouble if it was imminent. He smiled a sincere return to Chastity's goofy grin, but again it was Amber who felt the spark off of it, not Chastity.

Whatever this insight was that Cash possessed, it was a leveler between Amber and Cash, parity. She shared it with him, and it was erotic beyond any feeling she had known. The slight, knowing smile of unaffected warmth resulted in a soft and gentle fold that ran down one cheek, from the side of his nose to the upturned corner of his mouth. It was almost singularly attractive physically. Amber nearly gawked, but she stopped. Amber had not planned on reuniting with Cash with her mother around.

Chastity knew it when she saw it, knew passion and lust and sexual attraction. Amber may have planned on keeping Cash a secret from her mother, but that plan was useless now. Chastity knew everything in her daughter's mind. She sharply and suddenly recoiled from it. She was confused by the revelation.

"What brings you out to PA?" Cash asked.

"I'm meeting my fiancée," Chastity said.

Fiancée? Did she say fiancée, Amber thought. She had never heard her mother use a word like that in her life. Did she mean Cap'n Bob?

"He's a boat captain. He owns the *Dolphin*. We was gonna meet him here. Maybe you know him? Cap'n Bob Reno. He's sorta famous around here for fishin'."

"No, I guess not. Not much of a fisherman." Cash turned to Amber. "I'm glad to see you. I thought about you quite a bit last night. I was going to call you."

Amber was panicked now. She needn't have been. If anyone her own age said such things, they were obviously being romantic. Cash meant only what he was saying. For him, it was a remark free of subtext or hidden meaning. Amber looked at her mother.

"You picked up my spirits," he said. He turned again to Chastity. "I took a guest turn with Amber's band last night and laid an egg the size of Houston. Amber rescued me." Then back to Amber. "How did the rest of the show go?"

"Good, I think. I think he wants me back."

Unseen by Amber, Henry Biggins was bounding across the street toward them. As he got close, he called out.

"I see you found him," Biggins said to Amber as hello.

Amber did not want her mother or Cash to know she had been looking for him. She stood there waiting, looking at Cash, then her mother, then down the street at the passing people. She would wait. She would say nothing. She could think of nothing to say anyway, but she would give nothing away.

"Henry. Hi. Found who?" Cash said.

Henry Biggins saw the quick rise and fall of Amber's chest.

"Oh." Biggins looked first at Amber. Inscrutable. He turned to Cash. "Hard to say," he said. "Each other, I guess. You gonna start a band?"

"I don't know if Amber's band will work with me again after last night," Cash said.

"Sure they would," Amber said, relieved, happy for the new tack.

"I don't know where we'd play. Folks at the Partaway might

shoot me if I went back," Cash said.

"No. You're wrong. You weren't bad like that," Amber stated flatly. She was on her own level field now, serious, an expert.

The authority of the remark, the suddenness of the change in Amber, surprised her mother, went beyond her range of comprehension. Chastity could not imagine speaking to someone of Cash's stature and age with such confidence and control, to be sure of herself so completely. A second ago Amber was practically speechless, an embarrassed child around one of her parent's friends.

Suddenly Amber had become a frequency of light beyond the range of her mother's seeing; whatever Amber had said was unknown to her, whatever was happening was the result of supernatural magic. If her mother hadn't been smiling inanely, she would have been slack-jawed.

Amber continued, "You were scared. So you scared the crowd. That happens. That's not the same as bad."

Henry thought this a good place to back out. He didn't want to comment on Cash's performance. "You come down for lunch?" he said to all three.

"We come down to meet Cap'n Bob that owns the *Dolphin*," Chastity blurted out. She put her arm around Amber, but Amber didn't feel it. She was looking intently at Cash. "Y'all wanna join us?" Chastity offered.

"No, I can't," Cash said. "My dad's in there having a talk with someone, and I don't want to bother them, which I'm afraid I would."

Biggins didn't know Bob Reno personally, but he had been warned to give him wide berth. "I think I'm gonna get a basket of peel-'em-and-eat-'ems and take it down to the beach. But thanks." Henry saluted the threesome and backed toward the front door of Jack's. "You comin' out to the Partaway again, Cash?"

"Not today. I might come out tomorrow for lunch."

"Braised short ribs. Special. Nice to see you, Amber. You too—?" Biggins nodded toward Chastity.

"Chastity," she said. "So nice to know you." Chastity smiled, still weird to the moment.

"Chastity," Henry said, and disappeared through the door.

"I'm not trying to jack you up." Amber took a step and was free of her mother's embrace. "But you could sing if you want."

"Honey, we better go in. Bob's inside, I think."

"You're a good spirit, Amber." Cash was trying to sort out the tensions between Amber and her—what? Sister? "I wish I was that brave. It was good to see you. You have a good lunch." Cash shoved both hands into his pockets, an attempt to close the conversation. "I hope we can talk another time, Amber."

Chastity started to back away, but Amber didn't move. "You don't need to be any braver. You need to meet Buni," Amber said, refusing to break contact. "You want some help singing and about music, Buni's the best."

"Amber. We should—" Chastity tugged at her shirt.

"Mom. Please." Amber meant nothing by the remark, but it was a surprise to Cash.

Cash tried to reconcile Chastity as being Amber's mother. Her mother? She was only a few years older than Amber. Wasn't she?

"I can introduce you to him, if you want. If you're serious, I mean," Amber said, oblivious.

Cash brought himself around to the suggestion from Amber. "This is a teacher?"

"No, Buni's this guy that plays. But he knows a lot. I never got scared like you, but I did some other things, and Buni helped me out with it."

"Sure, I'd like to meet him."

Chastity loved being a mother, but not now. She felt the confusion of her position. She tried to talk to her daughter like a peer, like a sister or a girlfriend, maintain the connection from there.

"We better go in and find Bob. You should come on now, Amber." She began walking away.

But it didn't work. A cord was cut. Amber ignored her. Chastity was in the way. This was her daughter's time. Like so many parents, Chastity had not seen this side of Amber, never suspected it existed, and wasn't sure what it was. She felt a mother's pride, but it was a mixture of sadness and elation that settled upon her as she left Amber with Cash and walked alone into Cap'n Jack's.

Amber watched her mother go and had no idea anything had occurred, other than the new and wonderful fact she was alone with Cash, on her own and free to pursue what she wished to pursue. She was back to normal. She turned back to Cash.

"O.K. When I see Buni, I'll tell him you want to meet him," she said.

"That was your mom?" Cash said.

Amber nodded.

"I thought she was your sister or a girlfriend."

"Well, yeah, she's real young. I mean, she was real young when I was born."

"I was watching both of you get out of the truck and thought how pretty she was. You both were."

"Yeah." Amber was uncertain. She knew she was pretty, that her mom was, too, but then she realized Cash was saying something different. Cash was appreciating her and her mother's beauty in a way that gave it an increase. He was not trying to capture it or to use it for his own ends. Suddenly it thrilled her like no compliment had.

"And yes. I'd like to meet your friend," Cash said.

"Where're you gonna go now?" Amber asked.

"Take a walk along the beach, and then back home."

"You wanna go meet Buni now?"

"Now? No, I can't right now. Maybe we could go later this week sometime."

"But I need to know how to call you or something."

Cash took out a business card and wrote his ranch number on the back.

"That's my office on the front, but I'm never there. That's home on the back, and I've got voicemail." Cash handed it to her.

"I'll call Buni, and then I'll call you," Amber said. "Maybe later today, or something, whatever. So. O.K., then."

Cash held out his hand, but Amber walked to Cash, reached

up, put her arms around his neck, and pressed her cheek to his. She wanted to kiss him full on the mouth, but she knew better. Cash did not return the full embrace but pressed his hands on her shoulders and squeezed. Amber took a small step back, and all the nuances of affection from last night were upon them again. Their individual circles overlapped, and they stood well inside the other's thought. Cash was grateful to Amber for her approval of his efforts. Amber was in the thrall of a powerful attraction that she wasn't sure how to handle.

* * *

The waitress came to the table where Horton and Leland sat and asked for their order. They ordered shrimp and iced tea. The pause gave each man time to adjust. Horton surveyed the room.

The waitress brought two giant paper cups of iced tea. Horton took a sip and squeezed some lemon in it.

The steaming hot shrimp came in two large plastic baskets lined with paper. Horton looked at them, bewildered. Leland picked one up, peeled the shell from it, pulled off the tail, dipped it into a sauce of catsup and horseradish, and ate it. Horton picked one up and tried to peel it, but the peel wouldn't come off except in little pieces. He laid it down on the paper plate in front of him.

"I appreciate your taking the time to see me." Horton struggled with another shrimp. "How do you get this peel to come off like that? You've eaten three, and I still can't get the peel off one."

Leland took the shrimp from Horton and showed him the technique that made the shell come off in one piece. Horton thought it clever.

"Amazing," he said. "Practical-folk skills, hidden to my hundred-thousand-dollar education. I would have starved to death." Horton peeled the shrimp perfectly and popped it into his mouth. "Hey, that's fun." He peeled another and then shifted into seriousness. "I came down to tell you something I've been thinking about and to get your advice. I have to say I've pretty well made up my mind. It may not be so much advice I need, as some kind of validation or—something. I don't quite know."

"O.K. Quite a buildup," Leland said.

"Sorry. Right. What it comes to is this. I've decided, I mean, I think I've decided, to strike out on my own. To leave Sandra Corporation."

Leland looked out at the back bay, at the slips, and at another fishing boat starting up and about to head out. The roar of the motors silenced the conversation for a few seconds.

"It feels like it's time for me to move on," Horton said. "And I'd like to try some things myself. Cash has made me a very rich man, as you know."

"It's understandable."

"I don't quite know what I would do with myself. I never thought I'd be this rich, frankly. And I owe it all to Cash. Which is—that may be the rub. I stood around and swept up all this money that fell off of Cash's truck."

"Oh, I wouldn't—" Leland tried to interject, but Horton

held up his hand.

"No. Weak analogy. I know what you're going to say. I did a lot. I know that. But I wasn't the one making the smart moves. I just tried to stay out of his way and execute his ideas. But I can't help but wonder if I could have done it on my own. I'm only fifty. I can still do a lot with my life. Call some shots on my own."

"If you need to prove something to yourself, I can understand."

"I think a lot of Cash," Horton said. "Like a real friend. He has meant the world to me. I can't walk out on that. I'm not going to walk out on that. But I don't want to run Sandra Corporation anymore."

"I don't think Cash ever knew he was important to you, as a friend, I mean," Leland said.

"That's something else I'm hoping to fix. Maybe, if I'm away from Sandra Corporation, I can open up something different with Cash, be more of a friend, understand more about what the two of you have between you. Maybe even keep up with Cash in some way. Be more side by side with him."

"Fair enough," Leland said.

"I suppose I should head out to the ranch and tell him. Was that where he was going?" Horton asked.

Leland nodded. "Said he was gonna walk the beach a little and then head out there."

"Can I ask one pointed question, Leland? Am I making a mistake? Am I wrong to leave this? This may be the greatest job in the world."

"You know, Horton, the real answer is: I don't know. I think some principles are at work, maybe just one principle, that you and I know very little about. Remember when Cash made that huge Japanese deal, and he made—"

"Remember it well. Changed my life. A genius move."

"Yep. Might interest you to know he didn't even slightly know how that was going to turn out. Cash didn't call that shot. Something else takes hold at times, and it's not you, me, or even the roulette wheel, it's—I don't know what it is—a force, a push, an impulse, a principle at work. I've seen some people confused by it, reduced to rubble, never knew what hit 'em. Then I've seen people easy with it, and things work out the way they wanted. Like Cash. But like I say, I don't figure it for something one can control in the usual way."

Henry Biggins walked up to the table with his own basket of shrimp.

"I won't bother you. I just wanted to say hi, Leland." Henry nodded hello to Leland and then to Horton.

"Oh, hey, Hank. Say hello to Horton Callaway. Horton, Henry Biggins. So, you goin' outside with those?"

"Yeah, gonna walk down the beach and watch the tourists get the tar off their feet." Biggins chuckled.

The Gulf Coast underwater oil deposits routinely washed ashore and left clumps of tar on the beach. Unsuspecting beachgoers would get a quarter-size glob on their feet and then try to wipe it off with a towel, only to have the tar expand until it covered their whole foot, the towel, and usually everything else in a campsite. The locals found the process entertaining to watch.

"Saw Cash outside. He was with the girl that sang last night and her sister or something. I got out o' there without commenting on Cash's performance, though. Anyway, won't bother you. Just wanted to say hi. Nice to meet you, Horton. Get ole Leland here to bring you out to the Partaway, and I'll buy you a beer."

"Pleasure. We'll try to do that sometime," Horton said as Henry walked away. "Cash was here?" Horton looked at Leland.

"Yeah, a few minutes before you got here. I told him I thought you needed some room, and he went back to the ranch, I think."

"Y'all 'ont s'mor ahstee?" the waitress called out as she walked by holding up a pitcher for them to see. Both men waved no, thanks.

"What did he mean, Cash's performance? Did I miss something?" Horton peeled another shrimp and ate it. He was getting good at it.

"Last night. Cash played and sang with a blues band, and it was, how shall I say it, pretty rough. Sort of off-key and all."

"Wait. What—you mean—he sang?" Horton leaned in, curious, alert.

"If you can call it that."

"I didn't know he sang. I knew he played the guitar a little."

"Yeah—well," Leland said.

"Is—does he do this often?" Horton felt there must be something as yet unspoken in Leland's account.

"First time, far as I know. He wants to play some more. Pretty sure of that. I get the feeling he may be thinking of getting in a band."

Horton held the shrimp before his mouth so long the red sauce dropped from it and onto the table, his incredulity unabashed. He grabbed a paper napkin from the chrome holder, wiped up the sauce, and wadded the napkin into the ashtray.

"I know, I know," Leland said. "But there are worse things to do than to trust Cash's instincts."

Horton looked at a passing boat. One of the passengers waved to the restaurant, and five people waved back. He put the shrimp back on his plate.

"Cash told me once not to trust instincts. Intuitions yes, instincts no. This was general advice. Not just aimed at me," Horton said.

"What I mean is, second-guessing Cash has never served me well. Seems as if he's looking for the next thing for himself, is all. Sort of like you are."

"Leland." Horton was trying not to act as amazed as he was. "You can't be telling me Cash Carruthers is going to join a band. He can't do that. This is not a real option for him. Something else, maybe. I know what this is. It afflicts men of Cash's age and wealth. Hot-air balloons. Race cars. Sports teams. He, he… he's… I mean, Cash Carruthers is—even if he could sing, sing great, world-class—you know—I mean, wha—he's not 'joining a band,' Leland. Not possible."

"I don't know what he's going to do. He played and sang with a band last night, which for him was a real reach, and he, uh, I think, he might like to try more. I don't know what it means. But you and I know, Cash doesn't do anything as a hobby. So—."

Horton picked up another shrimp and peeled it slowly. He dipped it in sauce, looked at Leland, and then looked out to the Gulf and shook his head slowly side to side.

"Not in this lifetime," Horton said as he ate the shrimp.

* * *

Amber stood at the rusting wall-mounted pay phone and fed quarters into it. The phone was in a narrow hallway between two flimsy doors to the restrooms. Each door had a sign attached to it made from a paper plate that read OUT OF ORDER, written in crude hand by someone using a big black indelible marker.

"Buni, it's me," she said when Buni Rumble answered the phone at Buck's Bubble Room.

Buck's Bubble Room was a converted mechanics' garage in Surfside, Texas, along one border of the Dow Chemical plant and across the street from Louis's Bar B Q Shack. Buck had started the bar with a moderate insurance settlement after an accident at the chlorine facility of the plant had left him partly disabled.

One Christmas, Buck had decorated the inside of the bar with bubble lights, Christmas tree lights with two-inch fluid-filled extensions on the top of them. When the light heated the fluid, it made bubbles, hence the name. He had crushed different-colored aluminum foil, put it over all the walls, and then finished it all off with a big Christmas tree in the middle of the room. One of the patrons said it looked like the inside of a Christmas present instead of the outside. Another named it Buck's Bubble Room because of the lights, and the name stuck. So did the Christmas tree. Now, twenty years later, it still sat in the center of the twelve tables in the bar—dry, stiff, and highly flammable.

Tucked in the corner was a small stage next to the exit, and next to that the pay phone, where Buni Rumble was standing when he answered Amber's call.

"Hey. Where are you? I just called your mom's," Buni said. Buni had reddish-blond hair in a ponytail, a Fu Manchu moustache, and a gold stud in the lobe of his left ear. He had on his usual outfit of an open-collared shirt, worn outside his khakis, and sandals with colored socks. Today they were yellow.

"I'm down in Port Aransas with her. What're you doing?" she said.

"I'm settin' up for tonight. When're you comin' up?"

"I gotta get a way up there." Amber looked around.

"You ain't got nobody to bring you up?" Buni asked. "You said your mom's with you."

"Yeah, but she's in there with Bob the Slob and some guys from Houston."

"And she can't bring you up?"

"No, Buni she can't. I just said so."

"All right. I'll come get you. Stay there."

"OK. I'll wait outside at Jack's. And why I called is I want you to meet somebody, O.K.?"

"Who? Now?" Buni asked. "Somebody there?"

"No. This person named Cash. He's wanting to get into some music, and I told him about you."

"What's he play?"

"Guitar. But he's not very good at it."

"He sing?"

"Wellll…"

"Write? What's he do?"

"He kind of is different, real weird, but good weird."

"Sounds great, A. He don't play good, don't sing good, don't write. And is good weird. Can't wait."

"Well, you know what I mean. I told him you might help him learn some things like you told me. I can't describe him, but…"

"O.K., baby. I gotta get in the wind if I'm gonna get down there and back. I'll see you at Jack's in a coupla hours. Go kiss Bob the Slob on the mouth for me."

"Buni. Eeewww. Stop that." But Buni had hung up.

Amber went into the bar to the table where her mother, Bob, and the fishermen, two wealthy Houston real estate agents, were sitting. Amber pulled out a chair and sat sideways to the table, leaning the chair back on its rear legs.

"Hey, gorgeous. Wanna beer?" Bob held up the pitcher. Amber shook her head.

"She cain't have no beer in here. She's underage." Chastity smiled at Amber, making a joke. Amber ignored her and looked out to the bay.

"I liked your friend Cash." Chastity said.

This made Amber stand up. "Buni's comin' down to get

me," she said. "I got a job tonight singing up in Surfside, in the Bubble Room."

"Surfside? You won't get home till real late from up there."

"I'll stay in Buni's extra room," Amber said.

Amber knew, and Chastity suspected, there was no extra room at Buni's. It was an odd truce the two women had worked out about the relationship between Buni and Amber two years ago.

"Well," Chastity said. "Pretty soon I guess you can stay wherever you want. I hate to see you grow up so fast."

"I'm gonna wait out front for Buni. I want to get some sun. See you later." She pointedly did not say goodbye to Bob or his friends. Amber walked through the restaurant to get outside and on the way passed Leland and Horton.

Leland didn't see her, but Horton did, and when he did he had a strange sensation. She walked with a confidence that was familiar to him, something that made him watch her all the way across the restaurant and through the door. He couldn't quite put his finger on it, and then it occurred to him: in an odd way she reminded him of Cash.

Chapter Five

O utside, Amber settled down to wait on the bench across from Jack's and next to what the locals laughingly called the city park. It was a small one-block square of struggling grass and crushed white rock, surrounded by a half dozen sun-faded benches. There were no trees. In the center was a plaque on a pedestal, with a walkway to and from it. Amber never looked, but she always assumed the plaque probably read PARK. Amber had chosen a bench that faced the Gulf and was sitting with her legs stretched straight. It was over a hundred degrees and densely humid.

Horton and Leland came out of Jack's and stood next to the Mercedes and its open back door. Horton shook Leland's hand.

"I'll take the chopper out to the ranch and see Cash. I may change my mind between here and there. Just so you know."

"Appreciate that, Horton. I'm sure it will work out, whichever way you turn. Something's bound to happen. I might see you tomorrow. Cash wants me to come up to Houston with him."

Horton folded himself into the Merc. "Take me back to the chopper, Charles. Then you can go back. I'm going out to Mr. Carruthers's from here." He turned to Leland. "Thanks again, Leland," he said as he waved and rolled up the window.

Leland watched the Mercedes pull away, and then he walked down the road to his motel-room home.

Leland was fifth-generation Texan, one of a family of six, with two sisters and a younger brother. His father had run a small liquor store in Dallas, which had helped them make it through the Depression years, while his mother kept house and raised the kids. Leland went through school and completed all but the bar exam in his training to become a lawyer. He met his wife, Marjorie, when she was a nurse at the emergency room of Parkland Hospital in Dallas. They married and moved to Austin, where Leland took a job as a law clerk for a State Senator.

When Marjorie was pregnant with Cash, Leland still had visions of becoming a lawyer with a small practice in Austin, serving legislators and doing some contract law, but when she died shortly after Cash's birth, Leland was so devastated he never took the bar exam.

He moved to San Antonio, eighty miles to the south, and tried to set up a small farm east of the town on a hundred acres of land. He quickly found the land was of little use for growing crops.

It was on this small would-be farm that Leland devoted his life to raising his son. Leland loved Cash intensely and wanted him to live as well and protected as possible. Leland hired himself out on a project-by-project basis for specialized legal research. When things got tough, he sold a small piece of the ranch, and it was from these intermittent sources of income that Leland fashioned a life for himself and his son that allowed him to stay home and care for Cash.

They lived in an old rock farmhouse of four huge rooms and a bath. Each wall had a huge window with views of the surrounding hill country, which was dotted with oaks and alive with deer and quail. The aged house was cold in the winter and hot in the summer; both seasons tended to be mild in the south Texas climate, so the two spent many months of the year outside, taking their meals on an old redwood picnic table, and often as not cooking over an open-wood fire. It would be too misleading to call the conditions camping out, but it was closer to the truth than the reverse.

Their actual physical living conditions didn't matter much, however, since Cash displayed at his earliest sensibility an interest in a life of the mind. Cash loved nothing more than constructing and examining interesting ideas with his father, and conversely, Leland loved to watch his child's mind at work. It was obvious from the first that Cash was prodigious, gifted.

He was quickly bored with his formal education, and Leland had to work hard to keep him in school. However, it became clear to Leland during Cash's final year in high school that Cash was far ahead of his contemporaries, so Leland gave in and taught Cash at home. After the year interlude, Cash agreed to give college a try. He scored so high on his college entrance exams that even with a GED, he was allowed to enroll at the University of Texas at Austin.

When Cash went to Austin, Leland sold the land, gave most of the money to Cash for school, and moved to Port Aransas.

Cash quickly lost interest in the university. He took his living allowance and made his first business deal by helping his roommate buy a local pizza parlor. The pizzas paid his tuition, as well as expenses, through four years, and just before graduating, he sold his interest and netted a handsome sum.

Cash's next trade was as the lead negotiator in the purchase of a small computer company, which made him a multimillionaire when it went public four years later.

He expanded his reach to New York and Seattle and Mexico City in larger and larger business transactions, and in almost every case made more money and friends, which made him more money and friends. So the cycle went.

The big financial jump came when he sold his interest in a medium-size biotech business to a large pharmaceutical firm for company stock.

It was a particularly tough transaction. The pharmaceutical company was run by titans of the drug industry. Cash's partners in the biotech firm—one of whom was Horton Callaway—were wary of the deal, afraid they would be subsumed. The pharmaceutical company proposed to buy their firm using stock, under an agreement that called for a "standstill," so Cash or his colleagues could not sell the stock for several years.

His partners felt the deal would emasculate them, and they balked. All the partners wanted hard cash, nothing else, except Horton, who, after working with Cash, sensed his business acumen and trusted him. He was willing to take whatever Cash took.

Cash arranged, to the satisfaction of all, for the pharmaceutical company to pay everyone in cash except for Horton and him, and the two of them accepted stock with a small premium for their share of the sale.

In less than a year, an Asian company bought the pharmaceutical firm for three times the stock price. In that one deal, Cash, with his already accumulated wealth, became a billionaire, and Horton had "hitched his wagon to a star."

Cash learned quickly that the media fame of his sudden billionaire status was trouble and decided he must build anonymity for himself if he was to continue as a successful businessman. Along the way, one of his smarter business acquaintances told him, "Spotlights fade your suits."

Horton, on the other hand, took to the spotlight well. It was an easy agreement between the two men for Horton to be the front man. From this alliance was born Sandra Corporation.

With Horton on the media line, Cash retreated. He bought the ranch on the Gulf and managed his money with Horton through Sandra Corporation, and as the years passed, the public and the media all but forgot about Cash Carruthers.

* * *

Buni's Volvo limped down the street, all chortles and growls, breathing hard after the journey from Surfside to Port Aransas. Amber bounced to her feet and waved as it wheezed to a stop in front of her. She opened the car door, brushed a few old French fries from the torn seat, and jumped in.

"Man, I hope you got some dough," Buni said. "I am totally out of gas. I think something's wrong with Rachel." Rachel was the name he had given his car. "I had a half-tank, and now it's out."

"I got nearly twenty-five bucks." Amber reached in her jeans and handed Buni a ten.

"Oh, sweet mama! That'll do it." Buni patted Amber on her knee.

Buni Rumble was poor, but he was nobody's fool. Born Friedrich Bundt, he had been called Buni since childhood, a sixth-generation descendant of the original German settlers of the area, and was raised in the Texas hill country town of Kerrville.

Buni's interest in music started when he joined the high school band, where his teacher encouraged him to try keyboard instruments. Buni was fascinated by the keyboard, the technique of playing, and found the intricate science of harmony thoroughly engaging.

Buni decided to pursue a career as a high school music teacher and enrolled in the requisite music-teacher courses at the University of North Texas in Denton. He knew the reputation of the music school and especially of the UNT lab bands. He was looking forward to playing in an ensemble that didn't march, something he thought of as a bonus.

What he didn't realize was just how good the lab bands were. They quickly moved from being a bonus of the music school to being the center of his musical experience.

His first encounter with high-level ensemble playing came at a Fort Worth club, when he and a group of friends from the lab bands did a one-night job for a party. The guests were typical drunks, so the band ignored them, hunkered down, and played for their own pleasure. In the presence of other gifted musicians, Buni felt what it was like to make music as part of a team with one mind. All of the science and math of music was marginalized in the sheer exuberance and soul of the band, the beauty of it, the artistry of it. He realized, intrinsically and for the first time, that there was more to playing than simply playing well.

During this gig, Buni began to play aggressively and rhythmically with his left hand on the lower keys of the piano, making it growl, adding an expressive signature to the band's performance. From that night on, he was called Buni Rumble.

He graduated with enough credits to become a music teacher and returned home, but his mind-set was altered from the UNT experience. He continued to play in local bands, looking for the same high space he had found with the lab band, and he never quite got around to applying for a job as a high school band teacher, getting drawn deeper and deeper into the Texas blues scene.

It was a few years later, at an open mic night in Austin, that he first saw Amber. For a musician to encounter a singer with the scope, presence, and expressiveness of Amber Fanfare is rare, and Buni recognized at once the opportunity that presented itself. It was also the night of the first fluttering of Buni's deeper artistic and poetic intuitions. Amber awakened a sense in Buni that went far beyond the music and provided him insight into aesthetics and motivations that were at once unique to him and generally profound.

At first they were playful friends, spending more and more time together, until they became romantically involved. That change in the relationship almost cost them their musical connection, and as each recognized where the importance of the other was in their lives, they came to an agreement to part as lovers but stay musical partners. Buni still had gentle tugs at his pride, but the pain faded over time and was now weaker than ever, in part because Amber usually shook off the advances of the parade of men who chased her, but mostly because Buni was not by nature a jealous man.

From this new perspective Buni slowly came to spiritually understand her. She was true and elegant, the essence of music, with a voice and a musical mind that were incomparable. Whatever else happened, Buni knew he would never leave Amber. She was what playing music was all about, and playing music had become his life.

While Amber's prowess was clear to Buni, it was not always clear to a bar full of drunken football fans whose main agenda was to celebrate a victory or lament a loss. There were many nights in certain venues when patrons had asked him to turn down the music, for Amber to sing quieter or not sing at all.

Working with her, his fortunes waned and he was soon living, like she was, from job to job. And soon Amber and the various bands were his only family.

At first it was baffling to Buni that such talent was unrecognized and unappreciated, but it became apparent that many different dynamics besides Amber's talent would need to converge for her to get a shot at wide recognition, dynamics which Buni knew very little about. It was frustrating to see such extraordinary capability go unnoticed.

They continued with the club jobs and party jobs, but Buni would not accept gigs at weddings or bar mitzvahs. He saw Amber's authenticity constantly challenged, preyed upon by the vicissitudes of life, the pursuit of money, the lack of opportunity, the desperation for popularity. It was at this time that the first faint inklings of the Elvis arc and the Personal Las Vegas unfolded in Buni's mind.

He saw this notion coiled, sleeping in its metaphorical base, waiting to awaken and push Amber down the paths of peculiar gardens. He talked about this to Amber, but she didn't understand. She understood the general idea but couldn't see it in her own life. Why, she would ask, couldn't she be just as authentic playing a wedding as she was playing a bar? What was this strange monster Buni saw waiting to pervert the music? Buni called it the America Gene. He ascribed to it a certain irresistible power.

Buni tried to explain that it wasn't the venue but the motivation that mattered. The America Gene wasn't about music or art but about self-concept, self-worth, confidence. He didn't want her, or them, to end up like Elvis. But the metaphor of the Gene usually failed him.

He had not developed a proposition for Principia Musicale, only an artist's glimpse of the first dim light of Amber's Personal Las Vegas. True to his theory of "invisibility to the bearer," he could not, of course, see his own. But he could see hers, there off in the distance, and he dedicated himself to protecting her from it, since he knew in which direction it lay and how far away it was. The conversations with Buni about her PLV usually ended in frustration, with Amber confused, but her intuition told her to trust Buni on this one, and she did, completely. So she played no weddings, no bar mitzvahs, no graduations.

Amber didn't know just how right Buni was.

* * *

Cash was in the center of his library, a large room with floor-to-ceiling bookshelves. He was sitting forward in an easy chair, elbows on his knees, chin on his hands, looking up at Horton, who had stopped pacing and was looking at him for a response.

"I understand, Horton. It makes sense you would want to strike out on your own," Cash said. His apparent easy willingness to accept Horton's resignation belied his real concern for the tremendous impact that Horton's leaving would have on Sandra Corporation. Horton was, by Cash's accounts, one of the most important parts of the operation. He was irreplaceable. True to form, he did not want to burden Horton with the thought, so he stayed silent. He did understand.

"I wanted to tell you," Horton said. "And announce it at tomorrow's meeting. Of course, it's up to you, in case you wanted to make any special arrangements. And also if you wanted to have someone else run the meeting, or have me introduce someone—whatever. For continuity of management." Horton crossed to a large sofa and sat down, looked at the floor in front of him, and squeezed his hands together.

"Have you given any thought to a replacement?" Cash asked.

"I thought maybe Mike. He's been with me every step of the way. I would need your take on him as far as executive material, but he certainly knows the operations, and he has great institutional memory."

Cash nodded, noncommittal, and looked out the window. Michael Sanborn was a Harvard MBA, a Horton hire, and Horton was his mentor, but as far as Cash was concerned he was the epitome of ineptitude. Whatever he had managed to learn at Harvard, wisdom was not included. He was a numbers guy with no sense of what the numbers meant, where they came from, or where they were going. On top of all this he was a bureaucrat, obsequious to those above, tyrannical to those below, territorial to a fault. Cash thought it was a bad idea.

"Wouldn't he want to go with you? He's basically your guy," Cash continued.

"I'm not sure where I'm going. I thought I would stay on full-time for three more months. Till the end of the fiscal year. Then, after that, I'll be around part time as much as I need to train him. Mike will want to stay at Sandra. I'll see to it. I really don't have any idea what I'm going to do. This is more of a spiritual crisis than looking for new opportunities, and I know Mike isn't going to want to wander in the wilderness with me."

This made Cash smile. Horton's biblical references were incongruous at the least, and it might have been the first time since Cash knew the man that he heard him use the word *spiritual*.

Horton's grandparents arrived from Germany in the early 1900s, and in an effort to assimilate, changed their first names to Scott and Evelyn, picked at random from the Dallas phone book, changed their last name to Callaway, after the golf club manufacturer, and began attending the Lovers Lane United Methodist Church to make friends and melt into the community. Whatever the past held they kept forever behind this line in time.

Their first son, David, met and married Horton's mother, Peggy, at the Lovers Lane church, and Horton, named after the Dr. Seuss character in the book *Horton Hatches the Egg*, was christened there. Still, the family never drank too deeply from this well, and soon after the christening, David and Peggy stopped attending the church altogether.

Horton excelled in his schoolwork, and in his high school freshman year his parents packed him off to Phillips Exeter Academy. From there he went to Dartmouth, then finally to the University of Pennsylvania's Wharton School, where he got an MBA in business.

Shortly after graduating from Wharton, he took over as the

chief operating officer of the biotech firm where he met Cash. The sale made Horton a millionaire and set him up for further gain when Cash asked him to take over Sandra Corporation.

As far as Cash knew, Horton's ideas of spirituality were either nonexistent or lying aground in his shallow streams of Protestantism.

"I'll make sure whatever you do with Sandra Corporation will go as smoothly as possible," Horton finished.

Cash did not have any idea what that might be. Horton's departure would be the end of a certain stage of the company— something would leave with him, something important. Cash would continue, but whatever new business entity emerged would not be a simple continuation of the one he had now.

"I don't think it would make much sense to say anything to-morrow," Cash said. "I'd like to think it through and get a better sense of what I'm going to do with Sandra before we announce that you're leaving. Does anyone else know?"

"I told Leland. That's all. I hope that was O.K."

Cash nodded. He knew precisely why Horton had told Le-land. Leland was the North Star, a bellwether.

"Of course. What did he say?" Cash was curious.

"That forces were at work we didn't understand. And to watch myself." Horton now looked earnestly at Cash.

"I hope you know how grateful I am to you, Horton," Cash said.

"Cash. I have 968 million dollars; 967.9 of it is directly due to you. If everybody said 'thank you' like that to me, I'd...I'd be... uhh—"

"Rich," Cash said, and the two men laughed.

"I'm going to take the chopper back up. What time do you want it down here tomorrow?" Horton said.

"Eight's fine."

Horton stood up and offered his hand to Cash—an unusual gesture, since the two hadn't shaken hands in years. There was never any need. The handshake quickly turned into an embrace, finally diffused with a series of pats on the back.

Cash stepped back. Horton looked at the floor, then at Cash.

"It's not my business, but can I ask what's going on with you and this music thing? I know you enjoy playing. Leland told me you played to a crowd last night."

"At the Partaway, yeah. It was a nightmare on wheels. Never had anything go so wrong."

"Leland said you were thinking of doing more, though."

"Thinking about it. There was a singer there, Amber. She had a real effect on me. Something in the way she sang, her approach."

Horton looked at Cash with an expression urging him to say more.

"She knows something about the music that I don't. The reason it's right, when it is. I want to learn about that. But I don't want to go through any more of what I went through last night, if I can help it. So, who knows?"

"Well." Horton walked to the door. Cash walked with him and out into the late afternoon light. The chopper was sitting on the pad fifty yards from the house. "Eight o'clock," Horton said.

Horton walked to the helicopter, and Cash waved hello at Sam the pilot, who put down the magazine he was reading, jumped from the pilot seat, and held open the back door for Horton.

As the helicopter disappeared into the afternoon sky, Cash wondered aloud to himself, "Now what do I do?"

* * *

All the windows were open in Rachel the Volvo as it grumbled along the highway toward Surfside. The papers in the back seat and the candy wrappers and crushed beer cans on the floor danced in the eddies of wind buffeting through the car. The papers stuffed into the visors fluttered, when suddenly a gust of wind from a passing truck blew the visor down and all the papers flew out the window, skittering into the oblivion of the roadside grasses.

"Aww, man. That was the title to the car. Now I am screwed," Buni said, watching the papers in the rearview mirror as they dissolved into the wake of the countryside.

"You haven't registered Rachel since I've known you," Amber said, leaning back, eyes closed, unperturbed.

"I don't guess I can ever sell her now either," he said.

"This car is almost a planter, anyway. I think you should park it out front of Buck's, rip the trunk lid off, and fill it with geraniums."

"I could leave it right here," Buni said as they parked in front of Buck's and Rachel clattered to a stop.

In the nearly dark, air-conditioner-cold bar, Buni pulled the door closed behind them. It took a moment for their eyes to adjust to the low colored lights. Amber was instantly at the pay phone, reading from the card Cash had given her, and punching in the numbers. Cash answered on the third ring.

"Hi. It's Amber Fanfare."

"Hi, Amber. I didn't expect to hear from you so soon," Cash said.

"Well, I'm up at Buck's with Buni, and I just thought I'd call and see if you wanted to come up, maybe something changed, and you could come up now or something. Maybe you wanted to sing or something." Amber was not used to being aggressive, didn't know the subtleties. She was blurting all this out but didn't know how to stop. "I'm gonna sing, and Buni's here if you want to see him. Be different than last night. Buni makes the band work better. He can help you out if you want to come sing."

"Amber, it's great you called, but I've got some things I have to deal with here, so…"

"Like what?" Amber asked.

"Well, some things that—"

"Because whatever it is, it's better with music. Buck makes a good steak. Covered with jalapenos, cheese, and stuff."

Cash laughed, a mixture of nervous and sincere. "I know. It sounds great, but I've got some things going on I need to think about tonight."

"You know how to get to Buck's?" Amber asked.

"Uh, no, but..."

"Your Jeep make it to Surfside?"

"Well, I...I wouldn't drive the Jeep."

"Come up Highway 59, turn left, wait...Buni!" Amber yelled across the room. "Is it left or right off that road that comes up from Corpus? O.K. Right on 35 up through Bay City, then—then what, Buni? Then 228 and ask at Lake Jackson. Buni says it's two blocks past the first signal in Surfside. Over by Dow. Buck's Bubble Room. We're going on about nine. Don't forget your guitar, though. Izzy's here with all his, but he's picky."

"O.K., Amber. I appreciate the invitation. I don't think I can come tonight, but you were sweet to call."

There was that word *sweet* again. Amber tried to shake it off but couldn't. She was new to rejection, but she was quickly learning to recognize it. She didn't like it.

"I'm not being sweet. I was just telling you something about where I was and that you could come up. And Buni's here, too." Amber was edgy.

"I meant it was a good thing that you called. I like it. It was nice for you—"

Amber cut him short. "Nice? You better get up here, or go somewhere, because 'nice' and 'sweet' is for, like, pies and things. You wanna wrap yourself around some music, though, and get your feet on the ground, then we're here if you can pull it together. Which is all I can say. Nine. And I gotta go." Amber hung up.

Cash looked at the phone in his hand and then slowly put it back on its cradle. He had been in the seat of absolute power for so long that no one had spoken to him quite so dismissively. It was odd, but it made him smile. Whatever Amber had, it was potent. He liked it. He liked her.

Even though the show wasn't until nine, at four Buck's started to fill with people. The word had quickly spread that Amber would be singing tonight, and it was well-known among the locals that the music was never better than when Amber sang in front of a band led by Buni Rumble. People were staking out seats next to the bandstand in a land rush. Buck's could only hold about ninety, and more than half were already there.

The bar at Buck's was selling plenty of pitchers of draft Shiner beer and plates of Buck's Hotburger steak, but no one was coming for the food—they were coming to hear Amber Fanfare and excited to be there.

"You wanna run some things down?" Buni asked Amber as he sat at the keyboard. Buni could play almost any instrument a bit, but his primary talent was for keyboards, and tonight it would be piano and organ. Because Buck's was so small, the band needed little amplification, and great sounding pianos sound even greater when left acoustic, with minimal or no microphones. The rest of the band was simple and light as well. Izzy Firegate, a twenty-year-old Muddy Waters disciple, was playing electric guitar; Lane Deitrich was on bass; and Norba Hyjeen, a woman from Houston who worked for FedEx, was on drums. The little unit ran of one mind under Buni's tight hand, and all were settling into place and tuning up.

The early arrivals had hoped to catch some bits of the sound check. Hardcore concertgoers who knew about such things knew it was the moment a band might find the jewel buried in a song. Watching inspired players dig out the good parts could be as exciting as the final performance.

Amber moved to the microphone in the center of the stage, took the mic from its stand, cradled the cord around her forearm, and sat on Izzy's amp. The crowd saw her, and all were instantly quiet, reverential. Buni started a slow blues shuffle in E. Lane and Norba fell in the groove, and the pulse of the music took over every heartbeat in the room. Izzy ripped open a standard blues riff to set the introduction, and then Amber started to sing.

Throughout the centuries, in some fire-lit corner, to the accompaniment of sad soulful instruments, the great singers have revealed the space Amber now opened once again for everyone at Buck's to experience. Eyes closed, head slightly forward, the mellifluous tones of her husky alto voice wound their way into the crowd. Amber stepped easily into the sacred land of the legendary singers, and every tone from her voice painted a new picture of this land, a far horizon, a nearby symbol, mind pictures of a spiritual world, the only window to it through Amber's soul, the central sun of a glorious world.

The patrons held their silence when Buni stopped the song midway through a second verse and made a comment to Firegate. Buni played a couple of notes on the piano and emphasized a rhythmic shift. Buni looked at Amber and she nodded. All started at the beginning of the second verse again, and when they came to the point Buni had noted, the ever so slight shift in the rhythm gave Amber an opportunity to find a vocal curl, an enhancement, that sent chills through the crowd, and they broke into spontaneous cheers. Amber looked up and smiled at the audience, then at Buni, then at the whole band. Unusual for Amber to recognize the approval and share it, Buni thought.

Buni drew the song to an early close. The groove was there. No need for more rehearsal. Amber set the microphone back on its stand and stepped off the stage into the crowd, walking back toward the bar.

When an artist finds the place Amber found—a singer sings that indescribable moment—the result is not a crush of people wanting to touch. It is the opposite. People stand back, make a path, give way, which they now did for Amber as she walked to the bar. The tightly-packed crowd opened for her. No one dared touch her or even speak to her. Just the occasional polite nod, which Amber returned with a slight gesture of her hand, a genuine smile, or a flicker of real eye contact.

When she got to the bar, Buck slid her a draft beer, and the chatter of the crowd swelled back to normal.

"You know a guy named Cash?" Buck asked.

Amber was startled and looked up, wiping a foam moustache from her upper lip. "Yeah."

"Just called. Said he was gonna try and make it. I told him we was full…"

"What!" Amber said, alarmed.

"Easy. I said we was full up, but he said he was gonna try and come up anyways and to tell you. I can't get nobody else in here, Amber. Fire marshal put me under the jail as it is."

"O.K. He can just sit onstage." Amber took another happy gulp.

"Yeah, if he can even get to the stage," Buck said. "But they ain't no seats. I'm not kiddin'."

Amber took the mug and nodded assent to Buck as she made her way back to Buni at the bandstand. She was elated, almost giddy.

"That guy Cash is comin' up," she said as she sat next to Buni on the piano bench.

"Mr. Goodweird?"

"This guy's O.K. You're gonna like him." Amber sat on the floor of the stage cross-legged, finished off the beer, and set it down. She looked through the already adoring crowd without seeing them, thinking only of Cash Carruthers walking through the door at Buck's while she was in the middle of a song. Such an expectation was wonderfully new.

Chapter Six

The cars were stacked like a logjam in the lot and the streets around Buck's Bubble Room. Cash drove up and down the street looking for a nearby parking place but finally had to park a few blocks away and walk back. As he neared the open door of Buck's, he heard Amber's voice bearing down, hard-edged, tense, in an unrecognizable song.

Dozens of people were swarming around the open door of the Bubble Room, bees around an exceptional flower, heads bobbing to see, their faces awash with a mixture of the black light from the bar and the colored lights from the stage, red eyes and blue teeth, all glowing with delight. Smells of Jack Daniel's and Marlboro, pomade and hair spray, mixed in the swelter of a Texas summer night.

Cash stood at the edge of the crowd, and through the open door, he saw her on the minute stage. With her eyes closed, she clutched the mike and growled the lyrics deep and low. Cash pressed forward, but the doorman held up his hand and shook his head to indicate his effort was futile. There was no more room. Cash's height gave him a clear view over the crowd to the stage, so he moved to one side and leaned against a wall to watch. Amber finished the song, and the crowd went crazy with applause, whoops, and hollers. She surveyed the room, accepted the thanks, and then threw a quick glance to the door.

Her eyes passed his way, then over him, in what could have been a perfunctory look—Amber watching her own show as she had instructed Cash to do—but Cash thought he saw a spark of recognition from Amber.

Amber turned to Buni at the keyboards and took a drink from a plastic cup perched on the edge of the instrument. She laid her arm across Buni's shoulders and said something directly into his ear, then turned back, eyes down. Buni held up his hand to the drummer and counted off the next song.

It was a strong but slow blues shuffle.

Amber grabbed the mike and signaled for the band to play softer, holding her hand out, palm down, before her. From a place mysterious and tranquil, up from the depths of her musical mind, her strong, sturdy voice breathed life into the senseless words.

"It's cherry blossom time. It's cherry blossom time," she began.

Cash flinched, as he looked to his left, then to his right, then back at Amber. "It's cherry blossom time," she sang, increasing the intensity.

The melody she was singing only vaguely resembled the

one Cash had sung; she was making up more than she remembered. Amber infused the melody and nonsensical lyrics with a fervor, trembling, high and narrow, a tight-wire walker at vertiginous height.

The crowd was silent, curious, motionless, and in her grip. Where could she be going? Slowly the definition of the words Amber was singing fell away. She was at the point when the repetition of a word robs it of meaning, and she was left with pure sound, pure emotion, pure beauty, a transparency for Amber's soul.

It was here the song began, as she sang over and over, "It's cherry blossom time," from a place of joy, of first love, of an indescribable happiness. Together, all in her presence were climbing the surface of the song, following her, rising slowly and clearly into higher and higher spaces.

"It's cherry blossom time. It's cherry blossom time," she sang, and called the crowd to look out from their new vantage, high on a mountainside, alight momentarily on a ledge, where they could see forever. They looked out but clung to Amber, held close to her as she led, pulling them further upward.

"It's cherry blossom time," she sang again and again. This time she shaded the emotion, and the joy of first love began to sink into the sorrow of betrayal, a resonant anger, bitter and hateful. Instead of the mindless drone of Cash's performance, each recitation of the words unfolded the song to its next level, a flower opening, then more and more, until it was nature itself, and a new life born upon the stage.

She sang "It's cherry blossom time" now with a severity, vital, urgent, and a new melody emerged, and the rhythm settled down deep and primitive so the band members were swept up, gathered together, playing different parts of the same instrument. They watched Amber's body as she pulsed to the beat, swinging her hips back and forth, in and out, rolling her shoulders up and down, the muscles in her arms tensing and relaxing to the throbbing drums.

Without thought, all were near the top, the band was playing louder, almost covering Amber's singing, while her control rode across the top of the music, a feather on the wind, floating, twisting, moving in the currents, never behind. At the pinnacle of the song, Buni Rumble exploded into a keyboard riff that stepped out front, solo, that drew deep from Amber's sexuality, sense, and soul, that issued from the dregs of the Delta, the New Orleans skies and weather, the Gulf hurricanes, the thunderstorms, the howls of the wind, and became the fulmination of the Gulf waters against the Texas shorelines that laid the grasses on the dunes flat.

Buni handed the song back to Amber, and with a subtle, delicate quiver she sang the song now heartbroken, a lost lover, and the song cried in anguish, pain. A wail of desertion, the sadness of a stricken child, until at last it emerged into a resolve to carry on, leave the pain behind.

The song subsided; everyone coasted downhill. "It's cherry blossom time," sang Amber, and the tension ebbed from her, all the muscles relaxed as her panting breath charged the words with husky release, a whisper, love words close to the ear. "It's cherry blossom time," she sang, and the song was coming close to its end, the song born only minutes ago now disappearing in her hand, and the audience could feel the final chord waiting, and they sat forward, and some held up their hand.

Cash looked left and then looked right again, to see what was in the room, to see if this power had gathered itself into visibility. It was as if a pen had drawn the room so everything in it was pointing to Amber.

She slid back from the microphone, head bowed. The sweat ran from her forehead down around her lips, down her neck, as she raised a hand and pointed at the crowd, then through it, to Cash, straight at him. Cash, his head against the wall, met her eyes, as the final chord sounded and the song rumbled to silence.

Silence, calm, stillness. A hush without measure, infinitesimal, the moment of understanding, the moment when the memory of the song lodged into the collective heart of the crowd and rested there, to live there forever.

Silence. Wonder. A new birth.

Then an explosion. Suddenly, from the silence, a roar of acclaim, an eruption. The crowd jumped to their feet, a cheer overtaking all, yelling, screaming, whistling, slapping hands and chairs and glasses, a shriek of joy as the crowd gave their approval, an outburst of all the love they could draw from their common soul—now full of delight, sated, enraptured—

and give to Amber. Fanfare, indeed.

Amber looked out at the crowd and smiled, then an open grin, then a laugh, then she held both hands above her head in a salute and walked from the stage, out the door to the back lot of Buck's, the noise of the crowd undiminished, lasting forever, limitless approbation. Buni followed her and took her hand as he placed his arm around her waist in a side-by-side promenade, and drew her to him, laying his head against hers in fealty. He knew what this was, this ability to transform the mundane, the maudlin and meaningless, into beauty, power, and life. He knew it, and he honored it.

Cash stood stunned, listening to the clamor of the crowd as they pounded glasses on the tabletops and roared for more. Nothing had prepared him for what had just happened. To watch a live creative force at work, to see something that had not been apparent before suddenly spring into view was almost beyond his ability to grasp.

* * *

Leland Carruthers's eyes closed, and he fell away peacefully on the veranda of the little motel. His parting breath drew him near to a new picture of life. He loved his son and could see for the slightest moment his son was never born and never dying, visible for the small span of time Leland had watched him grow as a glimpse of eternity. Then Leland saw this same truth about himself, saw the end of his so-called life on earth, as he walked through the illusion of a final barrier of time, the earthly realities. As he stepped outside the view of all who were left behind, he held his son in an embrace, drew him close, and whispered one last word of encouragement. Then he was gone forever to this mortal sense.

At precisely this same moment, Cap'n Bob Reno, Bob the Slob, was being led away in handcuffs from the house trailer where Amber and Chastity lived, where Chastity lay beaten to death, crumpled on the floor, her head the center of a dark sienna stain that radiated out and disappeared under the foldout couch where Amber usually slept.

* * *

Cash walked slowly along the street outside Buck's. A low coastal fog had moved in over the hour and there was a slight drizzling rain. The huge arc lights from the nearby Dow Chemical plant were a blunt auburn, their halation surrendering to the fog by turning into lumps of muted color. The streets were changing from dusty slate to shiny black as Cash walked around the side of Buck's to see Amber in Buni's embrace.

The vibration from Amber's performance was still visible, even as the muffled intermission jukebox throbbed through the flimsy walls of the Bubble Room. A shaft of light from the back door framed the couple in chiaroscuro as they slowly rocked in each other's arms.

Over Buni's shoulder, Amber saw Cash and stepped

away from Buni as she opened to Cash. She smiled at him. Buni looked first at Amber, then at Cash, a tall, dark figure in the mist.

"Mr. Goodweird?" Buni looked back to Amber. She nodded.

"Hey," she said to Cash. "You made it. I sang your song."

"I—I don't know what to say." Cash joined the circle.

"This's Buni, guy I was tellin' you about."

"'S happ'nin'?" Buni extended his hand, and Cash shook it. Amber embraced Cash, pulling him to her and pressing her cheek to his.

"That was incredible. I—" Cash began, but the chirp from his cell phone interrupted him.

The sound was a prodrome. It stopped Cash instantly and filled him with dread.

As Cash opened his cell phone, Buck appeared at the back door, somber.

"Amber, there's a guy from the sheriff's department wants to see you."

Amber turned intuitively to Cash. A chill settled over and around them, tying them together. They stared at each other for an instant and then blinked in unison. Amber walked without a word into Buck's as Cash turned his back to the club and huddled over his phone, hand to the mouthpiece, protecting a delicate flame. At that moment, without knowing it, they had been inextricably linked to each other as shelter from the coming tempest.

The next days and weeks were held hostage by a low-grade tropical storm, brooding and appropriate, close to the ground. A shroud.

Cash's mourning traveled under a tent of black umbrellas, filled with lines of black cars and forests of black clothes.

Amber's was marked by the solo procession of a red-faced, out-of-breath county official, leaping on tiptoe across the pools in the muddy yard to the trailer, coming to the door with papers to sign, shaking the raindrops off them with a snap of his wrist.

A month later Cash and Amber were standing in their respective houses looking out their windows, Cash across the endless land to the somber, gray horizon and Amber down the rutted, muddy road that ran through the center of the trailer park. Both were in an emotional fog of grief and continuance. Both were looking for a light of any kind, and each was thinking of the other.

The manager of the trailer park knocked on the jamb of the open door, through which he could see Amber sitting at the small counter in the kitchen.

"Amber, I gotta get you to move, honey. I'm gonna need this space. I'm sorry to keep botherin' you with your mom and all, but time is money, and I gotta do something with this space."

Amber looked in acknowledgment toward the door, but not at the person. She had her few things packed in a single cardboard box. The sound of Buni's Volvo, a contrabass kazoo, grew louder as it splashed through the brown puddles and stopped outside her door.

The helicopter on the pad outside Cash's house was waiting for the jets to cool down, idling, until at last the pilot shut them off, and they swirled into silence.

Inside the ranch house, Horton was sitting across from Cash, knees to knees, hunched over in earnest. "I need you to come to Houston, Cash. I've held off as long as I could, but we have some people here waiting since Leland died. Any possibility you can come back with me?"

Cash acquiesced. "I'll come up, but I think I'll drive. You go back in the chopper, and I'll be up there this afternoon." Horton patted Cash's forearm in acceptance.

Rachel the Volvo roared along the county road. Amber watched the fields slide by as she held Buni's hand atop the center armrest.

"You think Buck'll let us come play?" she asked.

"I figure. He said any time. We oughta get more money I think, but I don't know whether he will."

Amber let go of his hand and turned to him. "D'ja ask him for more?"

"Not in so many words. But I can." He turned to Amber. "I will."

"'Cause I gotta work now for real. If I can make money singin', I gotta make it."

"I know, baby. Your mom leave anything?"

"Only what I had to pay to get her paid off. That guy, Raul, bought the truck. There was two-hundred-eighty dollars in the coffee can and these." She held up a pair of earrings. "Not real or nothin'. I kept 'em anyway. That was pretty much it. I can't wear her clothes. I got about thirty-five dollars left."

"Let's go over to Buck's, ask him. We're here. Might as well."

Buni turned at the road that led to Lake Jackson and Surfside. The Texas heat made ripples of the distance, the faraway roadside buildings lazy, gray flames.

Cash turned into the underground garage of his building in downtown Houston and parked in the space next to Horton's, which now sported a new, black Bentley.

"Hi, Mr. Carruthers. Real sorry about your dad," the guard said as he unlocked the exclusive elevator for Cash.

Cash's building was a thirty-story, granite and glass, nondescript monolith nestled half-unseen in the bouquet of the Houston skyline, its only distinction the very chic and exclusive Texas Club that occupied the entire top floor. The building had five floors dedicated to Sandra Corporation; the rest were an aggregate of general commerce: real estate, lawyers, insurance, banking, accounting.

Cash stepped out from his private ingress into the lobby of the Sandra Corporation. The receptionist was new, as usual, and did not recognize him, though he knew Cash was important because of this entrance.

"Hi," Cash said. "Mr. Callaway here?"

"Yessir. In the boardroom. Can I let him know you're here?

"No, I'll just go—" Cash stopped, turned, walked the other

way. "Actually, yeah, would you? Tell him Cash is here. In my office." Cash strode away down a hall.

The receptionist nodded and placed the call.

From the two floor-to-ceiling windows that met in its corner, the office Horton had built for Cash had a commanding view to the south, toward Galveston Bay and the Gulf. It was lavishly furnished in large—large being the principle design key: a large desk, a large seating area, large decorative prints on the wall, and six large potted palms, with no signs of activity. A showroom. Cash hated it and was hardly ever there.

Horton Callaway and Diana Copeland swept into the room, one behind the other, respectful, anticipatory. Diana was wearing a cream-colored silk-and-mohair suit with an Hermès scarf at her neck and Chanel pumps. Horton was in pinstripes and wingtips, with a manicure and an antique Patek Philippe barely visible under his crisp shirt cuff. Cash was in contrast: jeans, boots, and a work shirt, rumpled with sweat from the drive up.

Diana closed her open arms around Cash, drew him close with genuine affection, and whispered in his ear. "I'm so sorry, Cash. Are you all right?"

Diana's honest concern reached to the roots of Cash's emotions, and for a second he was speechless. She was, after all, an intimate friend, a lover, and arguably the closest person to him since Leland died. He had spent the funeral proceedings aloof and introspective. This was his first personal contact with true sympathy. His throat went dry, the muscles clenched around the notorious lump; he took a deep breath, then released it slowly, a sigh.

"Yes, I'm fine. Sorry I didn't call you. I've been—" Again lost for words.

"Hiding out?" Diana said as she released him.

Cash shook his head no, then held still through an uncomfortable silence until he whispered, hoarse with emotion, "Letting go."

"Everybody's here," Horton said.

Cash walked to his desk and stood for a few seconds, drumming his fingers, and then turned to Diana.

"Horton tell you?" he asked.

Diana turned to Horton, then back to Cash and nodded.

"I hope that was O.K.," Horton said.

"Anybody else?" Cash asked.

"Mike, of course. But, no. Just Diana. It came up."

"It's fine, but I need to think this through a bit, and with Leland gone, it's taking me a little time."

There was a sudden hint of discomfort, a cool breeze. Diana and Horton looked at each other again, but this time more obviously for clues. Diana spoke.

"I've asked Horton to come to work for me. With me. As a partner."

Cash nodded and then looked at Horton to see if he would add anything. He did.

"Diana has come up with something spectacular, Cash. I was sure I wanted to strike out on my own, something entrepreneurial, but when I heard this it felt like a good step for me. I—I hope you don't feel strange about this."

Cash smiled. He knew "strange" was a euphemism for angry. "Should I?" he asked sincerely.

No," Horton said. "No. Not in the least. I think it's a way for me to stay in the family, in a way—to—I mean, I hope I'm not getting personal here. Too personal. I mean professionally, of course, the professional family."

"Do I get to know this idea?" Cash asked.

"I want you to come out to the *Marianna* after the meeting if you can," Diana said. "I have everything out there."

Horton crossed between Cash and Diana. "But to make it clear," he said. "I don't want you to think I am leaving Sandra Corporation to run Copeland Lines. It just happened this way. I believe you'll see what I mean—we mean—when you get a look at everything."

"O.K.," Cash said. "So on to Sandra. What's the agenda today? I saw the list. It looks like you have everybody here."

"Yes, they are," Horton said. "It's the whole crew."

The strategy for Sandra Corporation was simple. Under Horton's direction, Sandra Corporation was the business of business. Buy cash flow, improve it, and then sell it. The formula was simple enough, but many other corporations had failed at it.

The idea was replicated time and again, and soon Sandra Corporation was a holding company. Each of the held corporations was locally managed, and the managers would convene twice a year, usually in Houston. It was a gathering to see how large the empire had grown, get a feel for it, and meet the new additions.

Cash's particular skill was an impeccable sense of ethics in the most complex business situation, a Solomon-like wisdom that untangled the knottiest problems, and an ability to discern the right thing to do. At least until now. Without Leland, Cash felt much less sure of himself. It made him feel vulnerable, made him lose his confidence, and compounded the anxious feeling from losing Horton.

"And you still feel as if Mike is right for this?"

"I do. Yes. He's excited by it, sees a great opportunity, and he has a real knack with money. He's not as smart as I am, but nobody in the company is except you, Cash." Horton's attempt at irony was always a failure, usually making everyone uncomfortable, like now.

"So we're going to tell everybody today you're leaving and Mike's stepping in."

"That's the main agenda. That, and to take a look at the last two quarters. Business is up again. We've had some terrific returns and it's time to give out bonuses. It should ease things a bit. There's a lot of money involved."

* * *

"Five hundred dollars!" Buck stood up from the barstool. "Nobody gets five hundred dollars a night around here, Buni. Are you out of your mind? I can't afford that! That's fifteen-hundred dollars over a three-day weekend!"

"But the bar—"

"The bar don't make that. Not so's I can pay it out. There's a cost to the booze, too, y'know."

"Yeah, but, well, all the people—"

"Hell, Buni. Look around. All them people cain't get in here. They stand around the door outside in the lot and I don't get no money for that, cain't sell 'em booze, neither, and besides I'm back here sweatin' bullets the fire marshal don't drive by. As it is I put a few more in here than I should, but I gotta tell ya, Buni, you can only get so many in here, and so many's so many, and it won't pay no five hundred dollars a night. This place would have to be three times the size." Buck turned, arms outstretched; his thick stubby legs thudded a three-step pirouette, so he ended back where he started, with a "see what I mean" look on his face.

"'Cept there's five of us in the band; that's only a hundred dollars apiece, not countin' equipment and things we gotta buy."

"Buni. Buni. You gotta get real, man. I can give you two hundred. O.K., two-fifty, but that's probably gonna squeeze the fun out of it for me."

Amber had been quiet, and now she was sullen. Too much of this conversation swirled in her mind between questions of "Is that really all Buck can pay?" and "Is my singing good enough to ever be worth that much?" Buck was scaring her. If five hundred dollars was out of reach, then any hopes she had for supporting herself by singing were out of reach, too. She was getting depressed, and Buni knew it.

"I can't live on a hunded and fifty dollars a week, Buni. I can't," she said.

Buni turned to her and tried to exclude Buck with a hushed tone. "It'd be the two of us though. We could do that."

"It'd be the two of us stuck together poor, is all it'd be." Amber kept her voice loud, at negotiating level. Buni, hurt, withdrew.

"I'm hungry. I gotta eat," she said, and walked out of Buck's. Buck looked at Buni, wounded, and for a moment thought about upping the offer but decided against it.

"I guess we'll get something to eat and get back to ya on this," Buni said. He knew to leave the door open.

"'S best I can do, Buni. Just ain't there. If it was, we could talk, but it ain't."

Buni walked out of Buck's and saw Amber leaning up against the Volvo, arms across her chest, looking across the parking lot at nothing. She started talking without looking at Buni as he walked toward her.

"Buni, point is, if we get together where each of us can't live without the other, we don't have anything except the other. It's not like we both have something and put it together to make more. It's like we don't either one have enough, and we try to make it by hanging on to each other."

"But, baby, that's what people do. Two heads are better than one."

Amber turned to face him square, arms still across her chest.

"Not if they're on the same body. You're the smartest guy I know, but not about this. Why would I want to live wondering if your arm was gonna fall off? It's like that. If people who can't stand up alone hang on to people who can't stand up, either, and figure just because they're together then they're both gonna stand up, I mean—even if they get up a little, it's not never gonna work. Not never. That's not standing up. That's hanging on. So when the other person falls down, you fall down, too. Won't work, Buni. Not with me. We gotta stand on our own, then you and me can share if we want, but not 'cause we gotta. So we havta make some money—and we can't be lettin' Buck say no—or—we can't—"

"Whoa." Buni held up both palms to Amber.

"Look. I told you I had to sell everything to pay off Momma's debts, and I gotta get to work. And I can't be livin' like she did, boyfriend to boyfriend." There was an incipient quiver in her voice wavering between tears and anger.

"O.K. Baby. I know. I know."

She dropped her arms and then wrapped them around Buni's waist as she put her head on his chest. He stroked her hair.

"Buni. You. You're the best thing in my life. I'm not mad at you. Scared's all. A little scared." She squeezed him hard. She released a deep, resolute sigh and listened for a moment to the beating of their hearts.

"I gotta get a taco or something. I'm getting a headache," Amber said after awhile. "Then we got to figure out how to get enough money for each of us."

Buni coaxed the Volvo to life and pointed her in the direction of the nearest Tex-Mex café.

"Think maybe we should drive up to Houston and look around? Go over to Tudor's and see if they'll hire us?" Amber slouched in the seat, knees up, feet against the dash.

"Can if you want," Buni said. "But I don't think we're gonna do much good. Nobody knows us—you—much up there. Everybody's gonna be like Buck, I'm afraid. I think we gotta get set up somewhere somebody'll let us stay, let the word build up, and charge a cover, or something like that."

They drove in silence, the harsh light of the Gulf glaring down, making chevrons of hard-edged shadows, slicing the buildings and shops of Lake Jackson as they scrolled by. Amber suddenly dropped her feet to the floor and sat up straight.

"Let's go down to Corpus. I know a place to ask."

Chapter Seven

Diana unfolded her closed fist into Cash's upturned palm. Five black marble-sized balls fell into his hand. They were light, clattering together like plastic, but with high resonant pings like the sound of lead crystal goblets lightly touching. Diana and Cash had taken the helicopter out to the *Marianna* and now stood in the main salon of Diana's stateroom suite.

"Aren't they amazing?" Diana said.

"What are they?"

"They're hydrofoam carbon beads. It's an oil derivative, injected with a gas and a chemical that whips it into a foam; then it's hyper-cooled, and these beads form. Now look at this." Diana held up a jar half-filled with water and motioned for Cash to drop them in. He did. All the beads floated, dancing as Diana shook the glass. "They float. Strong as steel, and it floats. Can you imagine the kind of ship you can build with this?"

Cash was impressed. Yes, he could imagine. The standard rules of volume displacement were not changed, but the rules of the shape of the displaced space might be. He saw the potential.

"Cash." Diana was breathless with excitement. "I want to build a city. A floating city! Not a city that looks like a big boat, but a real city that sprawls out in all directions. I can do it with this."

The first and loudest thought in Cash's mind was, What on earth for? But he squelched it. Instead he said, "Really?"

"I've been working on it ever since I found this material. That's why I was at the Genoa office so long. I was at Fincantieri, talking about a new ship, and I met this kid there. He showed me this, said he was about to take it around to the builders there, and I just grabbed him. Unbelievable, really, he did it all on his own. I bought all the rights. Patents, everything." Diana shook the glass again. The beads tinkled and bobbed, trembling at every microwave in the glass. "This is the latest batch."

Diana reached for a lid to the jar, screwed it on, and handed the mixture to Cash. "Put this somewhere you can watch it."

Cash held the jar up, peering at the specimen within, and then with a toast toward Diana, he set it on a table.

Cash and Diana walked to a side balcony overlooking the length of the boat in both directions.

"I wanted Horton to help me, because I haven't been able to get the financing I need and, frankly, because he can solve a lot of management problems in building this. When he saw this, he said he wanted a chance to build it with me. I had no idea he was leaving Sandra, and I thought we would bring it to you together. We can still use a partner."

Cash wanted no part of it. Diana was harboring a grand vision that seemed to have no purpose other than its own monumentality. What would a floating city do? What would it be for? Why have it float? Cash was afraid what the answers might be if he asked Diana. The whole notion was unlike her. The cruise business was flourishing. A project like this could jeopardize everything. Cash was puzzled, speechless.

"I don't know what to say, Diana."

"Don't say anything right now. Think about it. We've started building the floats. I've got the naval architecture in place. We're going to build it all right here in Galveston, around a platform just outside the twelve-mile limit, and launch it from there, so there's plenty of time. And there is a lot to think about. Especially now. Do you want to have something to eat?" Diana asked.

Diana was a tall, handsome woman—not exactly zaftig, but almost; not exactly beautiful, but nearly. Her face had an active grace among the features and was vital even at rest, agleam with ideas and emotions.

Cash had always thought she was better understood in motion, like a galloping mustang seen from a distance, a line fluttering along a hillside, a wind through fall aspens. In any case, she was a sexy and romantic creature, whose first claim to beauty came from a raw energy. As she approached her maturity, Cash saw finer qualities emerging, expressing a certain elegance of thought.

She was intelligent and educated, never at a loss for something interesting to talk about, and she was creative. She repurposed her father's freight lines, designed the entire cruise business, had the boats made, and created the marketing programs. Copeland Cruise Lines was a smaller line compared with some, but it was profitable and fun for her. She had built it all, and she owned it all.

Diana felt she found a soulmate in Cash. When they met, it was the first time in her life she found herself giddy, neck-deep in a dreamy-eyed crush, but over the years the relationship between them stayed unsettled as to form, consisting mostly of Diana loving Cash more than Cash loved her. There was an absence of a final bond, a latch, and while all their surfaces matched well, connecting seamlessly when they were together, the moment they were separate their connection drifted apart.

For the first few years, they talked on and off about living together, about marrying and having children, with Diana doing most of the talking, but after all that time they were only here, on the *Marianna,* staring out from their different viewpoints, never having reconciled their feelings, and only wondering what to have for dinner.

"I'm not hungry yet. What would you think about going down to the ranch? Would you like to spend some time there?"

Whatever the difficulties, Diana was companionship, and Cash enjoyed it, even if it was only propinquity.

"We can take the chopper and be there in about forty-five

minutes." The helicopter was lashed to the landing pad at the rear of the *Marianna*.

"I'd love it. Don't forget this." Diana picked up the small jar of floating black bubbles and shook it at Cash, a snow globe without the glitter. "I'll get some things." Diana went to the huge closet to find just the right thing to wear on Cash's ranch.

The twin-engine Eurocopter Dauphine was a quiet helicopter as far as it went, but Cash and Diana had to wear headsets to communicate, and they were jostled as each looked from their side windows to the expanse of the Texas shoreline below. The trip took them along the barrier islands and bays that dotted the coastline from Galveston to Corpus Christi. Cash's ranch was south of Corpus and well off the main roads.

As Cash and Diana walked from the helicopter, Cash heard the electronic chirp of the phone coming from inside the house and made a lazy round-the-bases effort to get to it before it quit ringing.

"Cash, it's Henry Biggins out at the Partaway. There's. I, uh—ordinarily I would have called Leland, I guess. Because I know you don't like to be bothered with all this, but—"

"No, it's fine, Henry. What's going on?"

"That singer with the band you played with the other night is here, and like I say, I would probably just not even think much about it, but I thought you might—I mean, she, they want a place to set up and sort of play regular, you know, make a name and all, and I wouldn't do it usually, but something said maybe I should call and let you know. I have to tell them no because they're asking for more money than I can pay them, but before I did, I thought you might want to know they—well, that they were here and all."

Minutes later, Cash and Diana were in his Jeep driving to the Partaway.

"I can't see anything wrong with it. Everyone has a hobby," Diana said as the wind flipped her short hair around her face in the open Jeep. She felt the word hobby clunk against the metal floor pan of the Jeep as she said it. "An avocation, if you like. But. Horton, now. I have to tell you, Horton thinks there is something profoundly wrong with it. I suppose you know that."

Cash nodded. "I can see where he might."

* * *

Horton looked across the table at the Arrow Club at Mike Sanborn and held up a glass of Jacques Estève Ancestral Reserve XO Cognac in a toast. "I think you did well. I'll talk to Cash later this week. He's staying out on the Marianna with Diana, so I'll leave him alone for a few days, but I think it all went well."

"I want you to know, Horton, how much I appreciate what you've done for me here," Sanborn said. He took a gulp of the Cognac and stifled a cough from the sudden explosion of taste in back of his throat.

"Don't thank me yet." Horton took a sip of the Cognac, then swirled the liquor in the glass as he inhaled and savored the aroma. "I was thinking of giving myself a little going-away party.

Does that sound crass?"

"Not at all, not at all, I was going to suggest it, in fact. It's the least Sandra Corporation could do for you."

"No, no." Horton waved his hand. "I don't want Sandra Corporation to do it. I want to do it. What I'm thinking about, Sandra Corporation can't afford."

When Horton had seen Diana's design for the *Mariner*, it was almost too big for him to understand. A floating condo was easy enough. Some kind of huge boat. But Diana was way past that.

The island city she had in mind would not be a boat in any conventional sense. More like an immense weighted fishing bob. A group of huge, partly flexible hinged girders would extend underwater hundreds of feet. To these would be attached electric motors, the size of those used in high-speed trains, with propellers hooked directly to the armatures of each motor. The motors were suspended from azimuths that allowed all the motors to rotate independently 360 degrees, so their thrust could be aimed in any direction. Spreading out on the water's surface above this submerged core was a collar made from arrays of the new carbon hydrofoam panels, linked together like pontoons with hinges, so the platform they created could articulate and follow the swells and waves of the ocean. On this collar would be built the control center, with turbine generators and solar arrays to power the motors and the condominiums. Radiating out farther would be the day-use apartments, shops, theatres, restaurants, landing strips, and commercial buildings. As the craft grew, more fishing bobs would drop in the water and more collars would be built around them, and then the collars would be linked. Over time, the craft would resemble a jellyfish more than a boat. A jellyfish the size of Las Vegas.

It was not expected to travel faster than three or four knots in any direction under its own power, designed instead to float along the ocean currents. If needed, a GPS-guided control system could coordinate the engines against the current flows to create a de facto sea anchor, so the whole craft could stay in one place for months, or years, riding like a submerged cork. Or change the thrust, and the artificial island could move slowly in a prescribed direction.

The first city would be confined to the Gulf of Mexico, riding the loop current of the Gulf Stream off the western Florida coast north to the southern coast of the United States, then drifting west along the Gulf's eddies, like bouncing over the top of a series of spinning wheels just below Alabama, Louisiana, then south along the Texas coast into Mexico, eastward around the northern coast of South America, to the Western Caribbean, then rejoining the loop current, a giant carousel.

No, this was no big boat or cruise ship, Horton mused. This was a new way to think about building society and civilization. It all captured his interest and came at exactly the right time. Diana had raised some of the money and had started some of the first building efforts, but she needed more. She needed what Horton could bring.

"Then, perhaps, Sandra Corporation could contribute. It owes you that much. You've left quite a legacy there." The word *legacy* came casually and easily to Sanborn, the type to use *genius* or *gourmet* without a precise sense of the meaning or application.

Horton knew his legacy was nonexistent. The future would perhaps remember Horton's great wealth, but only for a short time, then after that, nothing. The world would close over his advent like the ocean over the wake of a passing ship. His desire to create and leave a legacy was one of the overriding reasons he had moved away from Sandra Corporation and one of the compelling things about working with Diana Copeland to build her floating city.

He hoped this project with Diana would provide him with something he could point to and leave with pride. More than anything, Horton wanted this, and more than anything, it confounded and eluded him.

"It's something I want to do personally." After an imperceptible pause, realizing he and Mike were thinking about two different things, he said, "I just didn't want it to seem churlish. Giving myself a party. Do you think it would?"

Sanborn made no effort to consider Horton's question, calculating instead with the ingratiating, "How many people were you planning on having?"

* * *

"I can only get about a hundred, maybe a hundred-twenty in here, even when I move all the tables back." Henry Biggins was walking slowly around the Partaway, followed by Buni and

Amber. "We had around one-thirty in here the other night, when you sang. That was unusual. And I got a lot of good feedback. I think you might build up something here, but seven-hundred-fifty dollars a night's high. Not sure you could ever get there from here."

Unseen by Biggins, Buni looked at Amber with an "I told you so."

"I'm not sayin' no, mind you—"

Amber arched an eyebrow back at Buni.

"—but I'd need to talk to Cash about it. He'll be out here shortly. You can come back or call or wait or whatever."

"Cash?" Buni said.

"Cash Carruthers. Guy that sang with you the other night. He owns the place, sort of."

"Wait a minute. Cash owns the Partaway?" Amber looked straight at Biggins.

"More or less. He owns the town, actually. This is all his land. I rent from him. But his dad and I were partners in the Partaway business, and his dad's gone, so I guess Cash owns his dad's share, and like I say, the town we're in. More or less."

"This is who?" Buni was lost.

"Mr. Goodweird." Amber said.

"Yikes. Mr. Goodweird owns a town? That's—that's. What can I say? That's seriously outside the normal operating range of my comprehension—is what I can say."

"Anyway, I gave him a call, and he's comin' out, so I want to talk to him about it. More money than I feel O.K. about okayin', if you see what I mean. So, you can wait or come back—"

"We'll wait." Amber cut him short. "We'll wait. We'll be outside."

"Suit yourself." Biggins walked back into the storeroom to count liquor bottles.

Buni and Amber walked out into the late afternoon sun and stood on the porch of the Partaway.

"This was the guy that sang with you that night, right?" Buni was troubled. "This don't mean he's gotta sing with us, does it?"

"He didn't sing with me. He did a number by himself. He was good—but in a—"

"Weird way. I know."

"No, he doesn't have to sing with us. But you should give him a try. He needs a little help, but you might could help him. Then, who knows, right?"

"Amber, the joke is 'the piano player has a girlfriend who sings so you gotta take 'em both'—not 'the singer has a boyfriend who's weird but gets to sing because he owns the town.' Which, as I say it, is funny in its own way, but still—not the same joke."

As Cash and Diana pulled up to the Partaway, Diana saw Buni and Amber sitting on two barrels under the portal of the restaurant and club. The sun was in Diana's eyes, and she couldn't see them clearly at first, but then Amber stood up.

To Diana, the most striking feature about Amber was her eyes, deep set and dark brown. Not just because they were beautiful, but because they were riveted on Cash, oblivious to all else. Amber held up a hand in greeting and eased down the single stair between the Partaway porch and ground level as Diana got out of the Jeep.

"I didn't know you owned this place," Amber said as she walked up to Cash. Buni was right behind her.

"Hi, Buni. Amber. This's Diana." Cash presented Diana with a gesture across the hood of the Jeep. Diana peeled off her Hermès scarf, shook her hair loose, and said, "Hi."

"I don't really own it—I. Well. Maybe. My dad and Henry were partners, so I sort of inherited it. My dad just passed away. So maybe I do—hadn't thought of it."

"Wow. So'd my mom. You remember her outside Cap'n Jack's?"

"Oh, Amber. Really? I'm so sorry to hear that. She was young." Cash was shocked.

"Bob Reno, one of her boyfriends, beat her up, and she died from it."

"My God, Amber. When was this?" Cash felt the awful adrenaline rush from unexpected bad news. Diana had moved around the Jeep and was listening intently. She was shocked as well.

"Sheriff come by that night. When we was playin' Buck's. Where you came. He told me. That's how come I run inside. That's how come I'm out here. With Buni. Lookin' for work. It was just me and mom. Now I got to work for real." Amber spoke in short jabs, getting everything out at once. Whatever gift she had for singing was not evident in conversation.

Biggins shuffled out onto the porch with his hand above

his eyes.

"Hey, Cash," he called in greeting.

"Henry. Say hello to Diana. Amber just told me about her mother. Did you hear?"

"No. What? Why'nt you all come inside where it's cool." Biggins waved them in.

As they all walked back inside the darkened bar, Cash said, "Amber just told me her mother was killed by Bob Reno. Did you know that?"

"No kiddin'? Man. I did not. I heard they sent Reno away. Didn't know it was your mother, though, Amber. Sorry to hear that."

They had all come to a stop and were standing in a circle in front of the bar.

"Well, it happened." Amber shrugged. "I told Mama he was trouble. Anyway, here we all are." Amber shoved her hands in the front pockets of her jeans and rocked back on her heels.

Amber's casual dismissal of her mother's death astounded Diana. She didn't know whether the girl was callous, stupid, or in some insane retreat from the truth. Diana had never been this close to murder. Not that she knew of.

"I need to make money singing. If I can. Buni can put together a good band. And if we can set up here regular, I could maybe get started. Build a crowd."

Cash looked questioningly at Henry.

"Yeah, except. Trouble is, well—" Henry said. "Maybe we should talk private for a minute."

"We can wait outside," Buni said. He motioned for Amber to come with him, and the two walked out the door.

Diana spoke the moment the door closed behind them. "I can't believe what I just heard—and saw. How well do you know those two? That poor girl." She was talking to Cash, but Biggins spoke.

"She's played here a few nights, but not with that Buni fella. She was playin' here night Cash came down and sang."

"That's the first night I met her," Cash said. "But I went to see her after that—on the night she's talking about, when her mother died. What a shock.'

"That's why I called," Biggins said. "I knew you had sort of connected with her—as a musician, or something. She wants to come in and set up and play regular, weekends, which is fine and all, 'cept she wants me to pay her seven-fifty a night, her and the band."

"And?"

"And!? Ain't no way. I can get about a hundred-twenty people in here. That's full, and even if everybody pays—course, with the bar it might come close—but seven-fifty is real wages. Real high. Nobody gets that around here. In a place like this. I paid one-fifty the night you sang. Anyway. I guess I'm sayin' if it was up to me, I'd have to say no—maybe not altogether no, but no at that price. But it really ain't up to me alone. S'why I called."

Diana, sensing the two men needed their freedom to talk, began a deliberate walk around the Partaway, examining everything as she tied and untied a knot in her scarf.

"Yeah, it's a hard one," Cash said, and pushed his hand through his hair. He didn't want his own new yearning, the thought of having a band he could sing with, to influence him, but he could not repress the thought. It overshadowed his attempt at reasonableness. Clearly it made no sense to hire Amber and Buni's band at those prices. The Partaway was not capable of sustaining such a cost.

"Think they would take less?"

"I reckon," Biggins said. "I can ask 'em."

"Well, wait." Cash had a sudden picture of Amber, wretched, on her own, though he suspected he did not know the reality of her situation. She was probably fine, living with Buni. Maybe even hustling the price up. Then, there it was again. The band at the Partaway couldn't say no to him, and Amber did say Buni could teach him some things. The fire of the music was burning in him now, and its main source of fuel was Cash's business sense, which it was now consuming at an astounding rate. "How long did they want to stay?"

"If we give 'em seven-fifty? Probably the rest of their natural life."

"O.K. So—how much could we realistically pay?"

"Like I say, one-fifty is about it, maybe two. Depends on the bar. An' whether anybody's gonna think of the Partaway as a music club and pay a cover, which right now they don't. Yeah. I'd say one-fifty—two, outside."

"I could make up the difference, perhaps. Give me a place to practice. Worth it to me. Cheap, in a way, given the value. But you couldn't tell them," Cash said.

"No. Yeah. I sorta figured that. Reason I called. However's fine with me, but just so's you know, we can't take more than one-fifty out o' the Partaway and keep goin'."

"O.K. O.K. I understand. One-fifty out of the Partaway. Let's do it. Offer the seven-fifty for, I guess, eight weeks. That's the end of summer. And—and I'll pick up the shortfall. The six."

Biggins nodded and went outside. Diana closed her inspection circle and ended up back at Cash. "Charming," she said. "Very real. Very."

Of course, whatever reality the Partaway may have enjoyed, whatever Diana was savoring, had just gone out the window with Cash's acceptance of the Partaway deficit. Cash had redefined the Partaway and changed it into something that was decidedly not what it appeared to be. It was a first for Cash, and he had done it without having any idea he had done it—another first.

Since Buni Rumble was nobody's fool, he could see the Partaway had no possibility of meeting Amber's request for seven-fifty a night, so when Biggins announced they had the job at that price, he also knew something had happened inside the Partaway with Cash and Biggins that went to more than simply hiring a house band. After Amber's stories of Mr. Goodweird, he feared the worst.

As Biggins shook his hand on the deal, Buni waited for Biggins to add the requirement that from time to time, Mr. Goodweird would like to play with the band. To his surprise,

Biggins said nothing about that, but Buni was certain he had not heard the last of it.

Seven hundred and fifty dollars a night may have been an impossibility in a room the size of the Partaway, but seven-fifty was what Biggins had agreed to, and it was certainly going to go a long way toward getting Amber on her feet. For that matter, it was going to go a long way toward getting him on his feet. No one was going to hear any complaints from Buni Rumble, not yet.

Cash and Diana walked out of the Partaway and stood on the porch with Buni and Amber.

"We were going to eat here," Cash said. "Would you like to join us?"

"We gotta get back," Buni said, at exactly the same time Amber said, "Great!" She grabbed Buni's hand and walked toward them, as Cash held the door open for them.

Above the door was a small electric sign that Biggins turned on at night. PARTAWAY was written in small glowing blue script that was being lassoed by a continually expanding and contracting rope of red neon, held by a bright yellow cowboy in high western boots. Had it been fifty times larger, it was the type of sign one was likely to see on the Las Vegas strip.

Chapter Eight

After dinner with Cash and the two musicians, as Diana referred to Buni and Amber, she and Cash spent two more days at his ranch. She did most of the talking; Cash was distant. Whatever subject, however she pressed, Cash remained unengaged, pleasant but perfunctory, like a word without its thought value.

They did what they usually did at Cash's ranch. They talked long about various things from their mutual and unique global perspective, informed and thoughtful as it was. They ate the local barbecue, took long drives on the beach, made love, and were solicitous and kind to each other.

For the first time, however, Diana felt there was a part of Cash she could not reach, especially during the two nights they went to the Partaway to eat and listen to Amber Fanfare. For Diana the outing was fun but trivial, an easy whiling away of an evening with some quirky music. There was much more to it for Cash. He was enraptured.

At the end of each evening, he made a special effort to see Buni and Amber, to talk about the show, ask about certain songs. He was careful to include Diana, but the talk was about things Diana hadn't the least notion of or interest in. Instead, she watched carefully to see if anything sparked between Amber and Cash. Whatever she saw came from Amber to Cash. Cash was a model of composure and rectitude, sending only a proper signal of open friendliness.

When Diana got back to the *Marianna* and was set to start work in earnest on the *Mariner* floating island, she tried to nestle the varied memories of her past few days with Cash in their usual cozy spot, ready to be relived like a scrapbook of old photos, but all she could think about was Amber Fanfare. Diana could see an authority in Amber, an intrinsic strength, and the way Diana figured it, Amber Fanfare was very likely undefeatable on her own turf.

Diana began looking at herself in the mirror more and more often, measuring, and wondering whether her beauty was fading. This was new to her. Diana's vanity centered itself first in influence and connections, then money and achievement, then at the very end of the list, her physical appearance. She always had a workable level of confidence in her looks, feeling attractive, if not beautiful. She did not want to be thinner or taller, she liked her face with its less than -perfect nose and less than perfect eyebrows, and she liked the color of her hair and eyes. She didn't much care whether men found her attractive, whether they looked at her or not. Sometimes they did, and sometimes was enough.

All that had changed.

As she stared into the mirror in her dressing room, the fine wrinkles in her neck suddenly appeared to be grim evidence of the passing years. She had never noticed them until now. With no change, they had become hideous. Then she noticed the ridge of her nose had an obvious hump in it, halfway down, not exactly a crook yet, but maybe, someday. Her eyebrows were thin and weak, making her brow look low. Around her eyes, a shallow web of wrinkles had begun to appear, and there was the first hint of folds in her eyelids, tiny pleats. Under each eye was a dreadful and precisely named bag. Perhaps, she thought, she would do something about the folds, at least.

When she found out the surgery to remove wrinkles in eyelids was the easiest, quickest, and safest of all the cosmetic surgeries, she set up an appointment to have it done. The blepharoplasty took place at a Houston clinic, where Diana went as an outpatient. It was over in a few hours, and her two black eyes healed in a few days. To Diana, her face appeared brighter and more youthful, less tired and old, but the casual observer would have been hard-pressed to see much difference in before-and-after pictures. Cash's only comment, unfortunately, was "Are your eyes all right?" Diana assured him she was fine.

He was not insensitive, but he was distracted. He had finally gotten around to asking Buni if it was O.K. for him to sit in, and to his delight, Buni welcomed him. In fact, Buni had grown to like Cash quite a lot. He still had his reservations about Cash's dalliance with music, but there was a sincerity to Cash that made Buni forgive him. Naturally the idea that Buni would allow Cash to hang around, perhaps even come to a rehearsal, was truly exciting to Amber, though she had managed to calm herself down a bit in Cash's presence, a mixture of Buni's gentle admonition and her own pride. To mark the event, Buni revamped the band.

It now consisted of Firegate on guitar, Norba on drums, and a new player, Marion Bluster, on bass. Under Buni's tight hand, they made a fine ensemble, all happily secondary to Amber's fantastic singing.

Usually the band would play an opening set at the Partaway around 8:00, then Amber would sing a set around 9:30, then the band would play another set, and finally Amber would close the night with a late-night set, usually a scorcher, since the band and the crowd by that time was loose, lively, and ready to play.

Buni worked it out with Biggins so that only the band would play Thursdays and Amber would join them on Fridays and Saturdays, and Biggins would only have to pay for the weekends. At that the band was making fifteen-hundred dollars a week, more than any other bar band for miles.

When Cash asked if he could sit in, it was after one of the early Thursday night band-only sessions, as he sat at a table with Buni. Cash made it a point to come to the Partaway at least twice a week, usually when Amber was singing, but tonight he wanted to talk to Buni alone.

After Buni said, "Sure, why not," Cash took a deep breath

and asked, "Do you think it would be O.K. if I sang a number or two? I mean, O.K. with you and Amber?"

"Hey man," Buni said, "It's your club and your town, and I guess it's your band. You can do what you want." He knew it was exactly the thing Cash did not want to hear. It made Cash uneasy.

"Yeah," Cash said. "I know, maybe that could—one could think of it like that, but I wouldn't do it if you thought it was a bad idea. I'm really looking to you here, Buni." Cash was ingenuous, a quality that made Buni like Cash more and more.

Buni smiled broadly, breaking the tension, and said, "No problem with me. And hey, you know what? I think it's a good idea. I don't think you should do more than one number, though—and from what I've heard, I hope it's not 'Cherry Blossom Time.' Most certainly not 'Cherry Blossom Time.'" Buni laughed.

Cash did too. "No, no cherry blossoms. I'll stick with the classics. So? Would you help me? Could you, you know, maybe teach me some stuff?"

Buni's smile faded. He looked down and rubbed his chin with two fingers. Buni squirmed in his seat, turned sideways to Cash, and then squinted his eyes and said, "I don't, uh—I'll try. But man, you got to know there is only so much of this stuff that, uh, you know, that can be taught. Know what I'm sayin'?"

Cash did not know what he was saying. He was of the mind that everything could be taught. He shook his head and stared inquisitively, unblinking, focused. "I guess not," he said.

"Umm. Yeah, O.K.," Buni said. "Well, that's—you don't know what I mean, and, umm, I don't know what to say. 'Cept I'll teach you whatever I can. Happy to. Yeah. But it ain't much can be taught, is what it is." He paused. "You wanna go up there this next set?"

"Oh. No." Cash did want to, but the moment Buni made the offer, the feeling of stage fright overtook him, and he retreated. There were about fifteen people in the Partaway, none of them there for the music, but it was enough to choke Cash.

"You sure? I can get you set up easy enough," Buni encouraged him. Cash looked down.

"Izzy's got nine guitars in the car. He'll let you play one."

"Well, I—" Cash stuttered.

"You might have to buy him a house, though."

Cash shot Buni a look and saw an impish twinkle in his eye.

"Right," Cash said, acknowledging the rib. "But I need to work up to it. So not tonight. I'll bring my own guitar down, and—I mean, I just wanted to make sure it was—that you were O.K. with it. Amber, too."

* * *

"Like I say, it's simply a question of economics." Horton was sitting with Diana in the foreman's office of the temporary shipbuilding facility that Diana had set up in Texas City, a few minutes from the berth of the *Marianna*. "The idea's good, but there are a lot of good ideas. This is a big play. If you have the engineering side and the marketing side worked out, I think we can get the economics working. I'm not sure, mind you, but I think we can. Have you been out with this to any of your investment bankers?"

"I called Stan at Goldman, but he's scared like everybody else right now. Are you thinking we can work this up as an offering?"

"No." Horton shuffled through the stack of papers. "I think we have to look at something more creative. I don't know what, right now, but until we have a model for the economics, we can't get anywhere. Are you funding all this yourself right now?"

Diana nodded. They sat silent for a moment, both staring at the pile of papers. Finally Horton spoke.

"I was thinking of giving myself a going-away party. A 'leaving Sandra Corporation' party. I was going to ask you if I could rent the *Marianna*. Maybe we could combine the party with some of this." He held up the papers.

Diana gently rubbed her fingertips in her eyes and relieved some of the tension and the residual pressure from the surgery. "That could work. Sure. She's scheduled to start cruises in a few days, but there's some checkerboard in the calendar. Let's talk."

Horton picked up a small pile of the hydrofoam carbon beads from a shallow dish and poured them from one hand to the other. "Did Cash see this?"

Diana nodded.

"What did he think?" Horton asked.

"Didn't exactly say. I think he liked it. We talked a little about what it can do. He was noncommittal, though. I think he—I think he liked it, but I don't know more than that."

Horton stood up and paced. "If Cash was interested in this, he would bring a lot of interest with him. I think it would be important to involve him."

"We have plans for me to go back out to the ranch this weekend. You want to come out? We're going to the Partaway for dinner and to watch this band Cash likes. I think he may even be planning on playing with them."

Horton stopped his pacing and thought for a few seconds. "This is the bar? This Partaway is a bar?"

"More like a little steakhouse lounge. The band plays there after dinner. But it's very rustic. Steaks are so-so. Nothing special. Cash goes for the music."

"Yeah. O.K. That's a good idea. Why don't you ask him if I can come down. I don't think he'll mind. I'll plan on coming down early. Give us some time to talk. If Cash were interested, would come to this party, that could get us started in a meaningful way."

The party Horton was thinking about would reverberate through the community like a seismic wave, especially with a carefully chosen guest list. When the word got out, particularly if Cash were there, everyone would want to come, most eagerly the politicos and grantsmen.

Horton had contributed to several political candidates, following Cash's early lead, and had ended up on everyone's short list. In addition, a half-dozen magazines listed him in the top echelon of the wealthiest people in America, a status he secretly welcomed, while professing annoyance. Cash, on the other hand, had managed to disappear from all such lists. A search engine on the Internet would turn up dozens of pictures of Horton, each with various assessments of his wealth, some more accurate than others. The same type of search would turn up nothing on Cash. This visibility cost Horton his privacy. He was routinely and constantly petitioned for gifts of money.

The worst and most insistent pests were the politicians, and Horton found a wicked pleasure in dealing with them, a particularly smug satisfaction in his access to the Oval Office. He practiced a studied indifference in the presence of the more famous or more powerful politicians.

"I'm to the point where no one impresses me anymore," he once said in an effort to impress someone.

He was happy about the buzz the party caused, and true to form, he pretended pique, pretended to be annoyed by the hovering, hopeful applicants.

It would be a long party over several days, set in two stages. The first would start near the beginning of the week with a certain guest list that Horton wanted to use as an investor pool in the *Mariner*. Then, on the weekend, he would bring in Cash, and more people would join in, the movie stars, politicians, the glitterati, when—he hoped—each would astonish the other in a frenzy of glamour, money, sophistication, and wit. The press would definitely not be invited. They would not understand such extravagance, such luxury. Horton was sure they would trivialize it, or worse, ridicule it.

In a truck stop motel on the outskirts of Corpus Christi, Amber Fanfare was lying in a tiny, shallow bathtub full of drugstore bubbles. She and Buni had set up house for the duration of the Partaway gig in one of the cheap units. They had rented the room for Thursday, Friday, and Saturday of each weekend for the next eight weeks to save the drive from Helensburg to Buni's apartment in Surfside.

Aside from Buni's apartment and this motel room, Amber had no place of her own to live, but she pushed the thought away. She would deal with that when the eight weeks at the Partaway were up.

She had never had so much money, never been in an environment even this plush, so she was trying to relax and enjoy it. She wasn't enjoying it as much as she thought she should.

She used her big toe to play with a drop of water from the tub faucet. The bath-shower-combo tub was a thin-walled fiberglass affair that would only hold a few inches of water. Even though Amber was petite, she was barely covered by the water, and the cheap, strawberry-scented bath gel had only created a stack of bubbles slightly lower than her shoulders, forcing her to stay within reach of the tub's obvious design to deter such extravagances. The main nuisance, however, was the mild abrasion from the archipelago of flower-shaped yellow rubber stickers lining the bottom of the tub, stuck there to prevent an occupant from slipping when taking a shower.

Regardless of how she maneuvered, they scraped against her skin. In fact, the nonslip stickers were going to win the bubble-bath wars in the crummy motel tub, and she knew it; she was simply trying to get in as much time as she could before she couldn't stand it anymore. The drip from the faucet provided momentary distraction, but when the water drop finally rolled down her foot and off her heel, she decided enough was enough. It was time to get out, get dry, and get dressed for the day. It was three in the afternoon.

The motel had two regular-size beds separated by a Formica wall-mounted shelf with a small open compartment beneath it. In the compartment were a phone book and a Gideon Bible; on top were one lamp bolted to the surface, a phone, and the remote for the television. The television hung from the opposite wall by a tubular brace that allowed it to swivel left and right, above a low chest of four drawers. The carpet was woven in tight loops from a synthetic fiber that was a permanent spill-and-stain color designed to camouflage everything from blood to motor oil.

From a wood-grain-patterned vinyl-covered ice bucket that sat on the chest, Amber grabbed a tiny piece of melting ice and began sucking on it as she pulled the towel around her. She went to the window, cracked the curtains, and peered out at the blistering hot asphalt parking lot outside the door. It was 102 degrees outside.

Amber dried off and then sat naked on the edge of the bed, staring at herself in the mirror. On a chest against the wall was a pile of her clothes, all the clothes she owned except for the two shirts hanging on the coat rack next to the sink.

She fished a pair of panties from the pile, drew them on, and then unrolled a pair of jeans and slipped into them. She pulled on a women's-cut T-shirt, then looked again at herself in the mirror.

For a second so brief, she thought she saw Chastity standing in the mirror looking back at her, saw her mother in her own eyes. The vision slammed into her, almost doubling her over, but she calmed herself, no reaction. She walked to the dresser, opened one of the drawers, and took out her wallet. It was a new, pink, plastic wallet she had bought with the small advance Biggins had given them. After two weeks of work at the Partaway, it was full of small bills.

She carefully pulled out the money and laid it in piles on the dresser. A pile for ones, fives, tens, twenties, and fifties. She had two fifties. In all she had four hundred and eleven dollars. More money than she had ever had at one time in her life.

More money than her mother had when she was beaten to death by the vile Bob the Slob.

And before another thought could cross the threshold to her conscious mind, she was crying.

It was not a wail, there were no sobs, only a stream of tears far beyond her control. They flowed from her eyes, across her cheeks, down her chin, and then dropped off onto the wretched carpet. Her arms hung straight at her sides, falling from her shoulders like the tears from her eyes, from the well of her heart, which was meek and sad, and if she had to admit it, afraid.

They were simple tears.

The tears of a little girl who missed her mother.

Chapter Nine

B uni's Volvo sputtered away, talking to itself as it came to idle outside the door of the motel room. Buni grabbed the stack of CDs and cassettes he had brought from the apartment in Surfside and started in just as Amber wiped any trace of tears from her face.

"I got something Mr. Goodweird can sing, I think," Buni said as he came through the door. Amber disappeared into the bathroom to finish dressing.

"I think you should quit calling him that," she called out. "He's cool."

"He doesn't seem to mind, but O.K. You're right. He is cool. It could have gone the other way—" Buni stopped short. He was still not ready to tell Amber his suspicions about Cash paying their wages. "But you're right."

Of all the skills Amber had acquired in her short life, none was more impressive than her ability to draw herself up into her own beauty, expressing it fully, without one cheap trick. She had lived with the shabbiest clothes, hand-me-downs, ninety-nine-cent-sale items, and a mother whose sense of finery consisted of glossy costume jewelry and leather. In spite of it all, Amber always managed to find a way to make herself resplendent. Such a transformation was taking place now in the bathroom as she scrutinized the color, scale, drape, and silhouette of every article of clothing she had to create exactly the right look for today. This was the first time she would actually spend several hours close with Cash in her own territory. She was excited and wanted to look right. Though she had nothing to choose from but two well-worn shirts and some jeans, with the addition of a belt and a scarf she managed to dress herself so well that Buni said "Wow" when she came into the room. Her dark lustrous hair was drawn back off her face, and she looked more mature and extraordinarily pretty.

"You're looking special. This for Mr. Good—Cash?"

"Yep." She walked to Buni and kissed him affectionately and spun around. "How can he resist?"

"You're breaking my heart, A."

"Yeah, right," Amber said as she plopped down on one of the two beds. For the past few weeks, Cash's presence at the shows had kept Amber on her toes and her libido wide awake.

It was a simple case of chemistry, she thought. There was not anything she could point to about Cash that specifically lit her fire. If there was any one thing more than another, she would say it was his courage, but that didn't say it all. Chemistry. Courage. That was the best she could do.

This was the day Buni and Cash had agreed to rehearse to get Cash ready to sit in for an entire show. Cash would play rhythm guitar for most of a set and get to sing one number about halfway through—depending, Buni had told him, on what kind of a roll Amber was on.

They were working hard to build up a clientele, to get a good word-of-mouth going, and they were succeeding. The last weekend had been full—Henry said there were a hundred and twenty people in the place—and most important, they had come for the music and stayed for all sets. The bar business was booming.

As nice a guy as Cash was and however much he was paying, Buni didn't want to throw all the new goodwill away on Cash's nutty desire to sing the blues. If Amber was on fire, if the crowd was with her and there wasn't a space for Cash, he was going to keep Cash from singing however he could.

On the other hand, if things were all good, if Cash couldn't screw things up, then Buni was going to let him sing "Dust My Broom."

"Dust My Broom" was a great song by Elmore James, a singer and writer from Mississippi who made his mark in Chicago. It was one of his most famous songs and contained a signature slide-guitar lick. Firegate played a mean slide, so even if Cash cratered the same way he had the first night, the band could put enough music in play to keep the room alive.

Amber was shuffling through the CDs strewn over Buni's bed.

"I was gonna teach him "Dust My Broom," Buni said to her and pointed to the Elmore James CD that contained the song. Amber looked at it, then up at Buni, surprised.

"For real?"

"Well, he ain't gonna be able to cop the same space as Elmore, that's a no-kiddin' fact, but Izzy's gonna play slide, and the song is a natural blues. So it'll be good businessman blues—billionaire blues."

Biggins had filled in Amber and Buni on Cash's holdings, though most of it was wrong, full of rumors and distorted information. Inaccurate, but impressive.

"Leave him alone. I was asking as a singer, you think he can really sing this?"

"You already know what I think, baby. I think this whole thing is his Personal Las Vegas. He's got all the symptoms. So the usual rules of music do not apply. This is the simple awful-to-behold imperative of the America Gene. There is not a legitimate act anywhere in here."

"You are so harsh." Amber said. "He's not—"

"O.K.—O.K. Then let's just say I, only Buni Rumble, me, don't know for sure what the guy wants with any of this. If I got to throw him in somewhere, "Dust My Broom" is pretty warm water, the song has got all the stuff, all he has to do is sing it. I ain't lettin' him sing something he wrote, I'll tell ya that. He played me some stuff when we was alone last week that, man, I just—whoa—so if he wants to sing with us, he's gonna have to step up to some fastballs. "Dust My Broom" comes in straight and level over the plate. He should be able to hit it. A little."

"And you'll help him, right?" Amber said.

"He keeps askin' that. You keep askin' that. No. I can't help him, Amber. How the hell do you help somebody play the blues—or rock and roll? You either play it or you don't."

"You helped me," she said.

"We gotta get goin'. I told him we'd meet him at the Partaway at 4:30." Buni went to the closet and started changing into his performing clothes. Black jeans, black shirt, bolo tie. "And no, I did not help you. Maybe I was helpful to you, because you knew what you needed. I was afraid of you. You got more blues power in your little fingernail than I've seen in a whole chain gang."

"Don't toss this guy to the wolves, is all I'm sayin'," she said.

"I'm not. I'm not. I'm gonna teach him 'Dust My Broom.' If he needs more help after that, then you help him."

Amber knew Cash was never going to be a blues singer, and she knew why, though she couldn't explain it in words. What puzzled her was why Buni reacted so. Over the past few weeks, Cash had proved himself to be at least a normal guy, normal enough. It could have been different. He could have been slimy—but he wasn't. And he wasn't dangerous. So if Cash was a good guy and all he wanted to do was hang out and play along with a blues band, why was that bad?

"You act like you're mad about this," Amber said with a "you better not be" inflection.

Buni turned from the mirror, where he was working on putting in his dress earring. "Amber, look, I don't wanna do this with you. All I said was if there is an America Gene, this guy is the poster boy for it, and his PLV is so close and so big we might all get sucked in there and never get out, but no. I am not mad. O.K.? I like the guy. I do." Amber looked at the stack of CDs and tapes on the bed. She held up a tape.

"You brought your Tyrone Edwards tape?"

"I was listening to it in the car. I needed a hit of the real stuff. A, I'm not sayin' I won't help him. I will. But there's only so much I can do. If he ain't expecting nothing except to sing along with the blues, that's fine with me. Anything more'n that's twisted. Please, A."

Amber hugged Buni tight and kissed him on the cheek.

Cash was already at the Partaway. He had been there since 2:30 that afternoon. This time he had his instrument—a 1962 Fender Stratocaster guitar—and a two-piece Fender Tremolux amp. They were wildly expensive when he bought them, collector's pieces, and they were becoming more valuable as time went on. For good reason. It was an excellent instrument and amplifier, with exquisite sound.

He set himself up on a metal folding chair next to and behind Firegate. He sat, noodling, in anticipation, playing this tune and that, and trying to sing for an hour, but he couldn't take his mind off the booths that lined the back wall, under the windows.

All the booths, save one, had a window over it, and it made Cash wonder.

Henry Biggins came up to the edge of the stage. "Nervous? Excited?"

"Little of both, I think. Henry, why is there one booth without a window?"

Henry turned to look where Cash was pointing. Cash laid his guitar up against the amp and jumped from the stage and walked to the booth. Henry followed him.

"Used to be door there," Henry said. "I got these booths from a sale and closed it up in order to get them all along this wall."

Cash stared at the booth, arms folded across his chest.

"So there are what, six booths, they hold—four each."

"I can get six in if it's a party, and they don't mind. But I figure four."

Cash walked along the line of booths, tapping each one on its tabletop as he passed. "So that's twenty-four or thirty-six, depending." He stopped, turned, and looked at Biggins.

"Right," Biggins said.

Cash started to walk slowly from the main room to the bar, which was in a small anteroom through a large portal. "Then you—have you got a second, Henry?"

Henry held up a stack of papers. "Lemme put these on my desk. I'll be right back." Henry walked to the office, which was in the back of the kitchen.

Cash walked a slow loop around the room the bar was in, about twenty-five feet long and fifteen feet wide, not including the space behind the bar. He walked out into the open floor of the main room of the Partaway, where there were eight tables randomly situated in configurations for two to six people, in all, thirty-two chairs. Biggins returned and stood beside Cash.

"What are you thinkin'? he asked

Cash paced around the tables, looking at the stage. "I'm thinking about getting more people in the place."

"License is for one-twenty," said Biggins. "I been pushin' that by about twenty."

"Aren't you turning people away?" Cash asked.

"Sure am. People like this kid. She's good. Lotta kids comin in, too—by kids, I mean nineteen, twenty. College types. Families leave around 6, 6:30. But for the band, place has been filling right up. I don't know how to get any more in here though."

"May be a way." Cash rubbed his forehead and walked to the side of the stage, an empty area, with no seating or a table. He pointed to the wall beside the stage. "What's on the other side of this?"

"Parking lot."

"Henry, I think if you put a door there—where is the fire exit now?" Cash looked around.

Biggins pointed to an exit through the kitchen.

"I think if you made this a fire exit, I mean, you can't put a table here, anyway, can't see the stage, so if you made this an exit, we could get a license in this room for three hundred."

"Three hundred?" Biggins didn't believe it.

"I think so, yeah. Room's big enough."

"O.K.," Biggins said. "Say we did. How do you set it up for three hundred?"

"I think you gotta lose two of the booths, one on each end, that'll leave four. With those spaces open, you can set up the tables long way to the stage. If you do that, then, leaving the tables the same size you can get eight, twelve, fourteen, eighteen tables of six in here. Because they're long ways, the dance floor opens up on each side, so you can put some two-tops around the edge, and get say six, eight two-tops around the edge of the dance floor. That still leaves a big aisle here for the fire exit." Cash drew an imaginary line along a wall. "Two big aisles for service and people moving around." He traced an arc with his finger from the kitchen to where they stood. "So what is that?" Cash did an instant calculation in his head that was like a magic trick to Biggins. "That's a one-forty-eight there. Bar seats ten, plus thirty standing, that's forty, so you got one-eighty-eight. You're still not charging a cover, are you?"

Biggins shook his head. "Don't think I can, Cash. People around here are poor."

"Not a big cover, say ten dollars. Think people will pay ten dollars to see Amber Fanfare?"

"Might. Ten's not so bad. That's a—let's see—a—like, a thirty-dollar date, if you buy two drinks. Thirty. Well. Thirty's tough. Maybe. Don't know."

"I think they would, Henry. People like to pay for things. Free is always a trick. People like to trade. I think 10 would work. Just a hunch."

"We could try it."

"O.K. But wait. So, we got, let's say, we got a a hundred eighty in here at ten bucks, is eighteen hundred dollars, and we set it up for two shows, dinner show at 8:00, late show at 11:00.

That's the way it is now. Right."

Biggins nodded. "There's no break or nothin', but that's how—they play that many shows, if that's what you mean."

"Right. So we bifurcate the night. Split it in two pieces. Two shows, early and late. If they're full, not to plan on it, but just for the math, that's thirty-six hundred a night for the band."

"For the band!" Biggins almost shouted.

"Right. You don't want the door, the cover. You want the bar and the food. The cover is found money because of the band."

"But why should the band get—thirty-six hundred dollars. That's more than the whole bar makes. Almost."

Cash had heard this lament before but with many more zeroes on the end of the argument.

"Don't you want the band to get rich, Henry?" Cash let the question settle in.

"Yeah. But thirty-six hundred is—is—" Biggins was lost.

"What they're worth. If people will pay it, let the band have it. Don't forget, if nobody comes, they don't make anything. They're at risk, too. We make ours off the bar and the food. And if you go from one-twenty a night to three-sixty, just do the math. We win big. And so does the band. Isn't this a good idea?"

Biggins was flummoxed. Cash had, in a simple stroll, with a few simple changes of a door, some rearranged furniture, and a few new low-cost and no-cost elements, just managed to make the Partaway's business increase several hundred percent. Of course, this was the Cash magic, his almost superhuman ability to see the best path, how to maximize the elements of a business so everybody won. He had done it routinely for years. All his business associates watched him with awe when he was in this mode, and they all had made millions because of it.

For Biggins, Cash might just as well have picked up a truck by its back bumper and lifted it ten feet in the air. He didn't know how to react. Sure, it was a good idea. It was a great idea. There had to be something wrong with it.

"So. Wait," Biggins said. "What—I mean—how do we set the tables?"

Cash looked at the clock in the bar, with its big white hands and large band of blue neon. It was nearly 4:30. He knew Buni and Amber would be arriving any minute. "I'll write everything down for you. Kind of a plan. Nothing complex. Can you get somebody to put a door in here? That's the most important thing right now."

Henry nodded. "I think I can get somebody out next week."

Cash had heard this before too. He dealt often with people who had no sense of time as money, which, if they were adversarial, always gave Cash a winning advantage.

"I was thinking this afternoon. Latest tomorrow morning."

Another thundering shock to Biggins. He never thought this fast in his life. "Now? Not—no, I don't think so. It'll take a day at least to open that up, put a door in—"

"O.K.," Cash said. "Let me handle it. But you can be here, right?" Cash flipped open his cell phone and touched a number.

"I don't come in till about 11 on Saturdays, but—"

"Not tomorrow, Henry, tonight. After the show. You'll need

to stay here."

Henry was now wide-eyed and near total meltdown. He nodded, less in assent and more in astonishment. He felt like it was all impossible.

Cash spoke into the phone. "Hey, Brandon. I need a crew to put in a door at the Partaway tonight. Need to get it done in a few hours. Nonstructural wall, probably need a header and a couple of panic-bar doors. Regulation, fire code, metal. Six-foot opening, two three-footers. Heavy stuff, you know the drill. No, gotta do it tonight. Three a.m. is first you can get in here. You'll need a stack of guys. Gotta be up to code and out of here by 11 a.m. tomorrow. I'd call Gus and Tommy. Also call Lorraine and see if she can get the fire marshal out for a waiver tomorrow around noon. O.K. No. Just come on out. Yep. Later." He flipped the phone shut.

Biggins was speechless. It was the sound of Buni's Volvo wheezing into the parking lot that broke the spell.

"God, Cash. How much is this gonna cost? And, do you—I mean, will this work—I didn't, don't—" but Biggins was back in overload.

Cash put his hand on Biggins shoulder, gently, like an older brother. "It'll cost plenty, Hank. But it's not about how much it costs, it's about how much it'll make. And it'll work. I'm sure of it. I've been watching the crowds, too. Plenty of people want in here."

There was a rattle at the stage door, and Amber and Buni walked in from the heat and the light without the slightest notion how much their fortunes had just changed.

They strolled up to Cash; Amber gave him a friendly hug, and Buni shook his hand. "Hi, Hank," Amber said. "You O.K.?" It was an offhand remark, but as soon as she said it, she saw Biggins was in a strange state. He wasn't unhappy, but it was almost like he didn't know where he was. Amber waited for the answer more intently than the question warranted.

"I'm good, I guess," Biggins said, and walked toward his office.

Buni watched him go. He turned to Cash after a second. "So. You all set?"

Cash swallowed hard. His heart picked up several beats per minute, and his breath came shorter and faster. "I think so."

"I'm gonna get a drink. You want anything before we start?" Cash shook his head no.

"Bring me something, I don't care. Soft," Amber said.

Amber and Cash walked to the bandstand and stepped up. Amber went over to Cash's guitar, bent over, and looked at it. "Wow," she said. "This is some hot gear."

Buni jumped on the stage with two plastic glasses and handed one to Amber. "I just hit the sprayer. Can't tell which is which. It's club soda or 7-Up. Man, look at this." Buni set the drink on his piano and bent over Cash's guitar with Amber. "This is a sixties, right?"

"Sixty-two," Cash said. "I bought it a few years ago."

"Lemme hear it," Amber said.

Cash flipped on the standby switch of the amplifier and threw the guitar strap over his shoulder. He took a few weak plucks at the strings and then exhaled deeply. He started a rhythm pattern between two chords, a kind of R&B pattern he learned from a Curtis Mayfield record. He was a better guitarist than a singer, that was certain. He had practiced hours on his own and could keep up with complex chord changes and rhythm patterns. Even if not inspired, the guitar sounded superb.

"Well done, sir. Most fine," Buni said. He sat down at the piano and started to play along with Cash, jamming with the same Mayfield rhythm. Buni's left hand set down the great basic feel he was known for.

When Cash heard it, he spontaneously smiled and relaxed. His playing smoothed out, and he started playing along with Buni. Cash didn't know he was following Buni. It sounded much more to him as if they were playing together, but it didn't make any difference. Buni could feel Cash's following lag, kept the time with authority, and pulled him along effortlessly. He smiled at Cash and nodded, and Cash smiled back.

"Yeah," Amber said, and sat down on Cash's amplifier, sipping her drink.

They played this way for a minute or two, and then Buni dribbled to a stop and banged the keyboard a few times, signaling the end of the jam.

These moments were the happiest time imaginable for Cash. He was ecstatic. When they quit, he chuckled, as did Amber.

"So that's cool," Buni said. "You could get a fire started with that rig. I brought you a song I think you could sing if you want."

Buni opened his case beside him on the piano stool and pulled out the Elmore James CD. "'Dust My Broom.' You know this?"

Cash nodded and looked at his feet. He was almost childlike. "Yeah. I've heard it. Great."

"It's straight up, you know, just Elmore doin' his Elmore thang." Buni popped the CD into the player hooked through the sound system on the stage. The song blasted out at full concert volume through the Partaway. They saw Biggins close the door to his office in the kitchen.

The edge on James's voice lacerated the air around them, carving it up like a pumpkin. "I'm own gittup ina moanen, I b'leev I'll duss my broom." The voice blew the words out from the speakers like a hurricane, followed by the slide guitar lick, famous throughout the blues world, wherever rock and roll was played—fabled, honored.

Cash picked up the CD cover and was surprised to see the picture of James. He was sitting down. Cash felt his hands get clammy. When the song was finished playing, Buni walked back to the piano and sat down. He started the moderate shuffle in the key and tempo of the James record.

Cash wiped his hands on his pants as he stood up to the microphone. Buni kept the vamp going, playing the same chord over and over, waiting for Cash to start.

Cash took a deep breath and started to sing, but before he could, he stepped back from the microphone. His mind was racing. James's voice still rattled through his head. He tried to find the rhythm Buni was laying down, but his legs had started shaking, and he couldn't lift the heel or toe of his foot for fear of falling down.

Amber was sitting on the edge of his amp, looking down at the stage floor, waiting. Cash walked back to the microphone, took another deep breath and started singing a half-beat behind where he was supposed to. "I'm going to get up in the mornin'. I believe I'll dust my broooom."

By the end of the phrase he was in time—but by the end of the phrase, Amber was laughing hysterically. Cash stopped playing and looked at her. Buni kept playing a few more bars, and then he broke into laughter and stopped.

"Amber, goddammit!" Buni yelled, and laughed harder.

Amber stood up and walked to Cash, who felt faint and confused. She was still laughing hard when she put her arms around him, sliding her hands underneath his guitar, around his waist, hanging off him, still laughing.

Cash looked down at her, scrunched between his guitar and him. He didn't know what to do, but the laughter infected him, and he smiled. Amber looked up at him, bright-eyed, affectionate. The laughing faded.

"You b'leev you'll what?" she said, then started laughing again.

Cash laughed with her now. The three of them shook the moment down with barks and yelps of laughter for the next few seconds. Finally the laughter dispersed, scattering in slow moans.

"You believe you'll dust your broom?" Amber said.

"What?" Cash said. "Isn't that it? Aren't those the words?"

"Yeah that's the words, but—that's not what they mean." Amber, focused now, took a deep breath, put her head back. "I'm own gittup in the morning, I b'leev Ill dust mah broom," she sang softly, looking directly at Cash. She didn't use the same inflections or pronunciation James had; it was her own, but the words were infused with a sexuality, an intent, a passion that had to do with release. She whispered in Cash's ear, "What did I just say, baby?"

Cash looked at her and nodded, speechless.

"So," she said. "Sing that."

Buni, perfect accompanist that he was, aware of each millisecond of each moment onstage, started the blues vamp again, waiting for Cash to sing. Cash couldn't play the guitar with Amber hung around his waist. He tried to reach it, but she wouldn't move. He held his elbows out like the wings of a baby chick.

"Leave the guitar alone. What'd I just sing?" She nudged him.

Amber was tapping her foot in time to Buni's playing, and Cash felt the rhythm flow up through the base of his spine every time her heel came down. All at once, a landscape opened up to him. It was like a sexual embrace, but nonphysical. He could see where the downbeats were, like tombstones in a desert. He closed his eyes, and all he could see was Amber Fanfare and then, to his surprise, he knew exactly what the words meant, and he sang them exactly how he felt them. "I'm own get up ina morning—and I believe I'll dust my broom." Amber squeezed tightly. Buni's piano started to thunder.

"Yes, you will," Amber said into his chest.

"I believe I'll dust my broom," Cash sang again, and with those words, fell full into the song.

Amber released him and stood back, letting him float up. She kept one finger curled through a belt loop on his jeans. Cash started to play along with Buni, and suddenly he was airborne in a new world. He repeated the phrase, eyes still closed, leaning down, bearing down on the mic.

The shrill explosive sound of a slide guitar blasted across the stage at the point in the song where it was supposed to come in. It startled Cash, and he jerked up from his hunch over the microphone. Izzy Firegate had come in and set up and was playing along. He could see Marion was hooking up his bass as well, getting ready to join in. He felt his belt loop tug. He looked at Amber who gave him a look that scolded and cajoled "don't lose focus." Cash closed his eyes and started in on the second verse. It wasn't the second verse to the song as James sang it, but it was the way Cash remembered it, the way he felt it. "I b'leev, I b'leev. I b'leev my time ain't long."

And his vision was taken over by the image of sitting with his dad around the fire started for the evening meal outside the cold rock house in San Antonio. He saw his father from the back, bent over the fire preparing the food. In that instant Cash saw the weight of the world on Leland's shoulders, and he felt the weight, while at the same time he saw the world hold Leland up, like Leland had held him. The words welled in Cash, carried like tiny pieces of driftwood on an immense wave of emotion.

As the words flowed from his mouth, his hands strummed

the guitar in perfect time with Buni and Firegate, not following or leading but of one mind, one tempo, and the next thing he knew Marion was there and the bass started its huge thumping tones in time with the rest.

For the next few minutes, Cash sang each verse over and over, alternating between the two. Every time, the song felt better. Every time the meaning of the two verses came clearer, one potent, sexy, anxious; the other a lament, an inevitable end, but with a relief it will all be over soon.

Finally, Buni gave the musical clues to end the song. At the close, Cash spun to face Buni and Amber, Marion and Izzy. A family. They were smiling at him. Amber was back on Cash's amp. She was looking at Buni and nodding. Buni was the only one whose countenance was not one of complete acceptance.

"That's as close as you're gonna get to that, I think. That sounded fine. Well done, sir," Buni said as he stood up and stretched. None of the other band members said a word, but they acknowledged Cash in a way they hadn't before now. As Cash walked to his amp and swung the guitar from his neck, Amber stood up to allow Cash to lean it against his amp. She waved a "pay no attention" to Buni's remark with her hand and then placed it around the back of his neck and pulled Cash down low so she could whisper directly in his ear.

"Any time, Cash. Any time," she said, and kissed him ever so slightly on the earlobe.

Chapter Ten

The model of the *Mariner* looked like a garage door wallowing on the surface of the water in the oily estuary of Galveston Bay. Horton, Diana, and Vittorio Falucci, a dashing twenty-seven–year-old from Genoa who had invented the carbon hydrofoam, were on board a tender from the *Marianna,* watching the test of the first mini-model of the floating island. The center structure reached into the water several feet below the collar of carbon hydrofoam panels, with small electric motors on the underwater booms. There were eight other engineers and craftsmen present on two Zodiacs slowly circling the model, holding it up with short cables tied to the boats.

Something was wrong. The displacement of the panels would only support their own weight. Every time one of the engineers placed any extra weight on the collar, it would sink. Even with the panels linked together, as the main plan called for, they still would not support any substantial excess weight.

After a while, the engineers shored up the carbon foam panels with Styrofoam, so the collar would at least support the center and they could test the motors.

Falucci was visibly upset. He was calling questions to the engineers in the Zodiac about the manufacture of the panels, trying to determine if the Texas builders had followed his instructions perfectly. To Horton, the questioning was overwrought, and there was something suspicious in Vittorio's scurrying about.

The engine tests went well enough, and all agreed the basic concept of fully rotating motors affixed to a main spar sunk in the water would provide some propulsion. That was as far as they would get today.

It was late in the afternoon when Diana, Horton, and Vittorio sat on the rear deck of the tender and turned their attention to the disaster of the day. The problem was simple: the "floating steel" wasn't floating.

"I don't know why the panels are submerging. The displacement should be the same as the Styrofoam. Your confidence is high in these builders?" Vittorio emphasized his anxiety.

The question was to Diana.

"I'm confident they did as you instructed," she said.

"The only thing I can think is maybe this older process has a property we only now discover." Vittorio shrugged his shoulders.

"Older process? There is another process?" Horton said.

"Not another process. A different formula. I develop it after this one. The displacement so great in the panels made from the new formula, so strong, and I was able to float many grams of weight."

"When was this? This new—formula." Horton was sure this kid was up to no good. He didn't believe him. The process was, if not easy to build, easy to understand. Falucci could get very rich from the applications for this "floating steel." Horton had the feeling this upside was making Vittorio greedy.

"A few weeks ago. I tried something different, and it made the displacement increase by capturing more space in the foam. Bigger bubbles, you see. I thought it would be the same as you were building here. But I can see the new formulas are much different."

Horton now knew Diana was being set up. Vittorio was angling to get Copeland Lines to either pay more for something they had already bought or keep it for himself. He shot Diana a quick glance that she acknowledged by turning to the captain of the tender.

"I think we can go back now," she said. Diana and Horton stared out to sea for the short trip, saying nothing to Vittorio. As they pulled up to the *Marianna* steps, Vittorio said, "Perhaps I get my new formula sent to me from my laboratory, and we can create a new batch."

Horton looked again at Diana briefly and shook his head.

Once in the main salon of Diana's stateroom, Vittorio started pacing back and forth.

"The formula you have should have had enough displacement. But I never was able to do tests like today. So—"

"Vittorio. What do you mean the formula we have." Horton was trying not to lose his temper. "We own all the formulas—anything and everything that comes from the patents, and any process. You're not trying to say you have recently developed an entirely new formula—or a different process—however you wish to phrase it—are you?"

Vittorio was smart, well-educated, highly skilled, and a real inventor, but he was no businessman, and it was becoming apparent that he was tricky. Both were weaknesses Horton had exploited time and again, to the great dismay of his enemies.

"I have been doing much work, yes, but I don't think this would be a problem. I think it is different, yes. But it is not a problem."

"Let's be clear, Vittorio. Copeland Lines owns all the rights to all the patents to all the processes and all the formulas connected to the carbon hydrofoam, anywhere, anytime, anyplace, throughout the known or unknown universe, in perpetuity. Whatever this new formula is you are talking about is also part of those rights, and Copeland Lines owns it. Isn't that correct?"

Not only was Vittorio weaseling, he felt pushed, felt under attack. "Well—" he said, with an unfortunate trace of insolence.

"Get out of here," Horton said calmly as he walked to the door and held it open.

Vittorio looked at Diana, who averted her eyes to the floor. "Wait, there is no problem—"

"Get out, Vittorio. I'll talk to you later." Horton was furious, but he didn't raise his voice or give any outward signals.

"You are treating me with disrespect Mr.—"

"I respect people who honor their word, Mr. Falucci."

Vittorio glared threateningly at Horton.

"Vittorio, please." Diana said. "Just leave us alone. Horton—Mr. Callaway—and I need some time to talk."

Vittorio bowed slightly in Diana's direction and walked out the door.

"Unbelievable," Horton said as he walked to the small bookshelf bar and poured himself a Cognac. He turned to Diana. He held the bottle up to her in a "Want one?" gesture. She shook her head.

"You're tough," Diana said. "Are you sure he—"

"Diana, I've seen this a thousand times. You buy something from someone at the right price, and then they get seller's remorse. Their friends start telling them how rich we are, how they made a cheap deal—I know what this kid is doing, and he's not doing it very well, I might add."

Diana sat down on the sofa facing out the window through the veranda. She sighed. "Well, the panels we made don't work. That's certain. Do you think he has a formula that will?"

"Of course he does. And it's not new. This new formula is fictitious. He's trying to grind some more money out. He'll come back with stronger stuff, all right, but say you didn't buy that. Or he'll say you'll just have to pay more. That's his move. I know it."

Diana picked up a jar with the floating beads, like the one she had given Cash, and shook it. "But this really floats. Do you think the technology I saw in Genoa was a fraud? I had my two best guys there, and they—"

"No, no. The technology is not a fraud. I think he's done something to today's test to sabotage it. He's like all those kids that try to beat the wheel in Vegas. Everybody's got a scheme. He's got to learn to play by the rules, and he may need a lesson in what those rules are."

"I see. I see. Well, Horton, that's why I need you. He had me worried." She stood up. "I can't think about this anymore now. We've got to be at the Partaway in two hours to meet Cash. We have to leave."

Horton finished his drink. "Yeah. I don't want to do anything right now, anyway. Let Mr. Falucci stew in his own juice for a while. I'll go down and change, then meet you up at the chopper?"

"That's fine," Diana said.

Horton paused at the door after he opened it. "I don't mean to be impertinent, but—did you do something to your hair?"

Diana smiled broadly. "Why, Horton. Who knew you would notice? Yes, I let it grow a little, and I touched it up—took out the gray."

"Of course I noticed. I hope you don't mind my asking."

On the contrary, Diana was flattered by it. "No. No. I'm pleased."

"And you're wearing different eye makeup, aren't you? Again, not to be too—you know, too—"

Diana laughed like a child, all atwitter. "No. Horton," she said conspiratorially, "I had some work done."

Horton stepped back in from the door. "You're kidding. It looks great. Christ, maybe I should have that done. What did you do?"

Diana stepped close to Horton and pulled the lid down over her right eye. "It's called blepharoplasty. They take out the little wrinkles. All that's left is this little tiny scar, and they tell me sometimes that goes away too."

"Oh my God. Look at that. You just did this? Where? In Houston?"

Diana nodded. "A few weeks ago. I just decided to do my hair this morning. I woke up and decided I didn't want the gray."

"Did you have that much? You didn't have that much, did you?" Horton put his hands in the small of his back and surveyed Diana's hair from ear to ear.

"No. But, I don't know—I wanted to look nice for Cash. I bought a special outfit for tonight, too. Thought it might be festive."

"Well, you do look terrific. See you in about twenty minutes at the chopper." With that, Horton went to his quarters on the *Marianna* to change into something he had decided was more appropriate to the Partaway, something a bit more bluesy.

Diana was thinking the same thing. Right now she was wearing her usual work clothes, which consisted of designer wear from Italy, but with a comfortable, casual, working sense: dark slacks, a loose gray sweater, leather loafers, and no jewelry.

She looked at herself in her full-length dressing-room mirror and did a full turn. By the time she finished the spin, she was sure she looked old, dumpy, and tired. She peeled off all her clothes and saw too well her thickening legs, spots of sagging skin here and there, a mild stoop to her back, and a droop to her stomach, a slight paunch.

It was only recently, since she had been in Houston, that she paid attention with such detail to the way she looked. She usually waited till she was in the Genoa office to buy clothes, and she had excellent results by staying with well-known, conservative Italian designers. She would buy a spring and fall wardrobe each fall and spring in Milan, as well as some knockabout things, and that was the extent of her effort. Here in Houston she was starting to notice her age, and while forty-four certainly was far from over any hill in sight, she felt something slipping away with the years.

When Cash told her he was going to sing tonight and Horton had asked to come, she decided to make a party of it. The calamity with the floating panels had upset her, but she pushed all that away to focus now on what she was going to wear tonight, on how she would look, and how she would be perceived. At this moment, that was more important to her than Vittorio swindling her or even the specter that the whole floating-island plan might have to be scuttled because the technology was a sham.

She had shopped in Houston at a large department store and bought pants, a shirt, and a jacket from a high-priced designer she ordinarily would never have even considered. The designer made a name for himself among the younger set, though the clothes were hardly affordable for most twenty-year-olds. Diana saw the clothes in a new light and found them attractive. It was a big step away from her usual taste.

She showered, wrapped her newly blonde hair in a towel, and then dressed herself. A pair of tight-fitting leather pants with buttons up each leg and across her stomach, a tight fitting black-and-brown leopard–skin-print silk blouse with an open neck that emphasized her breasts, and an oversize distressed-denim jacket, with traces of Western design in the stitching. The shoes were open-toed three-inch high heels in brown patent leather. She topped it off with a dozen strands of bracelets and a pair of earrings with one carat diamonds dangling in a pearl-shaped drop from each lobe.

She brushed her hair back, in a style reminiscent of the way she wore it in college, and for the first time in years, she put on foundation makeup. She was thrilled to see the tiny blemishes and wrinkles disappear under the cover of the oily paste, to see her lips shine with the bright red color, to see her eyes enlarge and darken with the eyeliner and mascara.

The makeup drew a mask across the character of her face. The clothes, cut essentially for the young woman, accented her mature body in all the wrong places. The result was that she looked fatter than she was, shorter than she was, older than she was, and saddest of all, plainer than she was.

She stood before the full-length three-way mirror and surveyed herself carefully, turning around slowly, looking at her profile, her back, her behind. She saw none of the problems.

Instead, at the end of the turn she felt transformed, vibrant, and renewed.

Perfect, she thought.

Horton decided to wear black designer jeans with an expensive gold-buckled belt, a black close-fitting T-shirt, a black leather coat, and black ostrich leather cowboy boots. Like Diana, he had never worn such a collection in his life. The jeans were a touch tight, so Horton's fifty-year-old figure was pushed into an arbitrary and unnatural shape, yet Horton stood in front of his dressing mirror and had the same thought and reaction Diana did: perfect. Just perfect.

When the two met on the top deck, the chopper was sitting with the rotors idling, waiting for takeoff, and it was hard to hear, but Horton yelled at Diana.

"My God, Diana. You look fabulous. You look twenty years old."

She gave Horton a spontaneous hug. Until then, she had never shaken Horton's hand for longer than three seconds.

"That's a great jacket," she yelled back as the two of them walked, bent over at the waist, to the helicopter, climbed in, and slammed the door. Minutes later they were airborne over the Gulf Coast, on the way to their evening out with Cash at the Partaway.

A helicopter landing near the Partaway was not bizarre in the extreme, but it was bizarre enough. Everyone in the Partaway and the few outside first heard the noise and then turned to watch as the Eurocopter made its descent.

The lot outside the building was almost full of cars, but the gravel there would have made the landing impossible even if it were empty. Instead, the pilot sat down in a grassy field two hundred yards away.

Cash was surprised to see it. He did not expect Horton and Diana to bring the helicopter. As the two of them alighted from the chopper, Cash thought he might have made a mistake. Maybe it wasn't Horton and Diana; maybe it wasn't even his helicopter. He did a double-take on the tail number—it was his, all right. But who were these two people stumbling their way across the field? The shapes were foreign to him.

Neither Horton nor Diana had thought they might have to walk some considerable distance to the Partaway, and they were struggling with their shoes and the terrain. Horton was doing better than Diana, whose shoes plainly were not made for walking. They would hardly support standing for very long, being much more an ornament than footwear. She held on to Horton's arm tightly and took long, hesitant steps, bringing her feet together after each one. It was going to be a long walk.

Biggins walked out to the front and stood next to Cash, watching the approaching figures with all the rest of the Partaway customers who were outside. "That yours?" he asked Cash.

"Yeah, but I don't know who those people are. I thought maybe it was Horton and Diana, but it's not. I don't recognize them."

"That's Diana, for sure," Henry said. "I don't know who's with her."

"That's not Diana, Henry. It's someone else."

"Isn't the woman you came in here with named Diana? Wasn't that her name?"

"Yes, but—"

"Yeah, well, that's her. I don't recognize the guy."

For a moment the two figures stopped in the field, as the woman adjusted her shoe. Horton turned sideways to help Diana, and Cash saw his profile clearly. It was Horton. Cash's mouth dropped open.

"Henry. You're right," he said after a few seconds.

"Yeah, I know the lady, but—" Biggins started.

"That's Horton Callaway. My CEO. Ex-CEO."

"Oh," Henry said. "I met him with your dad at Cap'n Jack's. They comin' for your performance?" Biggins patted Cash on the back good-naturedly, but felt at once too familiar and drew his hand back.

Cash turned to him and smiled. "Yeah. I just can't figure out why they look so different, or what—"

Amber came out of the stage door and bounced up to Cash and Biggins. "Look, Henry, I've started drawing the helicopter crowd." She said brightly.

Henry laughed and looked at Cash, and then back to Amber. "I think you've had the helicopter crowd longer than you know. That's Cash's."

Amber blinked twice quickly but did not reveal more. She raised her chin, looked at Biggins and mouthed the word "oh" silently.

Buni held back, staying by the stage door, watching the helicopter and the two figures staggering toward the Partaway. Outrageous, he thought.

On the asphalt street, the traveling was little better for Diana, as the small bits of gravel pushed up through the thin leather soles. She had to stop and shake her foot to remove the pea-size stones that found their way in through the open toe. By the time they got to the door of the Partaway, Horton and Diana were sweating profusely. Horton had removed his jacket and carried it the last seventy-five feet, but he was still soaked.

"Hey, you two!" Cash greeted them. "Look at you. I almost didn't recognize you."

Horton was trying not to be irritable; Diana was panting. "Hi, Cash. Henry. Hey, Amber," she said through long drawn breaths. "That was some hike." She gave Cash a hug.

"You're looking very pretty tonight," Diana said to Amber.

"Thanks." Amber said. "You guys look really dressed up yourself."

Diana took it as a compliment. "I'm excited to hear you sing. And you too, Cash." Diana tapped Cash on the chest with her finger. Amber felt a strange knot in her stomach, an anxious frustration.

"Come on in, get out of the heat," Biggins said and made way through the line at the front door for all to follow him.

Buni watched all this but kept his distance. He had other things on his mind. Norba, the drummer, still hadn't arrived, and Buni was trying to think of someone he could call at this last minute, if for some reason she didn't show. He went back in through the stage door without noticing the new sign next to the front door announcing a cover charge.

Amber stood outside the door as Horton, Diana, and Cash disappeared into the crowd. She watched for a few minutes as the helicopter shut down and then saw the pilot step out, lock the door, and start his trek across the field. Finally she went in the stage entrance after Buni. Norba Hyjeen pulled into the parking lot just as Amber left.

Once Horton, Cash, and Diana were settled and had ordered steaks all around, Diana moved close to Cash and hugged his arm, kissing him on the cheek.

"Are you excited?" she asked.

"I am. I had a good rehearsal. Buni has a good way about him, and Amber is an inspiration. I actually feel ready." Cash did not mention the dim fear or the submicroscopic shake of his hands. He was learning to handle stage fright.

During dinner, the talk ranged from the day's testing of the *Mariner* model, to Horton's investor party, which Cash agreed to attend, at least for a day, to discussions of the *Marianna*'s three-day cruise to Mexico starting the next day. Diana was planning on staying with Cash.

When Amber's first set started, all seemed well. The crowd was responsive and the place was jammed, with more outside waiting to get in. The cover charge had not lessened the crowd to any degree that Cash could see. Cash soaked up Amber, as he had now for many nights. He didn't notice Diana's reaction to her.

For the first time, Diana understood Amber. Diana was not

musically driven, did not have music as part of her artistic or cultural environment. She attended the opera, tolerated it, but liked the socializing more than anything.

Tonight, Diana saw the force of Amber Fanfare. By the end of the first show, the crowd was exuberant with applause and appreciation, and Diana was pulled along with them. "She's good, isn't she?" she said to Cash near the end of one of her songs. Cash looked at Diana, smiled, and nodded knowingly. You don't know how good, he thought. "Yes, she is. She may be the best I've seen." Horton studied Cash's face to glean the remark.

Diana took off her jacket, laid it next to her, and arranged her blouse.

"Is the band good?" she asked. Cash looked blank. "I mean are they fun to play with?"

Cash looked down. He put his elbows on the table, arms outstretched, and squeezed his hands together. He raised his eyebrows and nodded. "It's kind of the other way around. I just hope I'm good enough to play with them."

Horton was on his third Cognac since arriving. "I have every confidence in you, Mr. Carruthers, as always." He held up the glass and toasted him. Cash was starting to feel like a giant sunflower in a first-grade play whose parents had come to visit. He stood up, made his goodbyes, and went onstage.

When the set began, there emerged a thick, heavy quality to the music. Something was wrong, but Cash didn't know what. He focused intently on playing his guitar, making sure he was as technically precise as he could be, but the viscid, gelatinous feel persisted.

Amber and Buni pulled the band along, but they were exchanging looks all the while. Cash worked harder at playing, blocking all other thoughts from his mind, but nothing would shake the weight from the music. It was lumbering along, and Cash was more and more certain it must be due to his playing, and worse, some element of his playing that he didn't know how to correct. He was sure Buni would not let him sing tonight, so he bent his head down, stared at the floor, and played the best rhythm guitar he could muster.

To his absolute surprise and consternation, Amber walked over after one of the numbers toward the end of the set, sat on his amp next to him, and nudged him to the microphone. Cash looked wide eyed at Buni. Buni gave him the same signal. Time to sing.

No introduction was needed. Throughout the set, Buni had sung a song, Izzy had sung a song. The crowd was used to the round robin. Cash stood up.

He could see Buni was not happy as he counted off "Dust My Broom" and the band started into the shuffle. The song started in a ponderous, soulless groove. Amber gave Cash a gentle shove, but just as Cash started to move, she said under her breath, "I'm gonna kill that bitch." Cash faltered and looked at Amber, frozen. What was she talking about? She glared up at him. "Get up there, Cash. C'mon. Tighten up, dude. Get us out of here. The bus is leavin'," she said as she crossed her legs and pointed to the mic.

Whatever fluid was coursing through Cash's body had suddenly dried up. He was utterly perplexed. He stood before the microphone, terrified. Buni was looking at him, and when he realized Cash wasn't going to start singing at the pickup, he led the band through another instrumental verse of the song. Izzy played an almost perfect rendition of Elmore James slide playing, and the song was back around for Cash's entrance. "C'mon Cash. 'Dust My Broom'!" Buni yelled out.

Cash felt Buni's words like a kick in the back, cleared his throat, and from an unknown place in himself, blasted out the first line of the song like a jump from an airplane. To his amazement, the crowd shouted back at him in approval. Cash dipped into the same resource for the second verse, and again the crowd yelled back. They were dancing, all eyes on the stage, heads bobbing in time. Cash felt the same sluggish, leaden pace, but he pulled forward on his own. Firegate answered Cash's singing with powerful guitar fills, and as easily as a child's birthday balloon, the song was in the air, hovering over the stage, and Cash could see the view. This was what Amber was talking about. He looked at Amber and she was grinning to herself, slamming the heel of her boot on the stage in time. Buni looked up from the keyboard and nodded and smiled. He looked at the crowd, pulsing in time, alive with delight. So this was the show.

Cash looked at Buni for a connection, only to see a darkness cross his face, a streak of anger as Buni lowered his head, bent down into the keys, and pushed the song along. Cash felt the authority of Buni's rhythmic pulse take over the music. Cash dove into the next verse with all his might, not shouting, but leaving no doubt as to intent. Amber stood up.

At the close, he got a solid round of applause, and Amber took over the microphone. Two more songs, and the audience went wild as Amber brought the set and the evening to a close. As far as they were concerned, this was what music was meant for.

As the final chord sounded, the house was on its feet, cheering. Cash was particularly gratified to see Horton and Diana on their feet, whistling and shouting, though they were still unnervingly like Little League parents at a game.

Buni and the band were gone before Cash had shut his amp off and laid the guitar down. The Partaway was emptying slowly, the crowd savoring the evening. A few patrons passed by the stage and paid compliments to Cash.

By the time the crowd was clear enough, Cash jumped from the stage and met Horton and Diana as they came hurrying to him.

"Outstanding," Horton said, drunk but well under control. "Never had a doubt. That was superior. Really was."

"Oh, Cash! It really was marvelous. I was surprised." Diana laughed. "No. You know what I mean. You were so much better than I thought." She laughed again. "Oh God, I better shut up. You know what I mean. It was brilliant."

"Thank you. But it was odd, there was something wrong— something going on I—" Cash said.

As soon as he said it, Cash knew Horton and Diana would have no idea what he was talking about and also knew he couldn't explain it. They were confused. "I thought it sounded fine," Horton said. "Did you see the crowd? They were dancing; they loved it."

Cash held up his index finger. "Right. Right. They did. Can you two hold on for a second? I really need to talk to Buni," he said. "I just need to go outside for a minute."

"Great!" Horton said. "Let's all go outside!"

Horton and Diana followed Cash through the stage door out into the parking lot. There was a small traffic jam as the cars jockeyed for position to leave. Cash looked around.

He saw the band on the other side of the lot, standing in a circle. The conversation was heated and he could hear the sound of Buni's voice pulsating up and down in volume, see him gesturing, but he couldn't understand the words. He started toward them. Amber looked his way, saw him, held up her hand, and waved him away. Whatever was going on, Cash was not invited.

Biggins appeared at the back door and joined Cash, Horton, and Diana. Behind him, through the stage door, the work lights went on as the few remaining people were leaving. The yellow lights lit the debris of the evening and revealed the scars and marks of the rustic building. It was 2:30 in the morning.

"Hey, Cash. That was some performance. I'm impressed." Biggins noticed the band members huddled together, saw the tension. "What's going on?"

"I don't know," Cash said. "Wish I did."

Chapter Eleven

A caravan, a mixture of six trucks and vans of various sizes, rumbled down the main street of Helensburg to the Partaway, turned into the lot, and parked side by side in a precise line. Brandon Taylor, Cash's top assistant, hopped from the first truck, signaled to the two workmen in the end truck, and then motioned to spots on each side of the lot. Within minutes, two generators with powerful work lights were stationed, flooding the entire rear of the Partaway with a blue-white halogen light as bright as day.

Cash excused himself and walked over to Brandon.

"Hi, BT. Thanks for putting this together," Cash said as he patted Brandon's back and escorted him to the spot where the door would go.

Horton recognized Brandon and knew what all the activity meant, though he had no idea what they were doing. He turned to Biggins and spoke as Amber and Buni walked over and joined them. "Cash up to something?" Horton asked.

"This afternoon he figured out a way to get more people in the Partaway, needed a fire exit, he thought—and here they are, looks like. Hi, Buni. You guys did well tonight." Biggins turned to him.

"We can do better. Thanks, though. This is a fire exit, you say?" Buni was curious.

"Here. Cash'll tell you." Biggins stepped aside as Cash returned from his walk with Brandon.

The lot was now bustling with twelve men setting up sawhorses, pulling power cables, and unloading lumber and two metal commercial doors. They moved almost wordlessly, with an easy speed, a team comfortable with the hour and the work.

Horton, Diana, Biggins, Buni, and Amber created a spontaneous circle around Cash. Cash, standing near the back of his pickup truck, lowered the tailgate and patted the metal, creating a seat. "Here Diana, have a seat."

Diana hopped up and sat, legs dangling. Cash spoke to Buni, but it was for all to hear.

"I imagine you knew I was covering the wages for the band's fee here?"

Buni darted a look at Amber, but she appeared unfazed by the remark as she watched and listened. Buni nodded. "I thought something like that might be going on," he said, wondering what might be coming.

"So, I thought—well, let me see—it's not that I minded paying, but it seemed better to me if we could set it up so the public paid. It was more—more—" Cash searched for the word.

"I'm there, man. I know what you're sayin'. I was, you know, havin' to deal with that, too," Buni said. He looked again at Amber. Still no external clue to what she was thinking.

Diana took off her shoes and shook the gravel out of one of them, brushed her feet off, and then slipped them back on. Horton hopped on the tailgate next to her, took off his coat, and laid it across his lap.

"Right. Good," Cash said. "Anyway, Hank and I figured a way to get some more people in here, and it looked like we needed a fire exit to make it legal, make it stick—so, that's what they're doing here. Putting the fire exit in. Then tomorrow, if I'm right, and if we can get a temporary waiver from the fire marshal, we can get a few more people in here and it'll be—there'll be more to go around."

"How many more?" Amber asked. Buni stepped back. Cash looked at Biggins.

"I don't know for certain," Biggins said, tentative and unsure what to say. "I guess, I mean, Cash, you—"

"Depends," Cash said. "If we can turn the house, basically get two separate crowds in here for each set, then three-seventy-six. That's full."

"Can we get more money?" Amber pushed forward a millimeter, pulled her shoulders back a touch, and leaned forward on the balls of her feet. Buni stepped back further with a touch of chagrin.

Cash looked at Amber and smiled broadly. He really was

starting to love this girl. Diana watched the two of them for any sign that might decipher what must be passing unspoken between them. Aside from Cash's delight with Amber, she saw nothing, but the delight was enough to be disquieting.

"That was the point. Henry started charging a cover tonight. What'd we do?" he asked Henry. "Twenty-one hundred, between people comin' and goin'. Two hundred and ten at the door, at ten dollars a head," Biggins said.

"So how much of that do we get?" Amber was direct, flat. Buni couldn't take any more discomfort. "Amber. Easy." He said, gently, with a slight admonition. Amber turned to him, but before she could speak, Cash said, "All of it." Amber spun back to Cash; Buni looked at him, surprised.

Amber transformed from stern to childish glee so fast it made Cash laugh. She almost shouted. "All of it?"

"Sure. You earned it. You take the door, and the Partaway gets the business." Biggins drew his cheeks together and swallowed. He still didn't like all that money slipping away. Horton watched him and knew what he was thinking.

"And no shortfall," Cash continued.

Amber turned to Buni with a huge grin, ear to ear. Buni shook his head in disbelief. She held her hand out to Buni for a victory slap, which Buni delivered mildly. "All right!" she said. Amber was as excited and jubilant as a child at Christmas. She nearly lunged at Cash and threw her arms around his neck. Cash turned his head aside just in time to avoid a full kiss on the mouth. This made Diana stand up from the tailgate, dusting off her behind, and straightening her blouse.

Cash hugged Amber and then patted her on the back, as she peeled away from him, keeping one arm around his waist.

Buni came forward and extended his hand to Cash. "What can I say?"

"And it was how many hundred?" Amber released Cash, took a step away from him, and looked at Biggins, who, though still not smiling, was getting happier by the second, caught up in the good and in Amber's unabashed joy. He reached into his hip pocket, pulled out a thick, unsealed envelope, waggled it, and then handed it to Amber.

"Two thousand, one hundred," Biggins said.

Amber pried the envelope open with her thumbs and looked at the stack of bills. She stared, mouth open at Buni, then jumped up and down, holding the envelope up. She turned to the other band members still standing across the lot and waved it at them. "Hey! Iz—" but Buni grabbed her hand and pulled it down before she could get their attention. He looked at her and shook his head. "Wait, baby. We got some things to do first."

Diana, smiling in spite of herself, walked next to Cash and took his arm. Cash stroked the back of her hand, which Amber saw.

Brandon Taylor approached the group, acknowledging everyone with a short nod. "I'll need someone to help us inside."

Henry excused himself and left the four as Horton jumped off the tailgate and stood in the circle. "So, I have a suggestion." Horton's speech was slow, the hyper-articulation of the thoroughly drunk. Cash knew he was well in his cups. "I'm having a party in a few weeks on one of Ms. Copeland's boats. A small cruise in the Gulf. Why don't you guys come and play? Be the band for the weekend?"

Cash started to say something, but Buni cut him off.

"Is it big enough for the whole band?"

"Hah!" Horton barked. "I would say it is, yes. Wouldn't you, Cash?" Horton tossed the question to Cash as repartee, but Cash sidestepped it.

"It's a cruise ship, Buni. Diana owns Copeland Lines," Cash said matter-of-factly.

Horton blundered on. "A colossal ship. Big theatre, casino, everything. You and the band could come out and play. Cash, you could play. Everybody's happy. Has a good time. It would be fun. And I'll pay you. Diana, what do the acts get to play in the theater on the boat?"

Diana looked at Cash for a sign about how to manage this. No response. She fumbled, "You know, Horton, I don't, uh, handle that—."

"But you have some idea," he said.

"Actually, I—not much. There's an agent who does it all."

"I know, I know. But you have some idea. Is it a million dollars?"

"No, Horton, it's not a million dollars."

"Well, there you are. Is it five dollars?" Horton was not going to leave this alone.

Diana sighed. She looked again at Cash, who this time gave her an "I don't know what to do" shake of the head. Buni spoke up, shuffling as if to leave.

"Maybe we should—"

"No!" Horton said, bullying. "No. Wait right there. Diana, it's a simple question. How much do you pay the acts in the theater? Not specific. Just general. A general number. What shows up on the financials?"

"Well, Horton, it varies. I think they get, you know, some of them get maybe twenty-five thousand a week—more or less—"

"O.K. O.K. O.K. There you go. I'll pay you twenty-five thousand. How about it? Will you do it?"

Amber looked at Cash. This was far beyond anything she had encountered, and she didn't know how to think about it. Buni was exceedingly ill at ease, also having no idea how to disengage from or disarm the situation.

"Horton. Let's sleep on it," Cash said.

Horton was alcohol-angry and starting to show it. "Cash, I love you like a brother, but I don't work for you anymore. And I don't want to be put off here. This party is important. It's my thing. My own thing, and I want to have Buni and Amber here come play. You said she was the best you ever saw." Amber looked at Cash, then back to Buni. "So, O.K., then I want the best you ever saw to come play. And I want to pay what I'm supposed to pay, which Diana informs me is twenty-five thousand American dollars. Is there a problem with that?" Horton's head described a series of tiny uncontrolled circles.

There was a long pause. Finally Amber broke the silence.

"We'll come play at your party, Mr. Callaway. We can decide the price later."

It was a good try.

"No, the price is settled. Twenty-five, and it's a deal." He held out his hand to Amber, who shook it, then Buni, who shook it after an uncomfortable lag. "Fine. Cash. Diana. I am going to take the chopper home. I've had a wonderful night, and I look forward to seeing you soon. If there is anything I can do, please do not hesitate to contact me at this address."

Horton pulled on his coat and turned to walk to the chopper.

"Wait, Horton," Cash said. "I can drive you out there."

Horton turned back, facing everyone in a grand formal pose, but with an underwater waver that started at his ankles and rippled up. "No. I'll enjoy the walk." He bowed deeply and then tottered away.

"Right," Amber said under her breath. "It's only about four miles."

"I'm sorry, Amber, Buni," Cash said. "I've never seen him like this."

They all watched Horton walk away when, just as he came to Buni's Volvo, he fell to the ground without so much as a stumble. One second he was walking in a manner that looked normal; the next he looked like a pile of rags. Buni ran to him, followed closely by Cash and Amber. Diana was imprisoned by her shoes, so all she could do was put her hand to her mouth and say, "Oh, dear."

Horton was picking himself up when Buni got there, and

Buni helped him the rest of the way, leaning him against the car.

"New boots," he said to Buni as he dusted himself off. Buni opened the door to the Volvo and helped Horton sit down on the passenger seat.

"Are you hurt?" he asked. Cash and Amber ran up.

"Only my pride. Which I can assure you I can pay to have fixed."

Buni walked to the driver's side, got in, and started the car. It shivered to life. Tyrone Edwards blasted from the radio speakers for a few seconds before Buni could turn it down." I'll drive you over," Buni said.

"Don't turn the music down for me. I like music. Turn it back up." Horton pulled the door closed and groped for the radio. He found the control and turned it back up, loud. Buni waved to Cash and Amber, who stood back from the car as it pulled away. They watched it for a few seconds before starting the walk back to Cash's truck, where they saw that Diana had reseated herself on the tailgate.

"Demon rum," Cash said as they walked. He noticed he and Amber fell easily into the same side-by-side stroll as he had with Leland.

"Don't need to tell me," Amber said. "Norba showed up cooked tonight. She went from being a drummer to being a groove assassin."

"Is that what was wrong? I felt something. I thought it was me. God, what was she drinking?"

"Drinking? Cash. Wake up. She was junked. Smack. Heroin.

She's been a junky off and on, and Buni took a chance, but she showed up tonight nodding off."

Cash couldn't help it. He was amazed. As they reached Diana, she could see the concern in his eyes.

"Buni fired her. Not gonna see Norba Hyjeen anymore," Amber said flatly.

"Was he O.K.?" Diana asked. "Fired who?"

"Two different trains of thought," Cash said. "Horton's fine. Relatively. Amber was just telling me Buni fired the drummer tonight."

"Oh. What for? I thought everything sounded lovely."

"Depends on where you're sitting," Amber said. "She showed up junked and tried to play, but she was, like, so off. Dope. Occupational hazard."

Across the field, Buni's Volvo was lurching back toward them as the helicopter jets whined, the blades repeating a slow *kachump* as they sped up. The sound of a circular saw screeched into the night, and the wall of the Partaway opened, revealing the innards, where workmen were measuring for the header, hammering, and trimming. An electrician was drilling, rerouting the wires in the wall. The ruined muffler on the Volvo added to the din as Buni came to a stop near the newly-assembled group. At 3:30 in the morning, downtown Helensburg was a hive of activity. The helicopter lifted into the sky in a blast of dust, weeds, and gravel.

Buni, Amber, Cash, and Diana watched it leave, and then Amber motioned to Izzy and Marion. "Yo! You guys can take off," she called out. "Buni and I will find a drummer." They waved good night and started to their cars.

"I'm sorry about Horton, Buni. He—" Cash began.

"No apologies necessary, sir." Buni held up his hand. "We played Tyrone all the way to the chopper, and he was still singing when he got on the ship."

"Thank you," Diana said. "He's not a bad person, just—"

"Really, say no more." Buni gave Amber a tug. "C'mon, baby, I gotta get back to the motel. I'm beat."

Buni climbed in the car, Amber beside him, when suddenly Amber flung her door open, jumped from the car, ran to Cash, and stopped inches before him. She deliberately and slowly moved closer, took his face in both her hands, stood on her toes, pulled him to her, and kissed him long and square on the mouth.

It was not a romantic kiss or even a sexy kiss. By some standards, it probably would not qualify as a kiss at all, just lips to lips. But it was a tender touch from her to him, heartfelt, and a real surprise.

Cash's arms hung to his side the whole time as he leaned forward and stooped to reach her. Diana's eyes got physically wider by half.

Amber stepped back and looked up at Cash. She put her hand around Cash's belt buckle and gave him two sharp jerks.

"You did O.K. tonight, buster. You'll do better with a good drummer playin'. And—I want—I appreciate what you did for us." She pushed him away. "And don't be turnin' your head when I go to kiss you on the mouth." She turned abruptly, ran back to the Volvo, jumped in, and turned the radio up loud. Buni made a U-turn, and the Volvo went past the work lights into the blackness.

Diana looked at Cash, who held up both hands in submission. "Don't ask me. I've never run into anyone like her. Let's go inside and check on Biggins." Cash walked to the new portal gaping in the side of the Partaway. Diana stood, watching the taillights of the Volvo as they dimmed into nothingness, and then she followed him in.

* * *

The roads were essentially empty, and except for a slight mist coming from the ground, the sky was clear. Buni and Amber rocked gently to the hum of Rachel the Volvo while Tyrone Edwards played softly on the stereo. The stereo was the only fully-functioning piece of equipment in the car, and it sounded good.

"What a night," Buni said after a few miles. "Did you check out Diana? Dangerously close to her own Personal Las Vegas, I fear. Did you understand the shoes?"

"Blues shoes, I think, for Cash. Not a PLV yet. She's not right for him anyway," Amber said.

"Careful," Buni said. "When you planted that kiss on Cash, I thought she might bury one of those heels in your head."

"Think so?" Amber turned to look out the rear window in mock fear. "Maybe I should get a burglar alarm."

Buni shook his head in resignation. "Don't be makin' fun of

this. You can't ever tell how they're gonna act when somebody hits their PLV. Dangerous times, sugar baby. Elvis carried a gun on stage toward the end. And from where I sit, it's not just Boat Lady, it's Mr. Goodweird too. I wasn't sure till tonight, but this guy is cruisin' the strip, just lookin' for the right hotel."

"Maybe." Amber said. "Cash is maybe hitting it—but you've got to admit he's not that bad."

"Not that bad?" Buni said. "Are you high? We got this billionaire up there singing the blues. Come on, Amber, don't scare me like this. This is not about bad or good and you know it. This is—"

"This is about you bein' jealous," she said.

"Oh, no. Oh, no you don't. Not gonna take me down that road. I may be jealous, but I can live with that. I'm sayin' Cash Carruthers is up there on the stage and hanging around with you—oh, yes, yes he is—hanging around with you, little one, because he has or is about to hit his PLV like a runaway truck. Stake my fingers on it."

"What do I have to do with his PLV? How can that be?" Amber knitted her brow and frowned at Buni.

"Aside from being the most beautiful female on the planet, and aside from having the wisdom of a sixty-year-old in the body of a child, you are one of the only true things I have ever found in life when you start to sing. Cash sees that. And when the America Gene wakes, baby, it makes you start looking for some kind of anchor, something to think or do or feel that's real. Why people go totally phony and nose job and funny clothes when this happens is just one of the mysteries of life. But Cash is smarter than most. Way smarter. That's why he's glommed on to you. I don't expect he'd kick you out of bed, but it's not the point, and you know it. He's lookin' to get real, and yet I fear he is about to go totally Vegas in a way I can't see right now. But you just watch, 'cause it's comin'."

Amber's frown faded, and she smiled lovingly at Buni as she put her feet on the dashboard and then gazed out the windshield at the Volvo's single palsied headlamp illuminating the flat, curbless Texas highway in jittery flashes.

"Maybe. More important," she said. "Do we do the cruise-ship party thing? What was that about?"

"That was all drunkspeak. I don't think there is a cruise-ship party thing. That whole twenty-five grand thing was a 'see how rich I am' riff. El Drunko. World of lies."

"What did Horton say when you drove him to the helicopter?"

"He sang along with Tyrone here. He wanted to know who it was, why I liked him, whether Cash was any good, but he never let me say much. Got to the 'copter, bopped out, flew away like those guys do." Buni turned the stereo on again. Tyrone Edwards started where he left off.

"That wasn't his helicopter," Amber said. "It was Cash's. Biggins said."

"I suppose. Biggins also told me Cash is the ninth-richest guy in the world. Says he's got like fifty billion dollars or something." Buni chortled, dismissively.

"Really? He's got that much?" Amber said.

"Biggins was just goin' legendary. Gilding the lily. I mean, yeah, Cash is buck's up, but you got any idea how much fifty billion dollars is?"

"I know how much two thousand, one hundred is." She set the envelope across her legs, opened it, and looked down at the edges of all the bills, which were breathing accordion-like in her lap. "How are we gonna split this up?"

Buni stared straight. "I think we give the band what we promised, plus, like, a little bonus or something, and keep the rest."

Amber pulled the money from the envelope, flipped through the bills, and then wagged them back and forth. "And how do you and me split the rest?"

Buni shifted in his seat and looked out the driver's side window for a second before he spoke. "I guess whatever you say. I gotta make some dough, but it's you they're payin' to see. I know that. You oughta close that up. Might blow away. You know Rachel."

Amber hand-fanned the money like a deck of cards. "I'd say fifty-fifty. For now."

"I can live with that." Buni nodded. "Fact, that's generous. I figured this would come up sooner or later. A reality check. Reality is, you're the one, so I appreciate the fifty-fifty. We'll change it when you want."

"Hey, Buns. It's only money. Wait till we make our first fifty billion." Amber folded the money back into a pile and stuffed it back into the envelope.

Buni laughed. "You don't know how big that is. Do this. Say you got a thousand dollars, right? How many thousand dollars is in a billion? Not fifty. Just one billion."

"I don't know. I can't do that. How many? A thousand? Ten thousand?

"A million."

"Wait a minute. It's a thousand million dollars?"

"Well, yeah, it is. But that's not what I said. I said it's a million thousand dollars. What would you do with a million thousand dollars? A billion dollars, Amber."

She thought for a moment. "I'd buy a convertible."

This made Buni laugh even harder as he pulled into the parking lot of the motel. "O.K. And you know what? You'd have $999,950,000 left."

"Then," Amber popped open the door and looked back at Buni just before she got out, "I'd buy you one, too."

* * *

Diana and Cash were in his truck as it whistled effortlessly along the country roads on the way to the ranch. Inside the truck, all was quiet, smooth, air-conditioned.

"That thing with Horton upset you?" Diana asked.

"Upset? Uh, no. Concerned. A bit. I've never seen him like that. Never saw him fall down. But I've also never spent this much time with Horton socially. Not since I've known him.

What did you think? He's your guy now."

"Oh, Cash, please. No," Diana moaned. "I'm glad to have someone like Horton right now, but he's hardly what you'd call my guy. And I assume you're speaking only in a business sense."

"Strictly in a business sense. I meant he's your team leader."

"Yes," Diana agreed. "He's helping with the financing and the build-out."

"That's the only Horton I know," Cash said. "At that he is very good. This Horton tonight, I don't know that side of him. I didn't even recognize you two when you got out of the chopper. You both looked so different."

"Do you like it? The new look? The clothes?" Diana asked, trying heroically to avoid sounding flirtatious.

"You mean you or Horton?"

Diana laughed nervously, "I meant me, but Horton's interesting."

"I don't think I've ever seen Horton in anything but a suit or some variation. The T-shirt is a big change. And you always look nice, you know. I don't mean any of this in a negative way."

"It is a change. You're right," Diana said. "For me, especially. I thought this would be good for me. I was feeling like I needed to shake things up."

"Yeah," Cash said. "You look fine. I'll have to kind of get used to it, I think."

Diana drew her jacket around her against the car's air conditioner. "Get used to it" had an unpleasant sound.

"But, you know Di—and this may not be the right thing to

say either, but I mean it to be the right thing. I've always been more interested in what you have to say than the way you look or the way you dress. You're pretty. I think you're pretty. But that's always been icing on the cake. And the cake for me is the way you think, the way you are. Am I saying this O.K.?"

"Yes, you're saying it right." Diana looked away from Cash, out her window into the blurry black of the roadside weeds hurrying past. "It's a good thing to say. A lovely thing to say."

Lovely or not, it hurt. Like it or not, she wanted Cash to think she was beautiful. Admit it or not, she was jealous.

"I think Amber is a very pretty young girl, don't you?" Diana said after a pause.

"Exceptionally so. I watch the men at the Partaway. They're all agog."

"She has a really cute figure, too. Sexy." She was watching Cash's face intently, taking advantage of the fact he couldn't quite see her, since he was driving.

"She's all around amazing. I've watched her now for several weeks, and, you know, I—I don't know anything about how all this works—but she looks like she could be very successful. Big time. A real star."

The remark cut Diana's faltering self-confidence to the core. The emotional pain was so great that she could hardly maintain her composure.

"And Buni is her what, husband, boyfriend? Seems like they're a couple," she said.

"No. Not that I can see. They're close, but Amber feels pretty available. At least she acts that way. Buni is more like one-half of a professional relationship. But I think they are, you know, extremely close."

Diana could take no more and leaned her head back against the seat. She drew her coat closer still, holding her arms. A few moments passed in silence. It was Cash who spoke.

"You cold? I can turn the air conditioner down. We're almost to the ranch." Cash adjusted the controls.

"I'm a little cool," she said as she pressed against the passenger door and adjusted the air vent. "This jacket's really just for decoration."

* * *

Two men were putting the final touches of paint on the door frame, while another two were vacuuming the construction debris from the Partaway floor. All the others were outside cleaning up, loading equipment, coiling cables, and packing the trucks. Biggins was asleep in one of the booths when Brandon gently shook him awake.

"Mr. Biggins, we're through here. Here are the keys to the new door." Brandon pushed the keys across the table to him. Biggins looked at the clock. It was 8 a.m. The sun was up.

"Thank you," he said through a yawn as he stood up. "Everything go O.K.?"

"Think so. Give me a call if you spot something." Brandon handed Biggins his card and left through the new doors. Biggins followed him and gave everything a cursory check as he looked around. The door looked as if it had always been there, perfectly plumb; only the fresh glistening wet paint gave away the new construction. Biggins pulled the door closed after Brandon, and it shut effortlessly, fit seamlessly. He pushed the door open and closed it again. The latch gave a solid, secure thunk as it fastened perfectly. It was the best-made, best-fitting door in the entire building.

He yawned again and stretched, looking around the room and then back at the finished door. It's entirely possible, he thought, that I could not have gotten this job done this well if I had a month.

Chapter Twelve

As anticipated, the announcement of Horton's party ignited the Houston social scene and reverberated around the global community. Horton chose the last week in October and booked the entire *Marianna*, all two hundred and forty-three rooms.

Diana immersed herself in work on the *Mariner* floating island and more or less moved her relationship with Cash off to one side of her thinking. It was easier than she thought. Her love for Cash, her expectations for it, had become anxious and unsatisfied. The diversion of building the *Mariner* was a genuine relief. In fact, Horton alone had become management-intensive and plenty to think about.

The day after he left Cash and the others at the Partaway, Horton flew Vittorio Falucci and several of the key execs of Copeland Lines to Genoa on his G5, where a series of difficult confrontations about the new formula increased Vittorio's intransigence and guile. Horton decided sterner measures were needed.

Vittorio's laboratory near the Fincantieri shipyards in Trieste was the repository of all the data and experimental work on the carbon hydrofoam. One evening, when Horton was sure Vittorio was gone, Horton and three of his assistants went there, identified the documents—any work even remotely connected with the carbon hydrofoam—and took it all. Once Horton was certain no other documents existed, no copies or backups of any kind, no prototypes, models, or examples that he didn't have, Horton destroyed every single item. Every incidence of the carbon hydrofoam or mention of it, anything even tangential to the carbon hydrofoam, was shredded, burned, smashed, or otherwise demolished and ruined. Nothing remained.

Regardless of the years of work, of whatever burgeoning ideas were contained in the work, the only thing Vittorio had left—or Copeland Lines, for that matter—was what Vittorio remembered.

The destruction of Vittorio Falucci's life's work was not entirely unlawful. Copeland Lines, by agreement, owned all the work it destroyed. Horton assured Diana that Falucci, even though he was young, would understand the signal that was sent and was now forced to work either with Copeland Lines or no one, since his personal lab and notes were ruined. It was extreme brinkmanship.

When Diana told Cash about the event, he was outraged. He said he thought it was the most reprehensible act he had ever heard of in business, or in life. Horton had crossed the line. This was moral turpitude.

Cash's high-value ethics had prohibited Horton's preemptive strikes on more than one occasion. Horton was free of those ethics now. He classified the carbon hydrofoam raid the same as preventive medicine: identifying and demolishing a potentially damaging individual before he could do harm.

Cash had argued there was more to prevention than just the repression of a threat. There had to be some measurable positive effect, some gain, otherwise such action was only negative and ultimately would produce nothing. He always prevailed at Sandra Corporation because he was the owner and boss. It was evident he never really won the argument with Horton.

The near-term result was to bring Vittorio around to Horton's control with a snap of abject acquiescence. Whether through cowardice, fear, or an appalling recognition of the kind of person Horton was, Vittorio meekly submitted to Horton's direction, and quickly rewrote and rebuilt the formulas and prototypes under the strict supervision of the Copeland engineers. Horton had been right. There was no new formula or process, and the reconstructed panels had displacement values allowing them to carry substantial weight, all more in line with the original specifications. Arranged in pontoons, they would easily create a floating island, and Diana's vision nudged closer to reality.

Shipbuilding in Texas was not high art, confined mostly to the repairs of tankers and other freighters that roamed the local waters and whatever naval architecture applied to the construction of offshore oil-drilling platforms. Diana and Horton put together a team from Italy and Texas for the fabrication of the *Mariner* and designated a spot in the Gulf, twelve and one-tenth miles off the Bolivar Peninsula, a barrier island to Galveston Bay, to create the first stage. Now all they needed was the money, hundreds of millions of dollars. Horton felt confident his soiree would be the primary conduit for the initial funds to flow to Copeland Lines.

The invitees to Horton's party constituted the world's rich and powerful, the famous and glamorous. Horton reserved dozens of private jets around the world to bring in those who did not have their own. There were more than six hundred people invited, which made the logistics difficult, but Horton assigned his best executives to organize it, and they knew to spare no extravagance. Horton had millions of dollars committed to the party before he sent out the invitations, and as the acceptances poured in, he was committed for millions more.

By any standard, it would be a party of all parties, but especially by the standard of excess. Custom-designed and custom-made jackets, shirts, and hats; gift bags with watches, perfumes, jewelry, and sunglasses; luggage stuffed with electronic gadgets, media players, and media, all individualized with names, cost hundreds of thousands of dollars. He took over two of the finest hotels in Houston for those who arrived before the cruise and booked all the limousines and helicopters in the city to shuttle the guests to and from the *Marianna* before and after the cruise.

Horton estimated that over ninety percent of the people he

invited would accept the invitation, and he was right, even though the majority were only casual or distant acquaintances. He had depended on the allure of great wealth and someone willing to spend it extravagantly to construct a party of people who did not know him, or each other, very well. It was a "see and be seen" affair, all of which suited Horton.

Attracting investors proved more difficult, and a bit of skepticism was in the air. Nevertheless, Horton's success and his investments were well-known, and the investment community took his recommendations seriously, so he was able to capture the interest of a few important financiers.

Diana's decision to have more cosmetic surgery came to her abruptly and, it seemed to her, only coincidentally, shortly after the drive to the ranch that night after Cash's performance at the Partaway.

It wasn't that her breasts were too small, she thought, but they sagged, so while she was having the implants to reestablish a degree of firmness, she also thought she may as well have them enlarged.

Her nose, which had a distinct character that contributed considerably to her looks, had started to bother her as well. She was sure it was too big, too prominent, and too hooked. She wanted it straighter, smaller, and thinner. She wanted a facelift, she wanted a firmer chin, and she wanted fuller lips. She wanted it all.

She had all the surgery done at the clinic that did her eyelids, and even though the wounds were cautiously and expertly inflicted, the process was much more complex, took much longer, and was more painful by an order of magnitude.

She withdrew from society and the public during this time, stayed in her suite on the *Marianna,* took all her meals in her room, and made no contact other than by telephone and email. When she finally healed physically, she looked different. The surgery did not have the minimal effect of the first one; now she was radically and extensively changed. She was a new person in her own eyes, with a significantly different appearance in the eyes of people who knew her.

Sycophants circled around Diana the same way they circled around Horton and Cash. When she first appeared with her new look, at a small dinner in her suite on the *Marianna,* Diana was kept from an unbiased, useful critique of the cosmetic change. The dinner guests reinforced whatever notions they perceived she was holding. In the end, Diana felt satisfied and prettier, and that was good enough for her.

She took the greatest pleasure and comfort in Horton's reaction. He was ecstatic, full of encouragement, and assured Diana it was an almost perfect makeover. In a response of camaraderie, Horton had one earlobe pierced and laced it with a tiny diamond stud. These assurances gave her the confidence she needed to meet Cash, her ultimate test of success. She planned on seeing Cash for the first time on the opening night of Horton's party.

Amber's attention was focused on her sudden wealth. The Partaway audiences had grown, and she was filling the Partaway Friday, Saturday, and Sunday nights, the result being thousands of dollars in receipts from the ten-dollar cover charge. By the end of the initial eight-week run, Amber had more than eight thousand dollars in cash, and Biggins asked her to stay on indefinitely, to which she and Buni agreed.

As to her life, she spent one whole day between Walmart and Target, two of the largest stores in Corpus Christi, where she bought clothes, shoes, and sundries. Buni encouraged her to buy a few necessities, like duffel bags for her new clothes and a large purse-like case for her money. Once the cash outgrew the little pink plastic wallet, Amber insisted on carrying her money around with her in her hand, rolled in strands of rubber bands. From a distance it looked like an old, treasured, tattered, talisman of some sort, but up close it was obviously a wad of cash, over four thousand dollars in small bills.

The purchase that excited her most was a very high-quality, elaborate stereo system, along with dozens of new CDs, vinyl LPs, and cassettes. She set it up in Buni's Surfside apartment where, with its big speakers and array of black wires in giant squiggles on the floor, it dominated his motley furniture. It did not bother her that she still had no home, or maybe it is more accurate to say it did not occur to her. She was uncertain what the future held, but the money and the steady gig at the Partaway were enough security for now, something she could appreciate.

Buni watched Amber in her new success with a sense of dread. He did not specifically know of Horton's destruction of Falluci's life's work, nor did he specifically know of Diana's radical cosmetic surgery, but he had all the important characters around Amber's new wealth generally in mind, and it gave his poet's heart a creeping sense that something was very wrong.

Buni did not yet consider these various players close to him or even to each other, but he felt an interconnection developing, especially as the Partaway, under Cash's control, grew larger in his life, and even though the orbits of Horton and Diana and the Partaway were distant, it made them each figure no less on his mindscape.

Buni's own capacity as a poet-philosopher was largely unknown to him. Amber knew it and Cash suspected it, but Buni thought of himself as a musician with no particular skills at insight. The America Gene idea had come to him during a session he was doing in Austin, a radio commercial for a local carpet store.

A producer he knew well had come in wearing a new hat, and to Buni, a very curious hat. The producer—usually in loafers, slacks, and open-collared dress shirts—was this day also wearing a beret.

It was, however, strange only in Buni's eyes apparently. The other musicians on the session even complimented the producer, but the beret was so obviously out of character, so startlingly strange, it set Buni's mind to work. He wondered how the choice had been made, particularly why it had seemed normal to the producer.

From there it was short and easy jump to Elvis. The choices Elvis made late in his career were strange like the producer's beret, Buni thought, and even beyond strange. It seemed to him such choices were well beyond the reach of any psychologist's explanation.

Though he knew little of the realities of genetics or recombinant DNA, the idea of an America Gene emerged as Buni's metaphor for these strange and unprecedented choices, and the metaphor was more apt than Buni knew. He thought the mutation might be generally hardwired somewhere in the American experience, and from this perspective began to notice similar behaviors among acquaintances, and then strangers.

Buni developed a sense for the Personal Las Vegas that kept getting keener and keener, and it was true, the PLV was a motivation far outside any analytical reach, unnoticed and unnoted by any scientist. He was learning to depend on it for explanations of all sorts of curious behavior.

Buni built a thought model for the Gene and its various effects that included, among other things, an almost magnetic pull from one person whose Gene had awakened to another whose Gene had not.

He was certain that when someone's PLV started to emerge, it was very likely to rouse others in its area of influence.

He saw something strange about Cash performing, as peculiar as the producer's beret, and now he deeply feared it was starting to pull in Amber. The Diana-Horton connection was still unclear to him, but it troubled him in the same way. He was more and more certain that this was a developing vortex of PLVs.

He knew everyone's PLV came along in a different way,

which was one of the reasons it was so hard to spot. To Buni's great despair, he hadn't the slightest idea what to do about it. For now he could only sit and watch.

Badgering Amber was not an option. He hardly knew Cash, and he didn't want to know Diana or Horton.

Besides, he had also learned not to talk about it too much, since most people dismissed it as a comic riff, and Buni was serious.

The jolt of Cash Carruthers in Amber's life surprised and confounded Buni. He admitted he was jealous. True, he had given up Amber as a girlfriend for a bigger relationship—more substantial, he thought—but that was an intellectual effort. His heart still belonged to her. But his jealousy of Cash was nothing compared with his wonder at Cash's effect on Amber. Since Buni had known her he had not seen this level of interest from her in anyone.

She would not discuss her feelings about Cash with Buni and had only once made a comment.

It was a comment made spontaneously, apropos of nothing, introduced as they ate a fast-food dinner. Buni had asked no question; Cash was not even a tangential subject of the small talk at hand. She looked at Buni, nodded her head, stopped chewing, and when Buni had given her his full attention she said, "This is a guy that can cope." True to their usual level of unspoken communication, Buni knew she was referring to Cash, and he knew what she meant.

It was a remarkable choice of words. It revealed an intuitive understanding of Cash's success, of his struggles, and of what had so enthralled her, why she liked him so much.

The insight reached deeper than either of them knew. If coping was what Cash did well, he needed all his skill right now. Sandra Corporation was coming apart at the seams.

Sydney Mansour, the head of the South American division in São Paolo, suddenly appeared in Houston to ask Cash if he was willing to sell the division to him, to allow Mansour to run it on his own.

It was not altogether unsuspected. Since the departure of Horton and Leland's death, Cash had grown less interested in the affairs of Sandra and had left the general operation of the company. He knew when he did it that it would only be a matter of time before the piper came calling. Not that Cash was dancing—he was mourning—but he knew this was more costly in the scheme of things.

The offer Mansour made was based on a fire-sale evaluation of the business, and it was plain he knew something Cash didn't about the financial health of the companies.

The truth was Cash no longer had the heart for Sandra, and he agreed not only to sell the division, but to sell everything to Mansour. Mansour was delighted, pulled the rest of the management of Sandra Corporation together, and responded with an offer to Cash that valued the enterprise at just over two billion dollars. A year earlier, it was worth four—six by some estimates. Cash knew this was the best for him, gracefully accepted, and started the process of transfer.

At every pivotal juncture like this before, Cash had reached out to Leland. That wasn't possible now. At first Cash tried spending time in his Houston office, but it was infected with falsity.

He tried staying at the ranch, but it was too isolated. One morning, in a wave of longing, he drove by the motel where his father had lived and went inside the apartment for the first time since the funeral. Rather than sad and troubling, Cash found it comforting and familiar.

He set himself up at his father's small desk, installed a few phone lines and computer links, and began transacting the minutiae of his personal business from there and taking long walks alone along the beach.

From this perspective, the sale of Sandra and the consequent diminution of his wealth became not just an acceptable idea but the only thing to do. Cash recognized he was opening himself up for other adventures. Pruning and repotting.

He and Horton talked off and on during the sale of Sandra, sometimes stridently, as Horton revealed more and more of a repugnant misanthropy, self-satisfied positions Horton vindicated by pointing to his riches. Horton was dismayed by these conflicts, mild though they were, even though he couldn't stop himself from asserting these mean spirits.

This outlook insinuated itself into the decision Cash had to make about whether to attend Horton's party, to lend himself and his prestige to proceedings that were to him at least strange, and at most anathema. In the last analysis, Cash made the decision to attend only one day of the cruise party, and that was because of Amber Fanfare.

Horton held to his drunken offer to have her play and to pay her $25,000. Diana had, of course, pleaded with Cash not to back out, but Cash had become suspicious of Diana's intent, especially as the *Mariner* project grew larger and larger, so her entreaties were feeble, holding little sway.

When Cash told Buni the offer of the cruise party was a solid offer and the pay was real, Buni did not seem as pleased as Cash thought he would be. Buni mumbled a small thanks and an equivocal acceptance, almost as if it were bad news.

Chapter Thirteen

Once the new semester started at the University of Texas at Austin, the news of Amber Fanfare and the Partaway spread over the Internet at light speed.

The Partaway was a perfect college-student weekend trek. It was an easy three hours by car from Austin, just the sort of thing that students were looking for to relieve the pressures of study.

Austin had its own vibrant music scene in the form of a string of music clubs along Sixth Street. Guy and Rose Marks, the owners of the Rafters, one of the lesser-known clubs, made the trip to the Partaway several times before making Biggins an offer to buy it for one and a half million dollars.

The Rafters was not particularly successful as a music club, but it had served well as a money laundry for Guy's marijuana trade, and Guy and Rose needed to do something with the money. At present the money was sitting in a dozen low-grade investment instruments, earning practically nothing. The purchase of the Partaway would put the money trail farther out of reach of investigators, should there ever be any. The Markses also thought they would enjoy the beaches of Corpus Christi.

It wasn't only Amber who had increased the value of the Partaway. Biggins listened carefully to Cash and hired a local chef who was exceptionally good at preparing catfish and steaks. Following Cash's advice, he bought high-priced, high-quality food and doubled the lunch and dinner business. The Partaway was now a local favorite for food, as well as a weekend destination for live music, worth the drive for people from Austin, Houston, and San Antonio.

Henry Biggins and his wife Teresa, childless, never expected to have so much money in their life. Only a few years earlier, Henry had been roughnecking on one of the Gulf Coast Oil derricks leased from Cash, and Teresa had been growing a little produce and selling it at the local farmers' market. They spent most of their time off watching television and eating cheese from a spray can.

When Biggins bought the Partaway, it was hardly more than a ruin, and Henry assumed it would be a place he and some friends could have a few beers and watch sports. The old building cost him eight thousand dollars in back taxes, paid to the county. He built the bar himself, Teresa made the curtains, and they slowly added to it over the years. When Leland bought in, it was to pay for the kitchen. The total capital investment in the Partaway was less than $25,000, not counting the Bigginses' labor. A million-five was a six-thousand percent increase. Their share of that was a million dollars.

The immediate question that came to Biggins's mind was whether or not Cash would be willing to sell. Technically, Biggins could force the sale. He and Teresa were the majority owners, but he had no intention of doing that.

His hands were shaking and his voice quivering when he called Cash. To Henry's amazement, Cash quickly agreed to the concept of a sale, but he asked Henry not to set a price, to let Cash negotiate the sale, and to let Cash inform Amber and Buni. Henry couldn't have been happier. Cash had offered to handle the two things Henry was dreading.

As it worked out, Cash made the deal with the Markses for the million-five they offered. Cash knew from his first meeting with them that they were unsophisticated buyers with a different reason for buying the Partaway than the one they were stating. Pro forma cash flows would mean nothing to them and financial statements would be dark magic, as would a complex evaluation, regardless of its accuracy or persuasiveness. As it was, Cash was having a hard time getting them to remember his name, so Cash accepted the offer as it stood. The sale was poetic, not practical.

The final deal did not include an arrangement with Buni or Amber, and Cash chose the Monday before the *Marianna* cruise to drive to Surfside and talk to them.

He arrived at Buni's apartment mid-afternoon to find Buni repairing the headlight on Rachel the Volvo. He was humming softly to himself under the car. Just beyond Rachel's grill, the open door to his apartment revealed Amber, barefoot and clad in only a T-shirt and shorts. She was lying on the floor listening to music through a pair of enormous headphones. Neither Buni nor Amber saw Cash drive up and park.

The door on Cash's truck closed with a thunk, and Buni squirreled out from under his car.

"Jeez, Cash," he said. "I didn't know you was here. Amber! Cash's here."

"Really?" Amber jumped up, dropped the headphones unceremoniously on the floor, and darted outside. The T-shirt hung to mid-thigh. "Hey, Cowboy!" she said as she ran to him, hugged him around the waist then kissed his cheek. "You slummin'?"

"C'mon in," Buni said. "See Amber's new super-deluxe stereophonic high-fidelity sound system."

Amber dragged Cash by the hand through the front door. "Want a drink? Buni just got this." Amber pointed to a new refrigerator.

"No. I'm fine." Cash sat down in a rickety easy chair that wobbled from a short leg.

Amber went to the main control of her new sound system and flipped a switch. Music burst out through the speakers at an extremely high volume, which Amber turned down so that she could talk over it.

The music was a thumping traditional old-time blues. "Tyrone Edwards," she said. "The best of the best. And with this"—she pointed to the stereo—"I can hear everything he's doing."

Buni turned to Cash, "Thus it goes. But that's not why you're here, is it?" He looked at Cash.

"No, but it sounds great."

Amber returned and sat cross-legged at Cash's feet.

"You don't drink?" Buni asked, waggling a beer at him.

"No," Amber said. "I've never seen him. You don't drink, do you?"

Cash shook his head. "Never liked alcohol. Cigarettes made me sick. So there you are. But I needed to talk to you about the Partaway."

"We told Biggins we'd stay. We won't leave," Amber said matter-of-factly.

"I know," Cash said. "But that's—it's different. Henry and I sold the Partaway."

Amber and Buni looked at each other, plainly surprised and concerned.

"I'm sure the new owners want you to stay," Cash went on. "They own a club in Austin, and I think you were a big part of why they wanted to buy the Partaway in the first place—they never said that, but they acted that way. Point is, you'll need to make a deal with them. I told them you were playing on the *Marianna* this week, so they aren't expecting you to be back for a while. That'll give you some time to think."

"So we won't be getting paid by—I mean do they give us the same deal—do they know we get the door? Or—wait, are we, like, fired now?" Buni asked.

"No. Not—at least I wouldn't think so. But the real answer is,

I don't know. I told them our deal, but they didn't respond, and they didn't want to make your deal part of the purchase—so—you know, you'll have to talk to them. But, yes, I told them you got the door."

Amber stood up, crossed her arms across her chest, and walked into the kitchen area, where she paced back and forth.

"I don't think you need to worry," Cash said. "My guess is they want you stay on, and they will want you to play the Austin club as well. Apropos what you said the other day, Buni, I think these folks might know some record people, too. They seem to be fairly deep into the whole Austin music scene, records and all. I see all this as a big plus for you."

"But for now we're fired," Amber said.

"No, Amber, that's—" Cash started.

"When do they take over?" Buni asked.

"Escrow closes tomorrow," Cash said.

Amber stopped pacing. "Who?"

"Escrow," Cash said.

"It's like when you buy a house or something. People hold the money until everything is right," Buni said.

Amber shook her head. "They're called escrow?"

"Not the people," Cash said. "Escrow is the name of the transaction. A third party holds the money until the conditions of a sale are met, then they release the money from the buyer to the seller."

Amber understood, and she appreciated Cash's assumption that she could understand.

"And that happens tomorrow—the—"

"Close," Cash said.

"—the close. So these new guys own it tomorrow. Wow. Just when I thought I had a home."

"Are the new guys gonna do anything to the place, you think?" Buni asked.

"It's a couple, man and wife," Cash said. "I think so. I think they are going to fix the place up a little, but they didn't say."

Buni shook his head. "Here we go."

"Should we talk to them now?" Amber asked.

"You do what you think best. If it were me, I'd wait." Cash stood. "You've got the *Marianna* job, which will be great money and probably exposure to the right people. Won't hurt the Markses to wait a week. They're busy, anyway, with other things having to do with the transfer. I don't think you have anything to lose by waiting till you get back."

Buni perked up. "You really think there will be something with the boat gig? I've been, you know, wondering how this was all gonna work."

"I know that Horton has invited some high-profile individuals from the entertainment business—"

"God, don't say 'entertainment business.'" Amber rolled her eyes. "It sounds like something for rich people to take their minds off their money."

Buni looked at her, surprised. Wasn't Cash "rich people"?

"O.K.," Cash said. "The what? The arts—the media—people who sell records and movies and whatnot. There will be some very active and successful people there in that line of work."

"And it is business," Buni said.

"I know," Amber said. "I know. I was just being bitchy. Money. Business. Escrow. Entertainment. Business. Got it."

"Can I have one of those?" Cash pointed to the plastic bottle of water Amber was holding.

"Help yourself." Buni pointed to the refrigerator.

Cash pulled a bottle from a shelf that held a dozen more. "I have to go now. But. I did have one other question for you. I don't know how you feel about this—but if you wanted to—I mean if you would like, I would be happy to let you take, uh—use the helicopter to ride out to the *Marianna* Thursday."

Amber, wide-eyed, turned to Buni. Then back to Cash. "You're kiddin'." She was excited.

"If you would like. Saves the drive."

"Saves the drive. Right," Amber repeated ironically. "It'd be a blast." She ran to Cash, wrapped her arms around his waist, laid her head on his chest, and squeezed hard.

The *Marianna* was at sea with the first part of Horton's party, the potential investors. She had sailed out to the platform off the Bolivar Peninsula and circled slowly around it as Horton, Diana, and Vittorio did a show-and-tell, a multimedia presentation outlining the design, materials, construction, and promise of the huge project.

Horton had gathered under a hundred investors, which was a third less than the affirmative "will attend" responses he had gotten. Times were tough. Big money had grown wary and much less frisky. The investors who did attend were not insignificant, but many of them were there simply because of the party and the networking opportunity it would provide.

Diana's floating island appeared to many of them like the dessert of the same name: exotic and a touch too rich.

By Horton's estimate, he thought he might have attracted around a hundred million dollars. Barely enough to complete the *Mariner*'s first stage, which included the operating tower, the casino, some shops, and eight apartments. Horton was not encouraged, but he was not unhappy. He, too, was caught up in his own party, having a good time and drinking a lot of expensive Cognac.

A helicopter landing officer, who was in constant touch with Houston air-traffic control, had been established onboard the *Marianna*. Over the next few days, they were expecting between thirty and forty different helicopters and as many landings on the *Marianna*. It was a heavy logistical load.

Cash's Dauphine carrying Amber and Buni was one of the first to arrive. Cash had called Diana to tell her he was sending them, and she had the ship's staff expecting them.

As the helicopter lifted straight up off the tarmac at the Brazoria County Airport, Buni looked down to see Rachel the Volvo sitting beside the terminal building, everything getting smaller and smaller in his view. Amber looked out and saw the unfolding expanse of the Texas Gulf Coast. She was elated. She punched Buni three times in the shoulder and pointed to the Gulf beaches as they stretched further and further. Buni looked up and smiled.

The flight to the *Marianna* was just over forty-five minutes. When the Chopper crossed the line of the beach and flew over the water, Amber's stomach fluttered. Away in the vast ocean distance she saw a white speck that was the *Marianna*. It did not occur to her at first that this was their destination, but when it did, Amber had a glimmer of what life was like lived at this scale. She yelled, much too loud for the headphones, "That's the boat!" The pilot smiled to himself. Buni nodded. "Unbelievable!" Amber yelled once more.

The landing on the *Marianna*, at sea anchor just outside Galveston Harbor, was uneventful. The helicopter landing officer and Horton's right-hand man were on hand to greet Amber and Buni, as promised.

They were escorted below deck to their rooms, which were in the same forward area of the ship as the rest of the crew, in an area designated for the entertainment staff—the band and performers who were part of the *Marianna*'s regular nightly show.

The two rooms were across a small hallway from each other and staggered apart by several other rooms. They were small, each with upper and lower bunk beds and a tiny shower and sink. There was a short upholstered bench against the bulkhead where Buni and Amber each threw their duffel. Buni felt cramped and wanted to get out of the room at once. Amber jumped from one bed to the other and explored all the cabinets and drawers. She was delighted and loved the idea that this was her own space, regardless of the size, which she thought charming. It helped, of course, that she was petite. It made the room feel capacious to her, easily able to hold all she expected a shelter to hold.

Buni knocked on her door.

"Wanna go up top?" he asked as she opened the door.

"No. I wanna move in," she said.

"I'm gonna explore a little. Check out the stage and piano. You be O.K.?"

"I'll be out in a while. Have fun." She gave him a peck on the cheek.

Back in her room Amber dumped the contents of the duffel on the bottom bunk. Then she took each item and either hung it up or folded it carefully and put it in a drawer. Once she was satisfied, she picked up her new purse, hung it over her shoulder, and set out to look around the ship. She was wearing a pair of faded jeans frayed at the hems and torn at the knees, boots, and a pullover blouse, and she was carrying over eight thousand dollars in small bills.

The *Marianna* had ten decks, but only seven were for passengers. Amber took the elevator to the top deck, where she found the spa and the beauty salon. The spa, with its array of exercise equipment, was small but lavishly turned out, like everything else on the ship. The beauty salon right next to the spa, Mr. Todd's, was opulent, clearly a province for women who wanted to spend time there. All the stations were empty except for Mr. Todd, who was sitting at one of them and reading *Vogue* magazine. He looked up when Amber poked her head in the door.

"Can I help you with something, dear?" He put down the

magazine. Mr. Todd was in high-fashion comfort clothes, in his late thirties and trim, with a shaved bald head and clear steel-blue eyes.

"No. This where you get a hairdo?" Amber inched into the room.

Todd Burrell had been with the *Marianna* since her first sailing and was a veteran of several hundred cruises.

"Yes, ma'am. It is. Best salon on the ship. I'm Mr. Todd. Wow. Look at you." Mr. Todd extended his hand and stepped forward. Amber shook it.

"So nice to know you," she said, trying to remember the phrase exactly as her mother had taught it to her.

Mr. Todd reached out and took the end of Amber's hair in his fingers. "Look at this hair. You're gorgeous, kiddo. You in the party?"

"Sort of. I'm a singer. The singer with the band for the party."

"Mmmmm. I don't think you're supposed to be up here, doll."

"Why not?" Amber stepped fully into the room.

"Staff's not allowed with the passengers."

"I'm not staff. I'm the singer. I was invited here."

"Really. Who invited you?" Mr. Todd was not aggressive. He sincerely didn't want Amber to get in trouble.

"Horton and Diana. Lady that owns it," Amber said.

This put Mr. Todd more at ease. It may have been a lie, but if she was willing to take the risk, he was too.

"Well in that case, come, let me give you a shampoo."

Amber hadn't counted on this. She didn't want to go in all the way, but she wasn't going to get pushed out.

"No. I—How much does it cost?" Amber had been to beauty salons with her mother and was afraid of them in some basic way. She washed and dried her own hair, and when she performed she let it hang naturally just below her shoulders, which was fine with her. It was a bit ragged, to be sure, but Amber was careful to keep it clean and combed. Most of the time, like now, she wore it gathered behind her head in a band.

"Nothing. Part of the guest services of the boat, which for the next two days are the compliments of Mr. Callaway." Mr. Todd was watching her now, looking for the lie. Nothing came. "You are really a beautiful one—what's your name?"

"Amber. Fanfare. Does it look dirty?" Amber was not used to professional flattery or any of Mr. Todd's moves. She liked being cosseted.

"Amber Fanfare!? My God, what a great name. Is it real?"

Amber nodded.

"Come in, Mizz Fanfare. Have a seat. I'm just killing time until the others arrive. Let's take a look. And no, it doesn't look dirty at all. I was just offering. What we could do, just for fun, is a shampoo with this—" Mr. Todd produced a bottle of exotic shampoo. "Then a condition with this." An even fancier bottle.

Amber plopped herself down in the salon chair. It was plush and cozy.

Mr. Todd pulled the band from her hair, which fell about her shoulders. Amber drew her fingers through her hair and shook it out as Mr. Todd stared at her in the mirror, the two of them looking at the two of them. He put his face next to hers for perspective.

"You are stunning, dear, I mean it. We just need to get rid of these." He held up the ends of her hair in a small bunch between his thumb and forefinger. "A trim."

Amber sat forward suddenly. "I don't want a haircut."

Mr. Todd patted her gently on the shoulder and back into the chair. He picked up a small pair of scissors and then held up a few strands of her hair for her to see in the mirror. They looked like a thatch of grass. He took the scissors and snipped a quarter inch off. The strands shimmered, all the same length. "These are split and uneven. Just a trim. See how much better. I know just what you need, Amber. You leave it to me. No haircuts. I promise."

Amber had been solicited and propositioned since she was thirteen and knew all those overtures, but she had never encountered this type of indulgence and attention. Her trepidation waned, and she settled into the seat. "I've got money," she said.

"Honey, let's let Mr. Callaway take care of all that. You just sit there and be beautiful, and let me work on you a little so I can take credit for it."

An hour later, Mr. Todd was blowing Amber's hair dry, gently using long, broad strokes of a brush and a blow dryer. Her hair shone from the light and was beautifully groomed, but it wasn't the same "Amber" hair. She was still undeniably gorgeous, but in a more predictable way.

The transition had been slow, and Amber had noticed nothing except the luxury of another human being pampering her. She liked what she saw in the mirror. It was better, she thought. Mr. Todd stepped back. Amber flipped her hair. It landed back in position perfectly. She shook her head. Same thing.

"You're goin' all the way, kid. I can't wait to hear you sing," Mr. Todd said.

"You coming tonight?" Amber stood up from the chair.

"I'm coming every night you're here, Miss Fanfare." Mr. Todd continued brushing a few more affectionate strokes while Amber stood there.

"O.K. I'll sing you a song." Amber felt wonderful. She bounced out of the salon of her new best friend and onto the elevator.

The next deck down was mostly rooms, but it had a large area that opened to the sky. From it she could see a helicopter landing well aft on the pad. Then she noticed two more helicopters out at sea, waiting for their turn at landing. The guests were starting to arrive.

Deck eight was the pool deck. There were only two people out, the day being far spent.

Deck seven was more staterooms.

Deck six was pay dirt. It contained the casino and all the shops, along a promenade that went the full length of the ship. Amber strolled along looking in the shop windows. She stopped at an "outdoor" café and ordered a beer, which she drank standing at the bar instead of sitting at one of the small café tables that bordered the promenade, and which, to her delight, she didn't have to pay for. Again, compliments of Mr. Callaway. Across the way, a woman was putting the finishing touches on a headless mannequin in a store window.

Amber stared as the woman dressed the mannequin in a pair of peach-colored satin pants and a light knit top with a design of rhinestones. When she finished the beer, she walked over and looked through the shop window. The woman saw her and beckoned her in. Amber was delighted at the presence of so many friendly and accommodating faces.

"This would look fabulous on you." Whatever Mr. Todd had done to Amber's hair had removed all evidence of her "staff" appearance. Her jeans were still ragged, her boots run over at the heel, her shirt plain, but her face and hair sparkled enough so that all the rest was rendered an affectation. The sales lady had no question Amber belonged.

"What size are you, dear?" she asked.

"I think I'm a two," Amber said.

The sales lady clucked approvingly. "Of course you are. Don't I wish we all could look like you. Can I start a dressing room for you? Would you like to try this on?"

The outfit was not exactly garish, being common fare for a shop in this setting; it was a type of daywear that was dressy enough to wear to dinner. The rhinestone design on the front was a single strand in a giant question mark. The sales lady walked to a rack and pulled a size two out of several different sizes of the same ensemble. She held it up to Amber in front of a full-length dressing mirror. Amber liked the newness of it, the shine of it, but had no idea whether it suited her or not. She had never shopped anywhere but large discount chains. No one ever held a dress up for her to see. She had always chosen from the rack.

"I'm Molly." The saleswoman extended her hand.

"Oh," Amber said as she shook it.

"And your name?" Molly asked as she led Amber to a small dressing room and pulled the privacy curtains aside.

"Amber Fanfare."

"What a fabulous name. Here." Molly hung the ensemble on a hook. "I'll be right outside if you need anything."

Amber was suddenly confused and felt very alone. She didn't know quite what to do. After a second, she took off her clothes and pulled on the satin pants and rhinestone blouse, then studied herself in the dressing-room mirror.

"Are you O.K. in there?" Molly asked after a few minutes. "Need anything?"

"I don't have any shoes," Amber said. It was not a request, merely a statement.

"What size do you wear?" Molly asked.

"I dunno. I wear a six boot."

A few moments later Molly pulled the curtain back discreetly and held out a pair of black satin pumps. "These might be too old for you, but just use them for now. I'll check to see what we have."

Amber slipped on the shoes and walked out into the store.

She looked in the three-way, full-length dressing mirror and was completely bewildered. She liked the brightness of the satin.

Her lifelong wardrobe consisted of jeans and boots and a shirt, all made for women, but men's styles nonetheless. She eschewed her mom's sexy outfits of short skirts and tight blouses.

This image was something else. Amber had never conceived of herself like this. She was waffling, struggling for a value base, when Molly said, "That looks fabulous on you. Look at the way it fits."

The tight satin pants emphasized the sexiest aspect of Amber's hips and legs. Amber turned around and looked over her shoulder at her rear.

"Try these." Molly held out a pair of low slip-on white espadrilles.

Amber put them on and the transformation was complete. She was following Molly's thinking like a baby duck following its mother.

"How much are these. Are they expensive?" she asked.

"Oh, no. Not really. The pants are two hundred and the blouse is three-fifty. And the shoes are one-ten. Would you like to wear them out?"

"I'll just carry them, I think." Amber said as she produced a wad of bills.

* * *

Buni Rumble sat at the Yamaha Grand on the stage of the two-story, four-hundred-seat Nautilus Theater. The theater took over much of the rear half of decks five and six. It was technically the finest facility Buni had ever been in, the piano was one of the best he ever played, and the lights and sound were unequaled in his experience. The theater was designed by a Las Vegas builder and was in essence a miniature of the lavish showroom stages of the Las Vegas hotels and casinos.

The seats tiered up stadium-style from the stage and wrapped around, so that every seat, overstuffed and covered in blue velvet, had a great view. The stage itself was large, with plenty of room to move—a real luxury for someone who played in a bar.

In all the splendor, Buni looked up from the piano to the back of the house, and a feeling of dark dread fell over him.

"There you are." A lady was standing at the top row of seats. Her greeting pulled Buni from his ominous reverie. He had no idea who she was.

"Hi," he said.

Navigating carefully because of her high heels, the lady made her way down the aisle. She was a lively, buxom blonde who was smiling broadly. "I see you made it out O.K." She click-clacked onto the stage and held out her hand to Buni. Buni stood up, smiling weakly, having no idea who she was or why she was being so familiar.

"It's Diana Copeland," the lady said.

"Oh my gosh, Diana, I'm sorry. The, uh, lights—I couldn't see. Yeah, uh, we made it out. Yeah. How are you?"

Diana knew Buni was covering his faux pas, and it was the first taste she had of complete nonrecognition since the surgery. It rattled her.

"Good. Amber here?" Diana looked around the stage.

"Uh, no, she was in her room when I left—well, she was. She may be out looking around. She's on the boat, if that's what you mean."

"And Cash let you use the helicopter. Wasn't that fun?" Diana said.

"It was. Sure was." Buni was getting more uncomfortable by the second. He had not recognized Diana at first, and now with her close, he recognized her even less. He was starting to doubt his acuity. This lady didn't look like Diana Copeland. Did he have something confused? He knew this type. She had a low-grade tension, a subparticle quaver. He felt as if she were about to jump out of her skin. This type wasn't the Diana he remembered. No. He had noticed none of this in Diana Copeland.

"Diana!" An unseen voice called out from the lobby of the theater.

"Horton!" Diana called back. "We're in the theater."

Horton appeared at the top of the auditorium and came down the aisle to join them.

"Hi, Buni. You made it out O.K. In fine style, I hear." Horton held his hand out and Buni shook it. Buni tried not to stare, but he couldn't take his eyes off the diamond stud in Horton's right earlobe. Buni unconsciously fingered his own gold stud. Horton was smugly aware of Buni's curiosity. "So, what do you think of our showroom?" Horton asked.

"Outstanding. Truly. Looking forward to it." Buni said.

The stage door opened, pouring outside light on the stage

where they all stood, and Amber walked in. She was carrying a large shiny shopping bag full of new clothes.

Chapter Fourteen

"And when you said, 'What happened to your face?' I thought, O.K., here we go…" Buni was looking at Amber sitting across from him at a table for two in the dining room of the *Marianna*, where they were talking about Diana.

"I didn't mean it like that," Amber interrupted. She was looking over the menu. The dining room on the *Marianna* was finished to the standard of the rest of the ship, and the general motif in this room was "Paris in the Twenties."

"I know. But 'What happened to your face!' Gobs of tension! Man." Buni could see three helicopters waiting to land off the back of the boat. The *Marianna* was close to shore, and the lights from the coastal cities were starting to come on. The air was hot and humid outside, but it was dry and cool in the dining room. A piano, drum, and bass combo were playing soft cocktail music.

The guests for the party were arriving in drabs and dribbles through the grand entrance of the dining room where Horton, with Diana at his side, were welcoming them.

"Well, she laughed," Amber said.

"I laughed too. But—"

"I wasn't being mean. I was just surprised. She looked so different. And she didn't act upset. She told me all about it. Which, I can tell you now, you do not wanna know."

"Oh, Mama. I know. I know. Do not tell me anything."

Buni and Amber ordered a Caesar salad, steaks, and draft beer.

Amber's innocent remark had caught Diana off guard, and it would have been an insensitive thing to say had Amber not been so obviously naïve, but it had not made the comment less painful.

It did make Diana realize how drastic the change was. Her onboard friends and staff had gotten used to it, and Diana was moving around the ship somewhat normally. She hadn't expected anyone to say, "What happened to your face?" but there it was. From the mouth of a babe.

Buni and Amber's reaction to the change in her were the first of a series of shocks that were starting for Diana. The rest were coming through the grand entrance of the dining room as she stood in a reception line of sorts with Horton, but the surprise wasn't only for Diana's new look. It was for Horton's as well. Most of the guests knew Horton as a straightforward businessman who was conservative, reserved, and private.

Horton was slimmer than ever and tan, with his remaining

fringe of graying hair in a buzz cut. He was wearing sandals, black slacks, and a black silk T-shirt. And of course, the ear stud.

As each new guest arrived, there was a new rendition of "hide the surprised look" played out on each of the faces. Some were tame, with only the slightest hint conveyed in a glance or a nudge, and others broke into laughter that they quickly disguised as merriment, random glee, or party laughter. Horton was secretly pleased. He liked his new edgy persona, liked the provocation of it. Diana was feeling more and more insecure.

After dinner, Buni and Amber went to the theater to meet the rest of the band and to check the sound. Amber had paid little attention to the stage earlier, when she had been talking with Diana. Now that she had a closer look, she found it daunting. This was no intimate bar, and there was pointedly no element of funk.

Standing at center stage, she looked out and up into the seats that surrounded her. She had played to packed houses, but they had looked different than this. The people were usually squashed together, gathered close around little tables, and the stage was usually raised so Amber could see over their heads. Here she was standing at the bottom of an imposing mountain looking up. It was enervating, disturbing.

Buni started the rehearsal, and Amber grabbed the microphone and heard the most superlative sound she had ever heard onstage. The monitor system let her hear herself and the band perfectly. It was far from the usual noise of the small-club sound systems. She could hear nuances, slight changes in the dynamics, all of which shored her up and relieved some of the intimidation of the big concert venue.

Amber had a contralto voice, low and deep, and when she reached into the higher registers to sing, her voice rasped in a pleasing and urgent way. Sonically, however, the range of her voice was always muddled in low-tech sound because it would get lost among the instruments. With this state-of-the-art sound setup, she heard herself clearly over the band, and her natural dominion gathered even more strength. She felt good, and she laid into the song with a vengeance. All the other band members, especially Buni, were amazed by her new level of clarity and command.

The doorways to the theater quickly filled with staff and passersby drawn to the indescribable voice, and at the end of the first rehearsal number, they all broke into applause.

Then it was Buni's turned to be shocked. Amber did something he had never seen her do since he met her. She smiled and then actually waved to all of them.

That night after dinner, the entire party made its way down to the theater to see the Amber Fanfare Show. They were drunk party revelers, giddy from the first-night excitement of being on the ship and seeing old friends. Horton had made a welcoming speech at dinner and told all of them to be sure to come to the theater tonight and tomorrow, so they were all here.

The number of party attendees had shrunk from the number of promisors by roughly the same third the investor pool had. Horton was expecting six hundred, but a few less than four hundred actually showed. As the news of the distressed sale of Sandra Corporation made its way around the global community that cared about such things, Horton's clout diminished.

It was nevertheless a pocketbook version of the party Horton had hoped for. The people who were there were dominant in their respective fields, from politics to sports, from science to the arts, from business to idle wealth. Despite Buni's running commentary, Amber was uninterested in most of these people and what they did or who they were or who they imagined themselves to be. What interested her was what kind of audience they would make.

In her room before the show, Amber carefully poured herself into her new wardrobe. Her natural skill at presenting herself in the best way was hampered by the new clothes. She didn't know what she was seeing when she looked in the mirror. Everything looked askew. Peach satin and rhinestones were a sartorial surreality to her, with no natural north.

After staring at herself in the mirror twice as long as she ever had, she was ambivalent, unsure of how she looked. She decided to trust Molly the saleswoman and leave it at that. Molly had faithfully promised to attend the show. Amber would at least have her there to lean on. She walked out of her room and down the hall to Buni's.

Buni opened the door and walked out before she got there. He saw her, and he stopped dead.

"What?" Amber said defensively.

"You—what are—?" But Buni was at a loss for words. He

made one full turn, then back to Amber, as if she might disappear or change while he had his back to her. She was still there, and he was still flabbergasted.

"Don't do that, Buni. Stop." Amber was fierce. "It's what I bought."

Buni dropped his mouth open in exaggerated astonishment and shook his head dramatically for effect. Because Buni avoided all confrontation, he did not have the grace or the poise to know what to say here.

"Amazing," he said, meaning *ridiculous*.

It made Amber angry. She knew what he meant.

"Buni!" Amber raised her voice. "Can't you just talk like a normal human? What is wrong with you? This is the way I look. Is that a problem?!"

Buni's modus operandi in all situations of this type was to withdraw, disappear if he could. If he couldn't, he clammed up. He was not going to comment on this. He couldn't. He didn't know how.

"Whatever," he said and walked away to the stage.

Amber fumed and stormed back to her room. She looked at herself in the mirror again. In her heart, she wanted to step up and out of blue jeans and boots, up and out of her ragged life, to know the finest and best, and in her heart she knew she didn't know how. This was the best she could do for now, and she resolved to follow that. Buni had betrayed her. She was on her own, and she had to make a decision. From here a rhinestone question mark looked like a step up to her, so she took it.

She slammed the door behind her and tramped purposefully toward the theater and the waiting crowd.

Horton was standing backstage when Amber blasted through the door.

"Amber. You're here. And you look fantastic," he said. "Ready to go?"

Amber looked at Buni and the band standing in a group. All of them were staring, in various stages of reaction, at her clothes. Izzy Firegate smiled and gave her a thumbs-up. Before she could digest Horton's compliment, he said, "How do you want me to introduce you?"

She looked at Buni. Buni looked away.

"Ask Buni," she said.

Horton walked to Buni, and they spoke quietly for a few seconds, and then Horton walked onstage. The crowd broke into a lazy applause. A few in the audience called out to Horton, teasing him about his pierced ear and stud. Horton bantered uncomfortably with the crowd briefly and then said, "This is someone Cash Carruthers discovered. He'll be up here tomorrow. But for tonight, she's all yours. Say hello to Amber Fanfare and her band, under the direction of Friedrich Bundt."

There was another lackluster round of applause as the band ambled on the stage and picked up their instruments. Amber followed them all onstage.

As Amber walked onstage and looked out, the crowd stretched away and up to dizzying heights. It was a monolith, dressed for dinner, some of it in black tie, some of it in gowns.

She was face to face for the first time in her life with a show crowd. She had no idea what to do. Her heart raced.

All of her usual patterns failed. She could not divorce herself from the crowd and simply watch the show she saw from the stage. There was nothing to see. This crowd had no dynamic. It was motionless. Hands folded. Waiting. Predatory. A blob.

Buni started playing, and the band sprang to life and the music rose up around her, but Amber was disoriented. She stood on the stage waiting for the internal pulse to overtake her, but it wasn't there. She became devastatingly self-conscious.

From the audience, Amber appeared twice as small as usual. A peach-colored, satin-covered mite on the stage. The band's music filled the auditorium with enough sound, but there wasn't enough show. The micro-moves she made in a club, the way the music was played—all were desperately inadequate here.

She forced herself to start the first song, but it was with half a heart. She stood motionless in front of the microphone and sang with her eyes closed, so the only thing the people on the back row of the auditorium had to connect to was a static sound source.

Amber's voice had the same remarkable quality, and the crowd noticed there might be something here, but this was a sophisticated, world-traveled audience. It would take more than a good voice to get their attention.

Amber began to sweat. She looked at Buni, who smiled and pretended all was well, but Amber knew him well enough to recognize a smirk.

At the end of the first song, instead of the explosion of approval she was used to, she only received polite applause, the damning of faint praise, indeed.

It was a catastrophic mixture. A bar band with no show. A singer that was insecure and tentative. A costume that came from a mannequin all of the audience had seen on the ship's shopping promenade.

Then, deep from the wells of Amber's soul, from the same still place she used to find the heart of a song, there came a calm call. She knew this music. She knew what it meant. She knew how to sing it. All the rest were trappings. The members of the audience were caught in their cummerbunds and corsets, but Amber was not caught. Peach satin or not, she knew how to fly on the wings of the music.

Before Buni could begin the next song, Amber walked to the mike and began to sing the song a cappella. It surprised Buni. He started to join in, but she held up her hand.

It was a familiar gesture of command to Buni, slight, delicate, but with clear authority, and the power of it, the control of this simple gesture, shot to the back row of the auditorium. They sat up a little in their seats.

Amber, sweetly, in her lowest and huskiest voice, began to sing, all by herself. She sang slowly and married the meaning of the words to their tones, then bled them across the stage and out into the crowd, now hushed.

She knew this space, knew how to navigate it. She held her hand higher, instructing Buni to wait longer. The song she had started was a powerful up-tempo blues the band usually blasted out loud toward the end of a raucous set, but she was singing so slowly and mournfully, the band was riveted in place. They waited.

She cried the words and brought their meaning out from her heart, and the crowd was with her. Listening. All eyes were fixed on this most amazing feat. They saw something coming to life before them. A few sat up straighter and leaned forward to see.

At the end of the first phrase of the song, Amber turned slowly to Buni and gave him the slightest look. Buni knew what she meant, and at her signal, the band broke into the rhythm and the power of the song at its full volume and its full and insistent dance tempo. Firegate tore open a blues-guitar fill, and as the song lifted off, the audience broke into applause.

A few in the crowd jumped up in the aisle and started dancing. Whatever bond held them down or made them suspicious or cynical was broken by the force of Amber Fanfare, by her connection to the music, a connection that set them free.

The rest of the audience cautiously consented to her.

But not entirely.

As the song unfolded, the audience began to break into clusters. Some followed, enraptured, others were charmed but wary, and still others had seen this kind of power before and were only amused. This was not a crowd that had traveled to see Amber perform or dedicated a night to it. This was a crowd bound by a party, not similar values. Amber could acquit herself well, but it would be impossible to sway all of them. The best she could hope for was to reinforce the positives and have the negatives move to neutral, and that was what she got.

More songs followed in essentially the same fashion. Amber held on to the audience through the power of her voice and her singing, usually only for a moment or two in each song. The crowd was mercurial, this way and that, attentive and distracted throughout the songs, but they usually ended up approving. By the close, Amber was exhausted.

At the end of the set, she received a solid round of applause. Some of the audience members even stood up; the rest were eager to get out of the theater and into the casino and disco. Amber accepted the thanks graciously and then dashed from the stage. She was badly shaken.

As the crowd dispersed, Amber looked around for a sign of Mr. Todd or Molly. Neither had come. Horton and Diana had watched the first number and left. She was alone. As the band came offstage, everyone seemed normal except for Buni, who was cool and aloof.

"Friedrich Bundt?" Amber glared at Buni.

"Simply trying to match the outfit, little one." Buni would not look at her. Amber stormed away to her room. She was on the edge of tears, and she would not give Buni that satisfaction.

Amber's angst was mild compared with Diana's. Horton and Diana were on the veranda of her suite. Diana was looking out over the stern of the boat loaded with Horton's merrymakers. She clenched the railing till her knuckles ached. The reaction of the guests to her new look had nearly overwhelmed her with self-doubt. Coupled with Amber's remark, it finally had over-whelmed her.

Horton was nursing a Cognac. He was still lucid but would not be for long. He was trying to be helpful and encouraging, but these were two emotional skills beyond his reach.

"She's a kid, Diana. She was doing what kids do when they have no frame of reference. The last time she saw you was before the surgery, and when she saw the improvement, she didn't know how to deal with the change. Kids do that. Especially homegrown ones like her. They're ignorant, you know. You can't let it make you feel bad."

Diana nodded her head in agreement, but in her innermost thoughts, she feared there was more truth in Amber's "What happened to your face?" question than in Horton's explanation of it.

"You're probably right. But it isn't the girl I'm worried about. I'm afraid it's a precursor to Cash's reaction. I am actually thinking of ways to avoid seeing him now. Isn't that terrible?" Diana's voice broke.

"Absolutely. Absolutely terrible, Diana. You look terrific. Yes, you have changed, but you changed to be the way you want to be. You have a right to do that. You. That's what this is about."

Diana paced back and forth on the veranda, her arms folded across her new breasts. "All that means nothing if Cash doesn't—" She couldn't finish the sentence.

"Then you should have asked him. If what he thinks is so important. You should have. I thought you were tougher than that. I still do," Horton said.

"I know. Yes, I shouldn't worry about what other people think." As she said it, Diana knew she had had the surgery precisely because she worried about what other people thought, but the idea was too painful to consider.

"And I don't. I don't care what other people think," she said. "Just Cash. That's probably wrong too, huh?" Diana was reaching.

"Diana. You never knew Darlene, my first wife—my only wife. We were kids. No business getting married, but—and kids say awful things to each other—Lord knows we did—and I told her she was as important to me as last night's salad. Because I didn't care what she thought. She was not important." Horton drained his glass of Cognac and walked to the bar to pour himself another. "I'll tell you what's important. Friends. Loyalty. People you can trust. They ask about you. They know who you really are. They call up. They don't say, 'Let's have lunch,' they really have lunch. Everyone else is not. They're not important, and you shouldn't care about them. They never have lunch." Horton was essentially free-associating, drunk, incapable of thinking coherently. Diana would find no solace here, and she knew it. She turned away from him.

"Looks like the party is rolling along." She pointed at the crowd milling about in the rear-deck lounge. "Maybe you should tend to them. I'll be down in a while."

"Right," Horton said as he held his glass up to her. "Here's looking at you, kid. Because you know why? Because you look great. That's why. Just like in the movies. When Humphrey Bogart was looking at Ingmar Bergman, he said that to her. And you look wonderful. Really." He took a gulp and left.

Of all the things he might have said, thought Diana, that was easily the worst. She had a premonition things were not going to go well with Cash. Maybe it was the little singer girl he was obviously so crazy about. Maybe it was his ridiculous new blues-singing career. Maybe it was because she did love him so much and wouldn't be able to stand the rejection. Maybe it was because she couldn't do anything about any of it now. What was done was done.

Whatever it was, from her own dark recesses she had seen it coming, and she had taken the unusual step of reserving Cash his own suite of rooms. Just in case.

* * *

Amber carefully folded her peach satin pants and her knit sweater like the treasures she assumed they must be and put them in the chest of drawers in her room. She shook out her old jeans, slipped them on, and put on her boots and a tight-fitting T-shirt. Buni was not going to get her depressed. She walked down the hall to his room and knocked. There was no answer. Izzy walked along the hall at that moment.

"He's in the staff lounge. You changed your clothes," Izzy said.

"Izzy don't give me any grief, O.K.?" Amber was hair-trigger.

She turned to walk away.

"Grief?"

"O.K. Tell me." Amber turned back, to face him squarely, making him stop.

"Tell you what?" Izzy knew Amber's moods but didn't recognize this one.

"What you thought of the outfit. Go ahead."

"I thought you looked cool. Great. Was there a problem?" Izzy was sincere, and Amber realized he was clueless about the rift between her and Buni, as well as the appropriateness of the clothes.

"Nope. Night, Firegate." Amber dismissed him and walked away to the staff lounge. Izzy shook his head, befuddled, and went on his way.

The staff lounge was empty except for Buni playing foosball by himself and drinking a beer. Amber stood at the door and leaned on the jamb. Buni sensed her presence but pretended he didn't see her.

"How can you do this to me?" she asked after she was sure Buni knew she was there.

"Hey, Amber." Buni continued playing. After a few moments he stopped, looked up, picked up his beer, walked over, and plopped down on a sofa. He stared at her. "Hey, you know what? I'm not mad anymore." Buni caught himself the second he said it. He had revealed too much. "I never was mad, really. It's your thing; you play it how you want to. It's all fine with me."

Amber walked in the room and sat on a countertop. "We're

supposed to take care of each other, aren't we?"

"Take care of each other? I thought you said we're supposed to take care of ourselves, right?" Buni said. He did not want to have this conversation.

"That was about money, about living together. I mean about the music and things like my wardrobe."

"Your wardrobe? Now it's your wardrobe? What are you doing, A? This is, you know, like—maximum PLV."

"Please, Buni," Amber said. "Don't start the PLV thing with me."

"Why not? It's important. I have no other way to describe what this is. And you hit it big-time. You hit it tonight like I never saw anyone hit it. What were you thinking?"

"I wasn't thinking anything. Molly the sales lady said it looked good, and it looked fine to me, and I thought it would be better than this, which is all I have, these jeans. And this is not a club. That is definitely not a club up there. So I dressed up."

"No, it wasn't," Buni said. "It was not a club. That was a Las Vegas showroom if I ever saw one. Whole different thing. So, your wardrobe was fine. Fit perfectly."

"Fine. Make fun of me. But if I'm gonna make money singing, I gotta play these kind of places. And I don't need you raggin' on me for what I'm wearin'. Either help me or don't."

"It's not the clothes, Amber. Satin pants are a symptom. It means you're thinking about something besides the music."

The remark so enraged Amber that she was speechless. She lowered her eyes and then looked back up at Buni and spoke in an urgent whisper.

"I never think about the music, Buni. Never. Music is what I am. I think about the clothes. I think about the money. I think about being alone and having to take care of myself. But I don't ever think about the music. Because it's the only thing I don't have to think about. It's who I am. I'm not gonna wear satin pants onstage again anytime soon, but it's not because I'm afraid I hit my PLV, or some other one of your brainy theories. And for certain it's not because they make me think about something besides the music. I'm not gonna wear them because I don't know whether they look good on me or not. And I just realized you don't, either."

Amber turned and walked out the door, leaving Buni to his beer and solo foosball. After she left, Buni had the ghastly thought it might be the beginning of the end. O.K., he thought. He had his music degree. He could always teach. He could go to Nashville or New York and play on recording sessions. He didn't need Amber. Especially if they couldn't talk to each other. He didn't need her at all. So he desperately wished.

"Mr. Bundt?" Standing at the door was a short, stocky man in his sixties. He was wearing an immaculate and expensive blue pinstripe suit, a pink shirt, and a shiny blue tie. Each cuff sported an enormous gold cuff link, and on his left wrist was a huge gold watch. He was ruddy-faced, blond, smiling, and ebullient. He was Sir Alfred Bates, the chairman and CEO of Bates Media Group, the world's second largest media empire.

"Actually, it's Buni. My friends call me Buni."

"Ah. Freddy Bates, Buni. Pleased to make the acquaintance. I must say, that music tonight was bloody marvelous. Just had to stop by and tell you. First-rate. Brilliant."

"Hey. Well, thanks. Are you in the music—uh, the—" Buni knew he recognized the name but couldn't remember exactly who he was. He didn't want to ask an impertinent question.

"Up to here in the music business. Yes," Bates said. "What with the Internet, I don't know how long that will be, but for now it keeps the lights on. Bates Group. Brussels."

That was it. This guy was a giant in the business. Buni stood up. "Oh yeah. Of course. I'm glad you liked it."

"Well, it's not the best place to perform, is it? Bunch of goofy drunks at a party. But I do have to say, I thought it was superb, given the limitations you were working with."

Buni didn't know what to say. "You want a beer?" is what he did say.

"Love one, actually." Freddy came in the room and looked around. "This is the staff lounge, is it?"

"Um, yeah." Buni went to the vending machine for the beer, then realized he didn't have any money. Now what? He felt in both pockets of his pants. Not a dime. He had spent it all. Freddy saw him fumbling.

"Here, let me get that." Freddy walked to the machine, produced a wad of bills, and fed one of them in. "Do you care for another?"

"Sure. Thanks," Buni said. There were worse things to do than have a beer with Sir Alfred Bates.

Bates pulled two beers from the machine, handed one to Buni, and sat his on the corner of the foosball table. "Care for a game?" he asked.

"Sure." Buni took his position at the side of the table. Bates took off his coat and laid it on the couch.

For the next twenty minutes, the two of them played foosball and never mentioned the music or talked of anything but the game in front of them, except for the occasional spice of Bates commenting with vicious precision on various aspects of Horton's party. All the remarks were clever and essentially harmless. Bates gave little hint of his opinions. He was a decent foosball player and soundly defeated Buni, which delighted Bates and made Buni anxious.

"These are fun, aren't they. I have one at home in the U.K. One of the things that keeps me going back there. Should move it to Brussels, really." Bates sat in a chair next to the couch. "How long have you been playing?"

"Almost all my life. I started in the high school band."

Bates laughed. "Oh, I see. No, I meant foosball. But since you bring it up. I did love the songs you played tonight. American blues. Just can't do better, in my book. And the girl. Amber. Just wonderful. You're the musical director?"

"Yeah. Amber and me, we started working in bars and around. This really was our first kind of sit-down concert."

"Have you recorded any of this?" Bates asked.

"Not really, no. I've got some board mixes, off the sound mixer, but they're not very good." Buni wished he had recorded more. That he had something to play for Bates.

"No matter, really. Guy Stevenson does the music side for us. He's the man you'll need. I just get excited and cheer him on. He's in Brussels as well. I'd very much like him to hear you and this girl. I have a feeling he'd love it."

You and this girl? There it was. No one had combined him with Amber until now. He was usually only referred to as her piano player. Buni did not realize Bates's diplomatic double-speak did not include him at all.

Bates was not the least interested in Buni, but it would have been too jarring for Bates to lunge at Amber without Buni, too uncivilized, not to mention bad business. After all, Buni might be important. He was still checking Buni out.

"I can get something together. I could make a CD and send it to him," Buni said.

"That would be splendid. I wish Guy had been here tonight. I believe you have something special. Is Amber around? I'd love to meet her."

If not having the money for the beer was ten on a ten-scale of bad moves, being in a fight with Amber right now was a million on the same scale. Buni squirmed. Bates noticed.

"Not if it's a problem. We can do it later. Tomorrow, perhaps. We're all sort of stuck in this together, aren't we." Bates stood. "I think I'll turn in. Long day. Thanks for the game."

"O.K. Yeah," Buni said. "That might be better. I think she's gone to bed. I'll walk up with you."

They walked from the staff lounge along the narrow hall past

Amber's room. Amber recognized Buni's footfall but not the one that followed. She wondered who it might be.

* * *

Cash spent most of that same night in his father's bed. He had been working late, on the phone to Switzerland, where his main financial advisor lived; to New York, with one of his money managers; and to Hong Kong, facilitating the transition of one of his Sandra Corporation executives. The time had slipped away. Instead of driving back to the ranch, he fell asleep on the couch and then finally moved to the bed.

Cash had not removed his father's clothes or personal effects. Biggins had come by shortly after the funeral and cleaned out the refrigerator, shut the place down, and secured it, but the apartment was in essence the same as when his father was alive. It felt good to be in his father's place, in his state of mind. Leland had no TV, radio, or newspaper subscription, so there was no connection to anything outside except through the telephone. Of course there was a wireless connection for the motel, but Leland never bothered to use it.

It gave Cash a look at his father in a way he only suspected till now. Leland was aware of the state of things, the state of the world, even local news and sports scores, but he got most of the information by talking to people. Through relationships—instant and casual, or stately and formal, sometimes loving, long-term, and close, or perfunctory, short-term, and distant—information flowed to him with the stamp of the last person he talked to.

Leland took it all in lightly, carefully measuring it against his own good sense, but he was most cautious about media.

Reporters in whatever media were always looking for a narrative track. A pursuit Leland had thought worthless.

Ordinary people rambled, talking about this and that, with no narrative structure, focusing on whatever they thought was important at the time. Leland could parse these meanderings well. They created a vital and real picture for him.

When Cash finally drifted off to sleep he remembered one of Leland's aphorisms.

"Life grows sideways."

Chapter Fifteen

It was late morning as Amber sat at a table for one in the huge Café Montmartre on one of the rear decks of the *Marianna*. When she first came in, many of the guests greeted her warmly. One table gave her a spirited round of applause. Several individual well-wishers shook her hand or patted her back and complimented her performance. Every one of them asked her to join them, but she refused.

Amber was nursing her broken heart. She would not have made good company. The fight with Buni over the clothes and their implications had overwhelmed her.

As far as she was concerned, Buni had let her down. He had withheld from her his counsel, had not provided access to him and his ideas when she needed them most. Without Buni, or someone like him, she couldn't work. She couldn't stand onstage and sing without a band, and she hadn't the least idea about how to assemble a band. Buni did all that.

Last night had changed everything. The whole line of thought made her sad, and it was starting to make her afraid.

In the distance Amber saw a helicopter approach. As it drew closer, she recognized it as Cash's.

Her spirits soared; her mood lifted. She finished her orange juice and dashed out of the café to the landing pad. She did not see Buni and Sir Alfred approaching her table and ran right by them without even noticing, before Buni could say anything.

Diana and Horton were already at the pad. She and Horton stood in the shelter of the stairwell to the pad as the Dauphine eased in for landing. Diana's heart was pounding, and her breath was short. She grabbed Horton's hand and gave it a squeeze. Horton smiled and squeezed back, but he was unaware of Diana's distress.

As the chopper landed and the pilot shut off the engines, Cash popped from the back, holding his overnight case and a large shopping bag.

Diana rushed to greet him, threw her arms around him, and kissed him affectionately on the cheek before he had a chance to look at her close. Within her embrace, Cash set his bags down and gave her a long and proper welcoming hug.

Horton stood behind Diana and held out his hand. Cash shook it while still holding her. When Diana finally pulled back from Cash and let him see her full face, she was in a near panic.

"Hey, Di. How are you, beautiful?" Cash took a long and focused look at the new Diana. There was a mask where her face had been, a stasis where there had been activity. Cash peered, straining to see her.

"Look at you. You've had some work done." Cash smiled warmly and was gentle, supportive. Not a hint of surprise.

"Do you like it? That's why I haven't come in to see you. I wanted everything to be perfect before I saw you."

"I think you look fine, yeah, great, really," Cash said.

"Doesn't she?" Horton said. "She looks great. She was so worried about what you would think."

Amber, breathless, appeared at the stair door. Cash saw her and his eyes brightened, as did his smile. "Hey," he called out. "Look at this. I've got the whole committee."

Diana turned and began to tremble slightly when she saw Amber standing at the door. Amber's hair whipped about her face in the wind; her clothes were rumpled and disheveled. She dashed out onto the landing deck and grabbed Cash as if she were a lost child. Diana stepped back and looked desperately at Horton.

Amber kissed Cash on each cheek. Cash was thrilled to see her, too. "And how is the lovely Miss Fanfare?" He gave her a warm hug. Diana drew close to Horton and held his arm.

"Awful. I gotta talk to you."

"Oh, no," Cash said. "What happened? Come on, let's get out of this wind." Cash led the procession away from the helicopter and down the landing to the elevator foyer.

When they stopped, Amber, seeing only Cash and unmindful of Horton and Diana, blurted out, "Buni and me had a fight. Bad one."

A tear rolled down one of her cheeks, but she made no sound and did not sob.

Diana stepped to Amber and put her arm around her.

"Oh Amber, honey, don't cry. I'm so sorry to hear that."

Diana's arm surprised Amber, and she suddenly saw Diana for the first time. She didn't want comfort from her. Cash put his hand on the small of Amber's back and rubbed it. Amber turned away from Diana to him and laid her head on his chest. Once buried there, she gave a pathetic shudder, a small whimper, and then the tears flowed through short choking sobs. Cash embraced her and stroked her hair. He looked at Diana. He assumed she was genuinely concerned for Amber, but there were no visual clues. The dynamics of Diana's face were hidden, immobile, painted-over, and rearranged. Cash knew a loving, compassionate side of Diana, but he couldn't see it.

"I'm sorry," Amber said. She pulled away from Cash and stood among the three of them. She wiped her nose with her hand and sniffed. Horton produced a handkerchief. "It just got hold of me," she said. "Please. I'm sorry."

"That's all right, Amber. Everybody cries," Diana said.

"I'm OK now, though. But can I talk to you? Sometime? Soon?" she said to Cash.

"Sure. Let me get settled, and we'll have a long talk," Cash said as Horton rang for the elevator.

Amber backed away, embarrassed now. "I'll be around the ship. I'm down on deck three, in 314. So you can find me whenever. Sorry, everyone. I'm gonna, uh, I'm gonna get some air."

Amber darted back up the stairs to the landing pad.

Cash, Diana, and Horton watched her go. Then the elevator door opened, and they stepped in.

"That was intense," Horton said. "What's the matter with her?"

"Buni is all she's got right now. A fight with him is a major concern for her," Cash said.

"Well, she's got you, too," Diana said. Cash looked for the intent of the remark, but saw only a mask, drawn tight and tucked in at the corners. It might have been a territorial remark of jealousy, or it might have been a tender remark of concern. Cash had no idea. He had lost touch with Diana. All he saw was a slight look from Horton to her that made him fear the worst.

As they walked along the hallway of Diana's deck, Diana pointed to the shopping bag. "Been shopping?" she asked Cash. Cash held up the bag. It was impossible to see what was inside.

"These are for Amber, actually. Didn't seem like the time to give them to her."

Diana continued walking past her own suite to the room she had reserved for Cash.

"Why don't you put your things in here for now," she said as she opened the door. It was a lavish space, almost the size of Diana's. It was the most expensive and elaborate of the rooms available to patrons, but it was not her suite, as Cash knew. It was portentous.

Cash said nothing, gave no clue to his thinking. He would not, not with Horton hovering as he was. Cash laid the bags down in the front room.

"I've got lunch set up in the dining room," Diana said, and led the way to her suite.

Amber stood in the hot sun on the landing pad until she was sure all had gone and then walked down the access stairs to the elevator. Inside the elevator, she saw she was one floor away from Mr. Todd, and on impulse, she pressed the button for the floor.

When she stepped out into the foyer on Mr. Todd's floor, she could see the place was buzzing. All the stations were full, and people were waiting. Mr. Todd was busy doing color on a portly woman in her fifties. Amber stopped at the door and looked in. Mr. Todd saw her.

"Amber Fanfare!" He almost screamed. Everyone in the shop turned to look; many of them recognized her from the show. "Come in. How did the show go last night? I'm sorry I couldn't make it, but after you left we got so busy, and by the end of the day, I wasn't fit for man or beast."

Amber stepped in the door. A woman in the station next to Mr. Todd spoke. "I can tell you. She was wonderful. We enjoyed your singing so much."

Amber smiled weakly. She had come to confront Mr. Todd about his broken promise of attendance. She hadn't counted on getting taken over by approvals.

The woman continued. "We were talking after the show. My husband said he wished you would sing more kinds of songs. I like what you were singing, but your voice is so good, you could sing other things just as well. Have you ever thought of singing standards, or some jazz ballads?"

"Thank you," Amber said. "Sometimes I think about it, but we don't know any. I just stopped to say hello. I gotta run."

"O.K., doll." Mr. Todd waved a paintbrush full of hair dye at her. "I'll get down there tonight. Take care, hon."

Amber held up her hand as she backed out the door. Almost the entire salon called farewell. She was still unsatisfied, still uncomforted, and now dazed.

She took the elevator to the shopping promenade and went to the shop where Molly worked. Molly wasn't there—another disappointment—so Amber strolled along, looking at the shop windows. She was trying not to think about Buni, not to think about Cash, in fact, not to think about anything, when, at the far end of the promenade, she saw Buni hailing her. She did not wave back or acknowledge him. Buni picked up speed and walked quickly toward her. She noticed Buni was wearing a blazer.

"You cold?" she said.

"Take it easy, A. I just had lunch with Sir Alfred Bates and his friend—a guy named Michael—and some other people."

"Good for you." Amber looked in a store window. Buni pointed to the sidewalk café.

"C'mon Amber. Let's get some coffee." He pulled her to a table and they sat down.

"Do you know who Bates is?" Buni asked.

"No."

"Bates of Bates Media Group. This guy is one of the biggest

record guys in the world. I mean he owns one of the biggest record companies." Buni waited for the remark to register.

"And?"

"And he loves you, is 'and,'" Buni said.

Despite herself, Amber broke into a huge grin. She made a useless attempt to suppress it for a millisecond but then beamed, unabashed.

"Really? What did he say?" she asked.

"He said he thought you were 'bloody marvelous,'" Buni tried to do an English accent. "He came to the lounge last night, like, seconds after you left. See? Gotta stick with the Bunster, A."

Amber's smile faded slowly, unnoticeably. Did he just say "Gotta stick with the Bunster?" Was that his notion of last night and all it meant? From the top deck of the boat till now, Amber was falling deeper into heartbreak. Amber wasn't going to fight with Buni anymore. She subtly shifted into her business mode with him. She didn't trust him.

"So what happens now?" she asked.

"He wants to meet you. I was with him this morning and we were coming over to your table when you ran out. What was that about? You acted like you didn't see me."

"Cash came in. I saw the chopper, and so I went to meet him. I didn't see you."

Amber knew Buni would not re-raise the issues before them from last night, though she was hoping. If he would just talk about things with her, it would mean so much. But she knew he would deny this access, the same as he had last night.

"This is something that can take us to the next step, Amber. Freddy says he loves the blues and thinks we can make a great record. He's up by the pool right now. Come on with me and say hello. You'll like him. He's fun."

"Freddy is Bates?"

"Right. But he says call him Freddy." Buni stood up from the table. Amber stayed seated. Buni looked at her and then slowly sat back down.

She said nothing, waiting. Buni said nothing. He was waiting, too, but not for Amber to speak. She was still mad. She would cool off. He could wait. It always worked before.

A waitress came to the table, and Buni ordered a latte. Amber ordered nothing. She would not sit silent forever. This was not a game of will. She wanted to make sure her analysis of Buni was correct. That was all. If he said nothing about last night, about her wardrobe, then his silence would tell her all she needed to know about him, about them. Then she would leave.

It may have been a good way to test the relationship with Buni, and it might have told Amber what she needed to know, but she lost her focus when Cash appeared, walking up the promenade. Amber saw him from a distance, approaching behind Buni. She had the same rush of emotion she always had when she saw him. She thought of it as a special type of joy, but even the most casual observer could see that it was love. She stood up, and Cash saw her and smiled.

Buni turned to see.

"Hey, it's Mr. Goodweird," he said.

"Hi, Buni. Hi, Amber." Cash sat down at the table with them. He handed Amber the shopping bag. He looked at Buni knowingly, then back to Amber.

"This for me?" Amber took the bag and looked in.

"Yep," Cash said.

"What is it?" She said as she pulled out tissue-wrapped clothes. Folded inside were two pair of new black jeans, two tight black women's T-shirts, and a box with a new pair of black boots. All in her size. Amber was amazed. She looked at Cash and then back at the clothes. She checked the bag once more. At the bottom was a small box. She opened it. It was a beautiful beaded belt with a small and delicate solid silver buckle.

"I hope they fit," Cash said. "Buni called last night and gave me the sizes, so I had to go to three different stores this morning before I found the right things." Cash picked up one of the T-shirts and held it up to her. "The belt's from me."

Amber was staggered by the complexity of the emotion she felt. Was this Buni's penance? What was he saying? But Buni had only the smallest part of her attention. The largest part was taken over in contemplation of Cash Carruthers's clothes shopping for her at Buni's request. An act so selfless, so generous, and so kind was almost inconceivable to her. Only her mother had come close.

Buni smiled bravely. "You asked me what I thought you should wear. So."

Amber stood up. She was not going to cry again. Even for joy. She was not. She took the bag of clothes, wrapped both arms around it, and held it to her chest. No, she would not say anything. Because then she would cry. And she wasn't going to cry. No way. She stepped to Cash and kissed him on the forehead, then to Buni, whom she kissed lightly on the top of his head, and then she walked away, down the promenade. She clutched the bag of clothes as if it were her child.

The two men watched her walk away.

"Have any idea what that meant?" Buni asked Cash.

"She was trying not to cry," he said.

"Good cry or bad cry?"

"Good cry, I think," Cash said as Amber disappeared into the elevator foyer. They watched as long as they could. Then the two looked at each other, and Buni shook his head in confusion. "Just leave it for a bit. Go see her later," Cash said. Buni nodded.

"So you saw Diana? You want some coffee?" Buni held up his hand for the waitress.

"Not for me. Yes, I did. Saw her when I got off the chopper. She was waiting with Horton."

"What did you think?" Buni was curious. He had described Diana's surgery in detail to Cash when he had called him the night before.

"You had me scared. It wasn't anything like you said. I thought I was going to see the Phantom of the Opera or some horror movie. I thought she looked fine," Cash said.

"Really?" Buni didn't believe him.

"Really. The only disconcerting thing was not being able to see behind her eyes. See the light, I mean. But I don't think that has anything to do with the surgery. It's spiritual. Hard for me to get the meaning of Diana these days."

"Cash, ole buddy. It has everything to do with the surgery. I've seen a facelift take out the best women. Women don't realize how pretty they are when they get old. They all say, 'Oh, after you're this old, nobody wants you,' and it just freaks 'em out. They start carvin' away on themselves, next thing you know—nobody's home. It may not be the facelift per se that shuts out the light, but whatever makes 'em get the facelift. They slam into their PLV. And there you are." Buni took a sip of the coffee.

"O.K.," Cash said. "You said you'd tell me about this Personal Las Vegas thing. So tell me."

"It's not science, you know, it's—it's aesthetics, I guess. But here's the theory. When Elvis was young, in Tupelo, Mississippi, he's making good moves. Goin' to the heart of things. Finding great songs. 'Heartbreak Hotel.' Like that. Then time passes and his career tanks—with the Beatles and the Stones and all—so he decides he's gotta make another move. Next thing you know Elvis is playin' Vegas, singing 'Battle Hymn of the Republic'—and that's not all. He's wearing these rhinestone capes and high collars, eating weird, and getting fatter and fatter, and just, you know, whoa. Well, Elvis is not alone in this. He's only the model for it. Because from where I sit, everybody in America goes through it. I mean, I've only seen it in America—I don't think, like, Polynesians hit their PLV—or maybe, but not in the same way. But it's like Americans come with this gene that wakes up, and you start doing these weird 'Elvis in Vegas' things at some, like, crisis point. Gettin' old is a crisis point for a lot of people. And you go and do, like, rhinestones and facelifts, and just go zonkers. It's the America Gene, and it sends you off to your own Personal Las Vegas."

Cash started laughing.

"It's true, man. People hit some major moment—like 'Oh no, I'm losin' it'—and they get strange. See, and the thing is, it's invisible. You know, they stand in front of the mirror, and they see this whatever, like a, a nose ring or something, or whatever they think is O.K., pants they wore in high school, but they're, like, fifty now, and they don't see them for what they are—the pants. It's like, 'Yeah, this hair style still looks good on me' or 'This dress is cool, shows off my butt,' and they don't see it. That's the mean part of it. It's invisible. You're still laughing, dude."

Cash was. "Well, it's funny. It's a great notion. And you're right—you're right on some level. Like you say, it's not science, but I've seen people hit their PLV, now that you mention it. I didn't know what it was till you just explained it."

"Like Diana," Buni said. "That's a PLV if I ever saw it. She's following the Elvis arc perfectly."

Cash's laughing subsided. "Mmm. Perhaps. But I think there's more to it now with Diana."

"You know, Cash, I'd like to agree with you, but I don't. If somebody'd jumped on Diana before she got her lift and said this is just a PLV, you know, calm down, she would have avoided the whole thing. Guaranteed."

"That's not the point, though. The point is nobody did say anything, and now she's done the surgery. She can't back out. Diana's looking for something, and I may not be able to give it to her, but at least I'm not going to keep it from her. I think telling her she hit her PLV would do that. However true it might be. It'd be too tough. Even cruel, in a way."

Buni thought of the conversation he had had with Amber. He suddenly felt terrible remorse.

"So, I have a question," Cash said. "You call it the America Gene, which is a great name, by the way, but if it's a gene, then when it wakes up, doesn't everybody act the same way? A gene is a replicator, isn't it?" Cash waited, but Buni didn't want to pursue the riff now. He was thinking about Amber. Then suddenly he was thinking about Cash and Amber.

"Yeah, well, the metaphor doesn't map exactly. But I think it gets the point across. A PLV is personal. A Personal Las Vegas. Everyone comes on to it differently. So it's different for each person. Very individual." Buni paused and thought for a moment. Should he say what he was about to say? He decided yes. "Like, I think this singing thing you're doing is your PLV. Your relationship with Amber, too, definitely has some PLV in it. I'm no expert on this, Cash. It's just a riff, anyway. I mean, it's true, riffs are true things, and I know a PLV exists, but it's just something to know, another knot in the great tangle of motivations. But it's not something to campaign about. I don't want to mess around with other people's lives. And, for certain, I don't want to be cruel."

Buni's words seeped into Cash. They had a much greater effect than he intended. Cash straightened in his chair.

"But I would want to do something about it if I still can. If I'm—if this is my own PLV—I don't want to start doing things and acting strange if someone can—"

"O.K. Wait." Buni held up his hand. "Yeah. You may be on the outskirts of Vegas here, but all you gotta do is be aware this thing is out there. That's all. It's like a nervous tic. Once you know you got it, you can stop it. Sometimes it helps for a friend to tell you that. Sometimes it doesn't—like you say."

Buni had lost his enthusiasm for the conversation and his exegesis. He was in anguish about scolding Amber, telling her she had hit her PLV when all she wanted was—Buni froze. He stood up and stared down the promenade.

Cash spun around to see what had startled him so. "What just happened? You went white."

"I think I just saw Charles Freeman. That was him. I thought he was dead. He walked right past there toward the elevator. I'm sure."

"I don't know who that is, Buni," Cash said.

"Charles Freeman was the bass player for Tyrone Edwards." Buni stood up and walked quickly away from Cash. His chin was up and he was straining to see over the crowd, to see into the past.

Chapter Sixteen

Cash sat alone at the table in the ersatz sidewalk café and watched as Buni dashed into the crowd that wandered the promenade. The past six months, from the first time he decided to sing in public until now, had just come into a new perspective. Even Horton and Diana took on a new dimension. Cash realized Buni was not wrong about the America Gene and was not wrong about Cash's hitting his PLV. In fact, Buni was almost entirely right. It was a startling thought. It was a funny idea, delivered in musician-speak, but it had an unmistakable ring of truth to it. Cash looked around him and drew the whole boat into this new viewpoint. It was its own Las Vegas.

After a moment he got up and strolled to the terrace on the far rear deck, where he had promised to meet Diana.

She was wearing tight shorts and a tight halter top, the same type Ann Margret had made famous in the sixties. She was stretched out on a deck lounge chair. She waved at Cash. It was a good thing she did, because Cash did not recognize her, nor would he have been naturally drawn to her. He came over and sat down in the deck chair next to her. The sun felt good.

"How did it go?" Diana asked.

"Pretty well, I think. Mended a fence."

"You really like those two. I don't think I've ever known anyone except Leland who had that much access to you." Diana was exploring and hoping Cash wouldn't notice. He did, but he didn't react to it, letting it pass.

"I do," Cash said. "They're easy. Nice change from the business types. Buni's a hoot. Very wise in his own way. Amber is a one-off. I appreciate Buni calling me in to help out. Altogether different experience from Sandra Corporation"

"You miss Sandra?" Now Diana was sincere, and Cash knew this as well.

"I did. But no more. It was the right thing to do. Without Horton, it wasn't the same."

"He said you two have had some disagreements over the last few weeks."

"Selling Sandra was hard," Cash said. "We both lost a lot of money, and Horton's going through some changes; I can see that now."

"Do you like the ear stud?"

Cash chuckled. Horton's ear stud had a whole new meaning to Cash. He knew that he couldn't explain this to Diana. Buni was right. She was well down her own road. "I don't pay too much attention. More important, does Horton like it, and he seems to."

"He asked me to bring you down to the theater when I saw you. He's got a surprise for you."

Cash looked at Diana. Once there would have been a knowing smile they would share that let him into her thoughts. The smile wasn't there, or if it was, he couldn't see it. It was covered with the full lips and the skin tightly drawn against the side of her eyes. He didn't know what Diana thought of Horton's surprise.

"He does? Great, let's go. I'm ready if you are," he said.

Diana looked for a familiar response from Cash but saw nothing. It was as if he was hiding from her, she thought, afraid to look at her the way he did before. The doctors and her friends told her this would happen. She tried not to make too much of it. The surgery had opened some doors for her, but it had closed the one she cared about the most. She hated losing the contact with Cash.

In the theater, Horton was sitting in the front row. He stood when Diana and Cash came in the door at the top of the aisle.

"What are you up to, Callaway?" Cash called out good-naturedly.

"I brought you a present," he said. "Should be here any minute." Horton's keen mind appreciated humor and wit, but he was uncomfortable with playful collegial banter. He didn't like Cash calling him by his last name. He thought about saying something, but it would ruin the moment.

As Cash and Diana reached the stage, the side door opened, and in walked an elderly black man, a bit stooped, taking careful short steps, not hobbling, but far from spry. Behind him were two other black men, both in their seventies, and behind them were Buni and Amber. Horton looked at Diana, surprised.

"Did you ask those kids to come?" Horton whispered to Diana as he gestured to Buni and Amber. Diana shook her head. "Jesus. Can't get rid of 'em." Horton said, loud enough for only Diana to hear.

Cash was puzzled. What was going on?

The oldest of the three men made it to a folding chair at center stage and slowly lowered himself into it. He was wearing new khaki pants, new trainers, and a red plaid western shirt. In the light, Cash could see the man must have been in his eighties. He also looked drunk. The man produced a flimsy smile—one of his eyelids closed and opened by itself as he scratched the palm of his hand—and looked at Cash, Diana, and Horton.

Horton stepped forward. Buni, Amber, and the two other men held back to the side of the stage.

"Cash Carruthers," Horton swung his hand in a graceful presentation flourish. "Meet Tyrone Edwards."

Cash's mouth opened. He looked at Diana but saw only a kabuki mask. Then he looked at Buni. Buni nodded affirmatively at Cash and then looked toward Edwards.

"Pleased to meet you, Mr. Carruthers. This gentleman here says you plays the blues a little." Edwards was slow of speech, cautious with his words, and was not looking at Cash. "Those gentlemen there is Mr. Charles Freeman and Mr. Roland White." The two men shuffled forward and held up their hand in greeting.

"Now you'll get to see what it's like to play with a real blues band," Horton said, insensitive to the insensitivity of the remark. Buni looked at the ceiling, held his arms, and shook his head ever so slightly.

Cash was amazed, caught in the most awkward of moments.

Horton was beaming, expectant. Cash was motionless until his sense of decorum overtook his sense of confusion. He walked on stage and approached Edwards.

"Mr. Edwards, I'm Cash Carruthers. It's a real honor, sir." Cash extended his hand. Edwards didn't see it and pointed instead to his colleagues. Another clumsy moment. Amber and Buni took a few short steps and stood on the stage with everyone.

"Them there is my bass player and drummer." Edwards looked to Freeman and White and then back to Cash. He was intoxicated, hardly coherent. "Mr. Callaway says you plays the blues some. That you'd like to play along." Edwards closed both eyes as he spoke, reciting the gambit.

Horton had, with little effort, found Edwards and his cohorts living in Paris. Edwards had moved there in 1967, a step away from a statutory rape charge that was consequently never filed, and was welcomed into the Parisian music scene like royalty, but the treatment quickly faded as Edwards's heroin use began causing no-shows and poor playing.

Edwards was also an inveterate swindler. On several occasions, he had made exclusive recording deals with three and four companies at once. Over the years, he had less and less success in the music business, and he was finally reduced to living from job to job around a second-rate club scene.

Work had been even scarcer the last year as the European Union opened free trade between the countries and a new infrastructure of live music emerged. It was all DJ mixes and dance clubs, so an eighty-six–year-old junkie blues player from the Mississippi Delta had nowhere to work.

When Horton found him, he was living in a rundown part of Paris, and he was hardly mobile. Horton had it in his mind that Cash would be excited and surprised to meet and play with Tyrone Edwards. After all, Buni Rumble was unequivocal about Edwards's status as the greatest blues player of all time.

As Edwards began to understand Horton's cost-no-object quest, he took the opportunity to affect a calculated intransigence, and with feigned reluctance quoted Horton a price of a hundred thousand dollars to come play. To Edwards astonishment, and even though Horton misinterpreted the price as a hundred thousand dollars per man, he agreed. As he told Diana later, "I paid more than that for my car." Horton liked the astronomical price of the gift. It was an indication to him of value.

All of which culminated here in the meeting with Cash, the unfortunate side effect being that Edwards was so out of it, he had little idea where he was.

Conveniently, Freeman and White were not in the same condition. Freeman, wearing a new brown three-piece suit, and White, in designer slacks, shirt, and new leather jacket, were both lucid and willing to talk.

"I see you have some instruments here we might play. Would

you like to play here?" Edwards never had it clear in his mind what he was supposed to do. Horton had talked about playing with Cash, and Edwards assumed this was the time. Freeman and White went to their respective bass and drum stations and began the preliminaries to playing.

Cash turned to Horton. Horton was smiling his broadest. Diana seemed less satisfied, but it was hard to know. "Horton, I don't know what to say." Cash said. This was the only thing that came to his mind, so he made the decision to say it, but it was far from communicating what he was feeling. Horton took it to mean that Cash was wild with delight and speechless because of it.

"You don't have to say a thing. You want to sing the blues in a blues band, Tyrone is the best in the world. That's where you belong, Cash. With the best. It's my pleasure. And I think everybody on the boat is going to be astounded when they see how good you are. I was. So I'll let you enjoy Mr. Edwards and friends here, let you rehearse for the show tonight. Don't forget the investors meeting at six, for cocktails in Diana's suite. We'll leave you alone. Enjoy, my friend." Horton took Diana's hand and motioned her to come with him. They walked up the aisle and out of the theater.

Edwards had picked up Firegate's guitar, turned it on, and was lightly strumming and tuning. It was clear he was going to play now, regardless of what anyone else thought. Buni ambled down to stage front and stood next to Cash. He said nothing. Amber was walking in small circles with her hands shoved into the hip pockets of her jeans and staring at her boots.

Then, because he thought he was expected to, Tyrone Edwards began to play, and Freeman and White fell in behind. Amber stopped walking and looked at Buni and then back to Edwards. The hair stood on Buni's arm.

Whatever magic Edwards had put forth on the recordings he had made over the years, it was nothing compared to what came from him now, live in front of Amber, Buni, and Cash.

He sang one of his most well-known songs, "Jericho's Farm." The sound system was not on, so his voice was unamplified, but it filled the stage. It was a high tenor voice, and with every word, it became more apparent why this was the music that changed the world.

As the players started the second verse, Amber walked over and sat at the feet of Edwards, who was still sitting in his folding chair. She stared up at him in wonder. This was the sound of all life; this was the singer of all songs.

No one was going to stop him or say, "We need to wait" or "You don't have to play now." Buni, Amber, and Cash were caught, held in the music that lifted the dying broken spirit, that gave reason to their life. Tyrone Edwards, singing without a microphone and torn apart on drugs, still controlled everything within the sound of his voice, the voice of the blues.

Then suddenly he stopped. He opened one eye, then the other, and peered at them. "I thought you all was gonna play." Amber turned to Buni. Buni sheepishly walked to the piano and sat. Tyrone still did not understand Cash's presence. He started the song again. This time Cash sat on the edge of the stage and watched.

Buni and Amber remained still. This was music very far above them, music they aspired to. Neither knew if this was music they could perform. At a certain point, Buni played a few rhythm notes with his left hand. Freeman looked at Buni and nodded approval, encouraging. Edwards looked, as well, and said, "Yeah, man." When he came to the chorus of the song, Amber joined in. Still sitting at his feet, she sang very lightly. Edwards eyes popped open and he looked at her, startled. "Hey, little girl. That's right." It was as far as Buni and Amber would venture. Just to be next to this awe-inspiring sound was enough. They were both afraid they would break the spell.

Edwards finished the song. Roland stood up from the drums and stretched. Freeman walked forward and spoke to Tyrone as if he was a child. "I think these people have a show they want us to do, Tyrone." Freeman was the only one with enough influence over Edwards to correct him. "I think that gentlemen there is who we're supposed to play with, but at a show." Freeman looked at Cash. "That right? We gonna do a show later tonight?"

The idea of singing with Tyrone Edwards was at once elating and terrifying to Cash. This was an opportunity that would never have ordinarily come to him, and he was sure it would never come again. To stand on stage and play with Tyrone, perhaps sing a song with Tyrone Edwards and his band backing him up, was a fantastic possibility, a chance to-when suddenly Amber jumped up and stood between Cash and Freeman. She spoke to Freeman, but she stared at Cash, controlled him, like jerking someone out of the path of a speeding car. "For sure your band will do a few numbers tonight, Mr. Edwards. You can rehearse if you want," she said.

Edwards spat, "We don't need no rehearsal. We's here for you, I thought."

"Right." Buni dove in. "Not rehearse the songs—she meant a sound check. I'll get the mixer." Buni ran from the stage. Freeman and White understood. Edwards did not. To the salvation of the moment, he also didn't care.

Amber grabbed Cash's hand, jumped from the stage, and dragged him up the aisle out of the theater, into the lobby. The ship was active with people.

"We gotta talk."

Moments later, the two of them walked into the room Diana had set aside for Cash. It was large, with a king-size bed, a big living area, and an expansive terrace to one side.

Amber spun around to Cash after they walked in.

"You can't do this, Cash."

Cash intuitively knew she was probably right but did not intuitively know why. "Do you mean I'm incapable, or that I'm not allowed?" he asked.

Amber paced a few steps and then plopped on one end of the couch. Cash sat down on the other.

"Both," she said. "But mostly because you—it—because it's not you, not part of you."

Cash did not accept limitations. His life was a testament to thinking beyond limits. He trusted Amber, but he would not let this go that easily.

"And I won't let you," she said. "I just won't."

"O.K.," Cash said. "I'm listening."

"You gotta know, Cash, you're not ever gonna sing the blues. Not for real. Tell me you know that." She looked at him. She was at her most beautiful, under the full control of the ideas that were expressing her.

It was a body blow for Cash. He blinked. It was as if all this time he had been training with a world-champion boxer who had been teaching this move, that dodge, encouraging but barely tapping him. Suddenly she had let loose with a grand-prize left hook to the jaw. She wasn't kidding, and she was right. He knew it.

"Well, Amber—" he stuttered.

"You have to know it, Cash. Think about it. You're this white guy with billions of dollars, and you think different."

"White guy? Your whole band's white. Is this a race thing? A genetics thing?"

"No, it's a spiritual thing. You and me do not have the—this music comes from a heartbreak we never had. Yes, some people who weren't there can understand it, if its handed down to them. I'm not a blues singer, Cash. I'm a singer. If I tried to sing the blues, I couldn't. I sing. Sometimes I sing blues songs. Tyrone Edwards is a blues singer. He's the real deal. And you can't get up onstage with him and sing along. It's too awful to think about. And it's not race. Tyrone Edwards is a blues singer, and he happens to be black."

"Amber, I've been looking to you. And you once said I could do this. What changed? Why now?"

"I meant you maybe could sing along, like I do. That's all. And you do that O.K., not great, just O.K. This whole thing, bringing Edwards over, and he's this present, or something— the whole thing sucks. I don't know what that Horton guy is thinking, but it's not about music. And if you get up there to-night, and you sing along with Tyrone Edwards, it's going to be so bad, so bad, and nobody will tell you either. I'm telling you because I love you."

Amber stopped. There. She had said it. She hadn't meant to, but there it was. What now? It was true, and Amber knew to stay with the truth.

"I love you, O.K. I have since I saw you. We're alike, or some-thing. So I can't let you get up there tonight and sing with Tyrone Edwards, that would—I don't know, it would be—just disre-spectful, is all. It's disrespect. To me. To Tyrone. And mostly to yourself. And I'm not gonna stand by and let you do it." Amber was on the edge of tears now, tears of effort, of frustration.

Cash opened his arms to her, and she slid across the couch to him. They embraced side by side.

There was a slight knock at the door, it opened, and Diana walked in. She was shocked to see them, and even though Am-ber and Cash quickly broke apart, the residual intimacy was still in the air.

"Oh. Excuse me. I—"

"No. Come in, Di. Amber and I were just talking."

Amber stood up and went into the bathroom.

"I see that," Diana said. Again there was no visual clue to the subtleties of the remark, but this time Cash felt the edge in her voice and knew she was upset and jealous. "I wanted to let you know we're going to have the cocktails in the lounge instead of my room. Vittorio wants to do a little update, and there really isn't enough space there. And there are people here who want to see you and say hello, so, all in all, Horton thought it would be best to open it up a little and have kind of a Cash-reception-cum-investors meeting." Diana raced through the words. She wanted to get out of the room. "Same time, but at the upper lounge. I'll leave you two alone." Cash stood to say something, but Diana whirled out the door without another word.

When Amber returned, Diana was gone.

"That was fast," she said.

Cash was still standing. He shook his head.

"Uh-oh. Bad?" Amber stood close to him.

"Yeah. I'm afraid so." Cash looked at her. "I should go talk to her. But, so you know, I never dreamed I would be onstage with Tyrone Edwards. It was never a goal of mine. I do know what you're saying, although I have to say it was not a distinction I made—singing along with the blues, as opposed to singing the blues. I know you're right about this. I know. I know I can't sing the blues."

It was a difficult thing for Cash to admit, but as he said, he knew she was right, and he did understand the distinction she was making. If that was all he got out of his time with the blues, that was enough. More than enough. An abundance.

"I really should go to her, Amber. I think she's very unhappy,"

Cash said as he opened the door.

When they were in the hall, Cash said, "What are we going to do with Tyrone Edwards, though, if we don't sing with him?"

"I think we let him sing a few numbers by himself. You heard him. He's amazing. Still."

"Wonder what Horton will think of that," Cash mused.

"Don't ask me," Amber said as she walked away.

Cash tapped on Diana's door, but there was no answer. He decided to methodically work his way down from the uppermost deck of the ship until he found her, but when he encountered the first of the partygoers, he found himself surrounded by old friends and acquaintances looking for the chance at small talk, about Leland, or Sandra Corporation, or any one of several things that pass for conversation at a party. Cash didn't get far, and the 6:00 meeting was on him before he had examined two decks.

Cash's attendance at the reception and investors' meeting was important to Horton. Cash's interest alone would have triggered several million dollars in investment funds, and if Cash actually put money in, the offering was a guaranteed sellout.

Falluci did a small presentation on the technology of the hydrofoam, and Horton talked about the larger vision of building a new world. Cash was not only distracted by the problem with Diana, he was also not interested in the enterprise, and as the presentation moved along, his disinterest appeared as skepticism. Cash asked no questions and gave noncommittal responses when questions were asked of him about what he thought of the project, how it would work, and what it would mean, leaving the potential investors in a quandary.

Cash stood next to Diana, but she was distant and cold. At a lull in the proceedings, Cash asked if he could have a few minutes with her alone, but she responded that there was no reason to. She trusted him, and if Amber and he were only talking, than that was good enough for her. The response could not have been more disingenuous, and Cash knew it.

As the investor meeting went on, Horton became more visibly distraught and more drunk. By the end, when all adjourned for dinner, Horton feared he may have lost some of the early investors he did have.

Cash insisted Diana and he sit at a table for two in a corner where they could talk. Not only was the evening coming to a head regarding the tensions between the two of them, Cash was going to have to tell Horton he wasn't going to play with Edwards. He understood what Amber said, and more importantly, what she meant. Diana chose a table that wasn't as removed as he would have liked.

Friends passed by and felt compelled to stop and say hello. It was a repetition of the trap he had been caught in on the upper decks, but after the meal started, the traffic died down.

"Diana, I'd like to talk a little about Amber."

"O.K," she said distantly. "Let's talk about Amber."

"I feel like you have an incomplete picture of her, and especially her relationship with me."

"I know what a young woman looks like when she makes

herself available," Diana almost barked. "I don't have an incomplete picture of that. And if you are starting this conversation to tell me Amber isn't doing that, then you're delusional, or looking at half a picture."

"Diana, Amber and I have no involvement with each other," Cash said. He was talking about sex.

"That may or may not be. I will never know other than what you say to me, but as far as I can see with my own eyes, you are very involved with her."

A frail woman about Diana's age approached the table. She was sporting the same facelift, or so it appeared to Cash. Diana didn't recognize her.

"Diana. It's Kitty. I just—"

"Kitty! Oh my gosh," Diana said with a flash of recognition. "I haven't seen you in a year and a half. This is Cash."

"Yes. I know. Hello," Kitty said pleasantly. "I won't bother you, but I had to tell you I think the work looks wonderful. You're just stunning. Did you do this in Houston?"

"Oh, thank you so much. Here. Yes." Diana was pleased.

"Just lovely, dear. Cash, my pleasure." Kitty walked away.

Cash knew he would not reach Diana now, or ever. Something had grown up around her that he knew nothing about. He understood a chapter had closed. As was his way, Cash would say little to offend, trusting instead the logic of circumstance to unwind the tangled emotions he had shared with this woman for so long, but he was sure it was over.

"You know, Cash," Diana said. "You've really changed."

In the context of the moment, Cash thought the comment astonishing. Before he could say anything, Horton came to the table and, uninvited, pulled up a chair. He reeked of Cognac and cigars.

"Have I done something to you, Cash?" Horton was drunk and aggressive.

"Please, Horton." Cash tried to deflect the attack.

"What was that display in the investors' meeting? I won't be surprised if some people back out. You could have at least been less dour, don't you think?"

"Horton, I had other things on my mind. I'm sorry."

"Sorry won't help me now, unless you're prepared to come in for some significant piece of the offering."

The remark was a big mistake. Cash was immune to guilt manipulations. Horton should have known this, of all people.

"Horton. I think the Mariner is a bad idea, and I'm not going to take any of the offering. It has little purpose, or use, and no way to add value. That's my real feeling. I want you and Diana to succeed, Horton, but I don't think this is it."

This was the last thing Horton had expected. He felt his anger rise, and with all his effort barely kept from going into a rage.

"I better excuse myself." Cash stood up, tossed his napkin into his plate, and walked away.

Horton and Diana exchanged looks. They were both angry. Cash's investment had been a foregone conclusion. Without him, the whole project might not work. Neither of them had spoken to this point before now, but both of them knew it as a matter of fact.

"He's really changed," Horton said as Cash left the dining room. Diana and Horton watched him the whole way, and then Diana spoke.

"What now?" she asked.

"I have enough investor interest to get us through the first part of the project. Not all the way, but most. We could build the island, the control pod, a nice casino and some shops—no condos. Not yet. But that might get us going. Stimulate the curiosity," Horton said.

A curiosity? Diana's heart sank.

* * *

"What did he say?" Buni asked. Buni and Amber were backstage, waiting to tell the band about Tyrone Edwards.

"He said he knew he shouldn't get on stage with Tyrone, and that he wouldn't. He acted like he wanted to, but he said he knew it wouldn't work," Amber said.

"Can you imagine?" Buni said.

Firegate, Blunder, and Kelly Day, the new drummer, popped through the stage door in succession. They were surprised to see Amber.

"Whoa. Yo," Firegate said to Amber.

"Yo. S'up," Amber responded.

"Band meeting?" Marion Blunder asked.

"A little one," Buni said. "Wanted to give you guys a heads-up. Tyrone Edwards and his players are on the boat and are going to play tonight."

"Instead of us?" Day asked.

"He's here?" Firegate said, impressed.

"No, we still play, and yes, he's here. I thought he'd come on sort of in the middle of the set. But they want to play our gear. That cool?"

They all nodded in agreement.

Cash opened the stage door. He saw the meeting in progress. "Am I interrupting?" He stopped before he came in.

"Come in. Just talking about Edwards," Buni said.

Cash came in.

"That it? Only wants to use the gear?" Firegate asked. "We gonna play with them or anything?"

Buni shook his head. "No. That's it for now." The band members went their way to turn on the equipment and tune up.

Amber sidled up to Cash. "Everything O.K.? She pissed?"

"Everything's not O.K., I'm sorry to say. I'm lost with those two." It was the most agitated Amber had ever seen Cash.

"This sounds bad," Amber said.

"I won't bore you with it. It's not your fault, if you're thinking that," Cash said.

"My fault? Never crossed my mind." Amber smiled big at him.

Cash nodded. "I see." He smiled back.

"Go get changed, little one," Buni said to Amber. "Those new jeans cost $50,000, you know. Apiece. Special made by—" He turned to Cash to finish the joke. Cash shrugged. "Some special maker," Buni said.

Amber made a funny face, flipped him the bird, waved, and walked off the stage.

"So how do we do this? Amber says you're not gonna play with Edwards. You gonna play with us?" Buni was one on one with Cash.

"Well. Wait. Let's talk about Edwards a little more. I—I think Amber's right. I probably shouldn't play with him, but, but—and 'grateful for Horton's present' doesn't really count as motivation," Cash said. "I have no obligation to Horton to do this." Cash hesitated.

"So, is there another question before the council?" Buni said.

"O.K.. Well. I want you to take me around it one more time. You're sure I shouldn't play with Edwards? I will never have this chance again, and—" Cash asked.

"What!" Buni cut him off. "How can you ask that question? Of course you shouldn't play with him. Absolutely not. No way in this lifetime. Never. It's wrong because of the whole 'present' thing, and wrong because you would be awful, and wrong because it would be extreme PLV. A triple whammy. Clear enough?"

"Is it, though? My PLV? I will never have another chance like this in my life, Buni. That counts for something. I don't believe I want to play just because I've hit my PLV—if I have—and maybe I have. I mean, I take your point—but my PLV is not the only thing at issue here. I mean, you said it's like a tic, once you know it you can stop, so I could stop after this one show—and for me it would be something, something real and—"

"Stop, stop. None of that counts," Buni said. "You playing with Edwards would be dragging him into your Personal Las Vegas, Cash. Yours. Not his. You can't do that to people, especially if you know you're doing it. That's all that's going on here. Amber saved you from it."

"O.K. O.K. Just help me through it." Cash said.

"Well. Cash. It's not a character flaw. There's not some therapy for it. It's just a weird option we all hit. Even corporations and institutions hit their PLV. It's not about rich or poor, not about gender, not about midlife crisis, not about age, race, or religion. Amber almost hit her PLV the other night, and she's only a kid. It goes to motive. Not what we do but why we do it. You're standin' at the crossroads here. For real. And what would be the motive for you playing with Edwards?" Buni left the question before Cash. He waited. Cash had to answer.

"It would be my only chance?" Cash tried.

"O.K. That's selfish. Is selfish a good motive?" Buni prompted.

"All right. I don't know. You tell me. What's the right motive? Is there a good one?" Cash was listening.

"Short answer, no, not for playing with Edwards. Not for you, my friend. Amber gave you the long answer. You can't get next to Edwards, Cash. You don't know how and never will. It's nothing you and I can ever learn. There comes a time when something gets sacred. People die and people live because of it. That's where we are with Tyrone. He's totally dialed into this. You can see he's a blues singer, and you and me gotta see the sacred in it, even if he doesn't. Which will tell you, you can't play along with Tyrone. Cash, there is a place for all of us. A place where the music we love fits in our life and where the music we play fits. It's not always music. It can be baking or laundry or gardening. Different for everyone. Its our Soul center. Our life. We know it when it hits. Not so easy to know what to do about it. If we let it, it leads us, shows us who we are. If we mess with it, it fades. That's when we find ourself in someplace we don't want to be. Gotta keep it real. You onstage with Tyrone? That ain't real, Cash. And you know that." Buni stopped.

The PLV might not make perfect sense to anyone but Buni, but it did make perfect sense to him, and he knew it like he knew his own name.

Cash looked at Buni and nodded acceptance. Both of them turned to the sound of the stage door as it opened and Tyrone Edwards and his side men came in.

The show that night went as well as could be expected, given the environment. Cash played with Buni and the band and sang a song by himself, much to the delight of the crowd. Everything he had learned from his time at the Partaway held him secure. The timid, stage-frightened Cash was replaced by the Cash everyone knew and loved, confident and charming.

Most important for Cash, the music he had loved for so long, that he had hidden away in his life as an executive and entrepreneur, was finally accessible to him as recreation. These were all friends, of course. It was a bit like a president or a prime minister playing at a party, and it got rowdy and fun as the crowd called out encouragement from the festive side of the music. Everyone enjoyed it, especially Cash.

When Amber performed, she increased her usual level of communication with the crowd, all of whom now considered her more of an acquaintance. She felt their support and even returned some of it in smiles and friendly talk from the stage. It still surprised Buni, but he admitted to himself he liked the less brooding side of Amber onstage. The extra access she provided to herself was endearing to the crowd, and her voice and talent had a new and resplendent setting from which to shine. Maybe, thought Buni, this wasn't Amber's PLV, but more of her growing up, into her art. It felt good.

Edwards played six songs, and from the second he started to play, the audience was much less than warm towards him, some even nonplussed. Edwards was hard-line Delta blues. As he played, the guitar went slightly out of tune, and he didn't bother to fix it, he didn't introduce the songs or his band, he sat down through the show, and after the merriment that accompanied Amber and Cash and Buni, his short time onstage seemed to most of the audience like an intermission. Add to this the fact that anyone who knew about such things could tell Edwards was wrecked on heroin, and Edwards's set was a failure to all but five percent of the audience.

Amber, Cash, Buni, and the band were part of that five percent, and they listened to every word, every phrase, every nuance. Edwards was the fully-realized incarnation of the blues. For them and the others in the audience with the same perspective, Edwards was magnificent. From the heart of his desperate life came the perfection of the passions and pain of this music.

Throughout Edwards's time on stage, Cash noticed that Amber and Buni did not move a muscle, not even to applaud. This was their church, their holiest of places. Cash appreciated Edwards, but not like they did. Watching them watch Edwards for those fifteen minutes taught Cash more about the soul of music than he had learned in his whole life. Cash silently thanked Buni and Amber over and over for snatching him from the brink, from even the contemplation of playing with Edwards.

After the show, a large group of happy partiers thronged the stage. There was laughter and good feelings all around, with much appreciation for Amber. Horton said nothing to Cash about playing or not playing with Edwards. Horton hadn't even been there. He had been outside trying to reel in an investor, and now he was working the crowd Cash had assembled and was content inside his own world of hustling.

"Just wonderful, Cash. Won't you introduce me?" Freddy Bates had finally cornered Cash, Amber, and Buni.

"Sir Alfred. Hello. You're looking well, as ever. Yes, my pleasure. Let me present Amber Fanfare." Cash said.

Bates extended his hand. Amber took it, but before she could shake Freddy's hand, he had hers to his lips and gently kissed the back of it. "Ms. Fanfare," he said. "It is an honor to be in the presence of one so gifted. Freddy Bates at your service."

Amber's mouth fell open. She looked at Buni, who was as surprised as she was, then to Cash. Cash gave her a single nod, with a slight smile that said, yes, he's for real. Enjoy it.

"Aha, Buni," Bates said. "My foosball nemesis. Good to see you. Great job tonight, again. Have you plans? Can we have a drink somewhere?"

"We were all going to take a drive," Amber said.

Bates laughed before anyone else. "It does get to feeling cramped on these things, doesn't it? Well, let me buy you a drink. Can you leave your adoring fans now, you think?" Freddy asked all three.

Whatever Sir Alfred had, it was perfect for Amber. She immediately loved him like an uncle. The four of them made their way from the stage as the group was dispersing. From the side, Diana, who was standing with a small group of friends, watched them go. An outside observer comparing the two groups would have seen a great difference in them.

Neither Diana nor Horton said anything else to Cash that night. Cash spent a bit of time with Buni, Amber and Sir Alfred, and then when he saw the chance, he left them together to plot Amber's future. Bates was smitten.

It was late, and only the casino was still active. Otherwise the ship was dark, settling down for the night. Cash strolled along the deck. It was a beautiful night. Clear, a full moon, and an expanse of stars, all reflected in the scallops of black water. The air was warm and damp, and there was a low breeze from the motion of the boat. Cash made one complete circle of the boat and then went to his room.

He paused for a second at Diana's door but moved on. There was nothing to say. He still cared for Diana, but this time the connection was fully severed, and as he drifted from that dock, he continued to drift into a landless expanse.

Cash sat on the couch in his room and looked out over the veranda. Leland had taught him the value of contemplation, of the quiet times alone with his thoughts. He sat there for a long time.

There was a light tap at the door. Cash knew it was Diana. He was not looking forward to hashing over events of the last few months. He didn't want to talk about her facelift or her new breasts. He didn't want to talk about the *Mariner.* He didn't want to talk politics. The sad truth was he didn't want to talk to her at all. He sighed and opened the door.

It was Amber. She was holding a beer and a plastic bottle of water.

"I brought you a beer." She held out the water to him as she walked in. Cash took it. What a surprise, and what a relief. He was glad to see her.

She walked to the veranda and looked out over the rail. Cash joined her. It was a beautiful night, made for romance.

"I think Sir Alfred is wonderful." Amber nodded her head and held an unusually long pause. "Of course, I may be just saying that because he offered to fly me and Buni to Brussels and give us a record deal." She leaned on the rail, looked at Cash, and beamed.

"I thought he might." Cash smiled at her. "That's fantastic, Amber. I'm so happy for you."

"Buni calls me A. You wanna call me A?" she said.

"If you want. I'll call you whatever you say."

"What I want is for you to call me. You like me, don't you, Cash? I know you do. You like me."

"I more than like you. You are dear to me."

"That's a good thing, because I'm staying here with you tonight."

Cash laughed. He was more uncomfortable than he thought he might be, than he thought he should have been.

"Don't laugh. I am. That's how bad it is. Is that O.K. for me to say? Can I tell you that?" Amber turned around, leaned on the rail, and faced Cash. She was yearning for him.

"Of course. You can tell me anything. But Amber—you know we can't do this." Cash was gentle, speaking low.

"Yes we can. Why not?" Amber moved close to him.

Cash looked at her tenderly. "You said this afternoon you wouldn't let me play with Edwards—and the reason you gave was that you loved me. You were protecting me. I'm saying the same thing to you. I love you too, Amber. But this won't work."

Amber walked away from him and sat on the couch. She was acting petulant, but it wasn't real.

"You don't want me," she said.

"Tonight only two things could happen. It would be either a one-night stand, or I would become baggage to what's about to happen to you." Cash came to the couch, sat on the floor, and looked up at her

"Is it because you're too old?" Amber said.

Cash laughed. "You mean because you're too young?"

Amber returned a shy smile. "O.K."

"There have been great May-December romances, but not many. That's hard for a love affair. But that's not what I'm saying. I'm in a strange place right now. You know this. You told me, and Buni told me. Told me what it was, and it's something I never thought of—something I have to think through very carefully. If we did this, I'm afraid I would just drag you into my—into something that wouldn't be good. So, please, not now. Maybe sometime, but not tonight."

"You love me? For real? Like I love you?" Amber said.

"For real."

Amber slid off the couch onto the floor. She took Cash's face in her hands, and with a touch lighter than a hummingbird to a flower, she pressed her lips to his. She pulled back and looked deep into his eyes.

"Good. Then I'm spending the night right here." She jumped up.

Cash was flustered and stood up. He tried to say something, but Amber held up her hand and stopped him.

"I won't do a thing. I won't touch you. We won't have sex. Fair enough. You said you loved me, and you said sometime maybe we could. You even said, 'Love affair.' But not now. O.K. So that's that."

Amber slipped off her boots, pulled back the covers from the king-size bed, and, fully clothed, climbed in.

"We can snuggle. But no sex. I trust you." She patted the space next to her. "But this is not the end of it, Cash. This is only the beginning."

Cash hesitated and then walked to the bed, took off his shoes, and, fully clothed, climbed in next to her. She pushed her back into his chest, making two spoons, and yawned.

"Wanna hear the best part about Sir Alfred?" she asked.

"Tell me," Cash said.

"He asked why I wasn't wearing the pink outfit from the night before. Said he liked it, thought the black jeans were 'a bit drab.'" She giggled.

"No. Really?" Cash started laughing.

"I swear to God." Amber started laughing too.

The two of them pulled the covers up to their chins and laughed themselves to sleep.

At three in the morning, Diana, in her sexiest nightwear, pushed the door open to Cash's room. She took a half-step through the door and saw Amber and Cash, heads above the cover, side by side, asleep. She stared in stunned recognition, and perfectly assured of what she saw and knew, backed out from the room.

The almost inaudible click of the closing door woke Cash. He knew at once what had happened. He raised gently to his elbows to not wake the sleeping Amber, but after a few seconds, he lowered himself back beside her. There was nothing he could say to Diana. Nothing that would comfort her. They had come to the same crossroads, and she had gone one way, he another. The part of his life he shared with Diana was over. He had to trust it was for the best.

Diana went to her suite, opened the bar, took two glasses and a bottle of scotch, and then made her way to the deck below, where she knocked on the door of Vittorio Falluci.

Falluci was awake. He had been in his room since the presentation, studying a report that had been emailed to him. This time there was a real problem with the carbon hydrofoam. It might float for several years, according to some calculations, even decades, according to one, but at some time it would founder. Nanometer by nanometer, the hydrofoam was waterlogging, like a sponge soaking up liquid, but at a rate so slow it had gone unnoticed.

He was surprised to see Diana standing at the door, but he fully understood her presence. She held up the scotch and the glasses; Vittorio smiled a sweet, satisfied surrender and held the door wide open for her to enter. He would say nothing of the *Mariner*. Certainly not now, probably not ever.

For now the *Mariner* floated as Diana and Horton had wanted, and it was maneuverable as they had wanted, but it would never become the floating city they had wanted. It would sink.

In the morning, before the sun was up, Cash called his pilot, and the chopper was there three hours later. Cash would not take the boat back to Galveston as planned. He would leave it all here. All except Buni and Amber, who climbed into the chopper with him, and watched as the *Marianna* shrank beneath them, and the whole world opened up.

Printed in the USA
CPSIA information can be obtained
at www.ICGtesting.com
LVHW052222050124
768155LV00002B/181